G000039082

ABOUT THE AUTHOR

Stephen Timmins has spent a significant portion of his adult life surviving in the "media" sector. Born and brought up in Surrey he now lives in a village near Bristol where he spends his time contemplating higher matters and planning trips to Lidl. He has been a fan of John Buchan's Richard Hannay stories since childhood and often wondered what would have happened to Hannay's descendants. This is the second book of the trilogy that tells their story.

Published in Great Britain in 2021
By Diamond Crime

ISBN 978-1-8384026-5-5

Copyright © 2021 Stephen Timmins

The right of Stephen Timmins to be identified as the author of this work has been asserted in accordance with the Copyright, Designs and Patents Act 1998.

All rights reserved.

No part of this publication may be reproduced, stored in a retrieval system, or transmitted in any form or by any means without the prior permission in writing of the publisher, nor be circulated in any form of binding or cover other than that in which it is published.

All characters appearing in this work are fictitious. Any resemblance to real persons, living or dead, is purely coincidental.

Diamond Crime is an imprint of Diamond Books Ltd.

Thanks to our NHS
Long may it be publicly owned
and publicly run.

Book cover design:
jacksonbone.co.uk

Also by Stephen Timmins

The Fortieth Step Thrillers
Volume 1 – Legacy
Volume 3 – Promise

And coming soon to Diamond Crime

The Stanwood House Chronicles
Flora's War
Kit's War
Flora's Peace

For information about Diamond Crime authors
and their books, visit:
www.diamondbooks.co.uk

To
Lucy, Martin, Daisy,
Nina, Zach, Ted and Joel
Daniel and Gabi and Alex

THE FORTIETH STEP

VOLUME TWO

REVENGE

STEPHEN TIMMINS

PROLOGUE

It had been a battle getting through the fog, mainly because the night was as black as the Earl of Hell's waistcoat. But the more I struggled past unseen objects, the worse the pain got. Somewhere ahead, though, I was sure I could see that it was turning into mist so if I could just keep going. Then, finally, in the distance – voices just on the edge of hearing. I fought harder to reach them. They disappeared. For a moment I gave up the struggle. The pain died away leaving just the darkness and the fog. I was beginning to hate that fog. I struggled forward again, feeling my way. And then one voice was clearer. "You don't understand him. He'll keep fighting unless we let him know he has to rest in order to heal."

It was a woman speaking. I was sure I knew her voice.

"If I bring him round, he might not be able to bear the pain."

That was a man's voice. Not one I recognised.

The first voice spoke again. "He can handle pain. If there's one thing he's known how to handle since he was eight years old, it's pain."

The voices faded. I struggled again to hear them and now it was working. The fog was thinning. I was nearly out of it and into the white mist, but the pain in my chest was appalling. The first voice had been right though, I did know how to manage it. I knew that pain came in different layers. At the top was a thin, shrieking layer.

1

That, I could push to one side. There was a deeper, wilder layer below it. Through that one too. And at the very bottom? Just exhaustion. I concentrated harder. I twisted and turned and burrowed and bit–by–bit, I found it: the route map from the unbearable to the manageable. And as the pain eased, the first voice was back again, insistent – faint at first then louder and clearer, the flat, fuzzy echo dying away.

"John... John... John Richard... John Richard Hannay, can you hear me?"

I did know that voice. I opened my eyes. It was white, bright white. I squinted. She moved. I saw her. She hadn't left me. She touched my face and I managed to croak. "Robbi."

She looked down at me and stroked my cheek. "John, listen. They've had you under sedation for more than a week and you're on a really strong opioid analgesics for the pain. I know it's very bad, but we had to bring you round so we could talk to you. The doctor says you're healing, but you must relax. You mustn't fight it. You need to heal. Do you understand me, John?"

I smiled properly this time and managed a slight nod. "I understand. Robbi?"

She leaned in to hear my voice. "What?"

"What names have you thought up for the Collies?"

She smiled. I remembered that mischievous smile.

"Spit and Spot"

Out of the corner of my eye I saw a man's hand reach out and twist the tap on the morphine drip.

"Idiot." I said as I drifted back down.

"Idiot... diot... iot..."

Down into the tumble of opiate dreams in which I could feel my grandfather reaching out a strong arm to me across the generations. Over my father cartwheeling, already dead, across the Manor lane in his burning Austin Healey. Over my mother, dead, rotting on her bedroom floor; through the kitchen in the flat where I had sat, aged eight, after I had found her body before a man and his son tortured me. The echoes of my visions faded finally from crimson to purple to black to nothing and the pain inside me slowly died.

CHAPTER ONE

A handful of letters had arrived in the post yesterday and I was only just getting round to opening them. Seven of the letters looked like junk mail for the same product. I binned six and kept one. I opened it. I read it. It didn't take long. Just one letter, 'E', typed on cheap, eighty–gram paper. I went to screw it up and paused. I picked up the wastebin and lifted out the other six letters: same London post mark, same cheap envelopes. I opened another one – a single piece of eighty–gram paper with the letter 'V'. The next was 'R'. Eventually I had seven pieces of paper in front of me with one letter on each. 'E V R G E N E'. I had never been much interested in solving anagrams...

Still distracted, I opened the eighth letter. This one was official – very official. I swore. I was summoned to appear as a witness before the House of Commons Treasury Committee. I was supplied with the committee's terms of reference and an outline of the matters expected to be dealt with during my appearance. I stared at the little portcullis logo on the top corner of the page hoping vaguely that it was a hoax from one of my so–called friends. I re–read the relevant paragraphs – to précis: the committee wanted to know what the hell had gone on in the trading rooms of BTD and Medina Ventures during the Sterling crisis between 20th and 23rd July of this year. Why me? Why now?

Two reasons to call Major Alan Cummins of MI5: two incidents of the exact type on receipt of which I was instructed to call Major Alan Cummins of MI5. But I didn't. If I called Major Alan Cummins of MI5 it really would start all over again and I wasn't well enough for that, not by a long, long chalk.

I stroked the screen of the iPad intending to read up on Commons Select Committees. Already on the screen, though, was an old email, from the person I was learning to call my 'wife', to Staff Sergeant Paul Browby's wife, Margaret, in her hospital bed in the specialist cancer hospital in San Francisco. I had found it in my sent-box and forwarded it to my own email account because it had made me smile.

Date: Fri, 29 August 15:51:13 +0100
To: margaret.browby@ussf-net.co
From: robbi@fosse.co.uk

Dear, dear Margaret,

I do hope you're beginning to feel better now. Your description of how the chemotherapy left you feeling made me cringe, but the hospital has the best reputation in the world and when you're better you can go and see the Golden Gate Bridge and send me photos of it. Talking of photos please see attached my favourites from the wedding. I'm so sorry you and Paul couldn't be there. It was such a wonderful day.

The ceremony was in John's village church and afterwards we went back to Fosse Manor where we'd had a marquee put up in the walled garden. Everybody that John knew from the village was invited and you remember Emma 'The Boss' Fitzgerald – the woman John worked for as a City *trader – well she asked after you and said to tell you that you had to get better as she wanted another of your puddings! She was looking dead gorgeous and flirting with everybody including Lord Clanroyden and Major Alan Cummins (was he Paul's commanding officer in the SAS?) and she didn't say f**k once the whole time which John said was a world record. But even though it's all over, Dominick Medina in some kind of secure asylum, John out of hospital, wedding and all, I still keep waking up in the middle of the night just to check John's still breathing. I even took his pulse last night while he was asleep, but it was fine – 60 beats to the minute; you could set your watch by him. I just really pray he's as tough as the doctor thinks he is because he has been through so much pain. Not that I need to tell you about pain...*

Anyway, that's all for now.

Lots of love and get well quickly wishes,

Robbi. xxxxxxxxxxxx

P.S.

Forgot to say that the builders have almost finished work on the lodge house now so it should be ready for you and Paul when you get back from San Francisco. I hope you don't think we're trying to bully you into living at Fosse, but we really do want to have you here because you love gardening and the kitchen garden needs a flame thrower and John thinks Paul would make the most brilliant gamekeeper.

Pleeeeease.

LADY *RJH xxxx*

The first ray of October morning sun struck the leaded window lights. Below me on the drive outside, the woman I still occasionally thought of as Robbi Lord was now 'training' the Border Collie puppies. She was wearing jodhpurs and riding boots and an ancient V necked sweater of mine back to front and the training appeared, to the untutored eye, to involve Spit and Spot jumping up and trying to lick her while she collapsed on to the damp grass by the drive, in giggles.

I stared at the seven crumpled pages in the wastepaper bin. I looked down at the letter from the House of Commons. I would have to phone Major Alan Cummins of MI5 and let him know, but if I did that... I sighed, picked up my phone to make the call that would start it all off again, sighed once more, put it down and looked out of the window at the ridiculous scene below.

CHAPTER TWO

I can't now remember the point of the particular charity committee onto which Robbi had been dragged not long after our wedding. But its coup was to have got her into our local Academy school as a last resort before the courts dealt with its most disruptive pupil, the fifteen-year-old Grace Harker. Grace's actions did not match her name. Grace had set fire to the chemistry block. Grace had assaulted two boys, two years her senior, reduced them to tears and nearly put one of them in hospital. Grace took no prisoners.

Day One: Robbi brought her to the Manor to meet the horses. (Just after our wedding we had bought two horses and a pony.) Robbi offered Grace the chance to learn how to ride on condition she mucked out and helped groom the horses and showed development in her studies. The threat hanging over her head was clear and unambiguous.

Day Two: Grace brought her best friend, Jasmine, and their boyfriends – a pair of unappetising and spotty youths. Little mucking out was done.

Day Three: I couldn't find my saddle. I mentioned this to Paul Browby whose eyes took on a faraway look.

Day Four: the saddle reappeared, the boyfriends did not, and Grace trod with extreme care anywhere in Paul Browby's vicinity.

Day Five and onwards: Grace learned to ride and was better behaved then anybody could remember – ever.

This has been a diversion. But it is not irrelevant. Grace is important.

* * *

I was still hunched up on the wide window recess on the landing wishing I had brought a cushion to stop the cold from the stone sill seeping through my jeans to my still too skinny posterior. The half opened mullioned windows reflected a slanting, early October morning sun and highlighted the tyre undulations in the gravel drive a floor below me. The last drenching fortnight of rain had passed and the morning echoed to the rumbling of tractors, their trailers bouncing empty, out towards the fields and then maize full, growling back towards the silos. Jack Cartwright said it had been a good harvest – and if an English farmer said that, it must have been spectacular.

I shook my head and seeing the movement Lady Roberta Jane Hannay ceased her dog training and raised a manicured middle finger in my direction and then made exaggerated beckoning and car driving gestures. Today was Wednesday, which meant shopping with Mrs Trudgeon, one of the old pensioners in the village. She had babysat me thirty–five years ago and was not backward in informing Robbi of how to take care of me. It was Robbi's decision to offer Mrs T some vicarious excitement and now the trip to the supermarket in Burford had become one of the highlights of her week.

Half-heartedly, I lifted my phone again, stared at Major Alan Cummins' name on the screen, looked back down at Robbi on the drive below me and pressed the off button.

* * *

In the supermarket car park Robbi grabbed a wheelchair from beside the front entrance for Mrs Trudgeon, leaving me to wander across to the cigarettes, lottery and newspaper section idly wondering if she wanted The Guardian. A shrill and angry voice broke through my reverie.

"How dare you drive that wheelchair into me and how dare you treat an old person like her with such disrespect? She needs proper care, not being bucketed around dangerously at high speed by some… some common little, over made–up, dyed blonde, Essex tart."

I looked round. A woman in her fifties with a crimplene perm and a surround–sound, beige trouser suit was haranguing Robbi. I stepped to one side to get a better look and nearly trod on a dirty trainer containing the foot of Grace's (now ex) boyfriend, Liam. He smirked at me uncertainly.

"Who's that, Liam?"

"Dunno S'John. Want us to find out?"

I looked down at them. A third member of the team was trying unsuccessfully to hide behind Jasmine's boyfriend, Tyler.

"And who's this, Liam?"

"S'my younger brother, Petie, S'John. He's infectious. We're looking after him."

"Hmmm. Of course you are, and better nursing I'm sure would be hard to find. Get her purse from her handbag, lads. No stealing from it. Just find out who she is. Twenty quid if you can. Paul Browby will come and see you if you nick anything. I mean it."

"Piece of piss." squeaked the infectious team member, receiving a cuff round the ear from his older brother, nurse and mentor. I stepped back into the shadows and watched. Robbi was listening to the harangue with an expression of calm bemusement on her face. I could see the store manager wringing her hands and behind her and to one side, a face I recognised, grinning unpleasantly, and talking to someone I didn't know.

Mrs Trudgeon had launched her own counter offensive at the glossy woman who was beginning to colour up. I texted Robbi one word: 'cry'. She heard the alert and glanced at her phone. Within seconds her face puckered up and she began to sob.

"I'm so sorry. I was only trying to help and I thought she might enjoy it and I don't dye my hair honestly and...." she sobbed and hiccoughed "and I'm not wearing any makeup."

Mrs Trudgeon twisted round in her chair.

"Now don't you take on, Robbi, dear."

"How did she know I was born in Essex, Mrs T?"

Robbi sobbed some more. Mrs Trudgeon turned back to Mrs Glossy and bellowed.

"Now look what you've done, you revolting woman. How dare you upset Lady Hannay, the finest, kindest woman it's been my privilege to know? I..."

As unobtrusively as I could I made my way out of the store and back to the Landrover from where I watched the exit. Tyler, Liam and Petie were first out. I stepped up onto the running board so they could see I was watching them. Reluctantly they dropped the untouched purse by the trolley park and trotted towards me. I waved the twenty–pound note slowly in front of their faces.

"Well?"

"She's a Mrs Mathilda – M A T H I L D A, that is – Robinson. She's got a Barclaycard and her driver's license says she lives somewhere in Derbyshire."

Petie joined in: "it were Buxton – B U X T O N."

The twenty–pound note changed hands, followed by a pound coin.

"How many does that make for each of you, Petie?"

"Seven pounds."

"And if I'd given you twenty pounds how much would that have been each?"

He stared at me suspiciously, suspecting a trap. Not seeing one, he answered.

"Six pounds sixty-six, with one p left over, Mister.

His broad grin was removed by another clip to the ear.

"He's Sir John, not Mister."

"John's just fine and perhaps you could go easier on the clips round the ear, Tyler?"

"Yes, S'John."

"Try going to school, lads. It may be boring, but you're way too bright to waste your lives on the dole and whether you like it or not, going to school's a way out."

"Yes, S'John."

I sighed. They scarpered. The wheelchair arrived. Mrs Trudgeon was still outraged. "Who did she think she was, John, that's what I want to know?"

"She's a Mrs Mathilda Robinson from Buxton in Derbyshire, Mrs T."

Robbi studied me. "How did you find that out, you crafty sod?"

"Robbi, language!"

"Sorry, Mrs T."

"Ever see her before, Mrs T?"

"No, John, but I shall make it my business to find out exactly who she is."

She muttered and harrumphed all the way to her home. After we had dropped her off Robbi sat sideways on her seat, waiting for an explanation.

"I do love a good cry, you know."

I smiled.

"You know her comment about me being a tart from Essex..."

"Yes, Robbi, I do. Remember Alexander Mallin, our erstwhile estate manager?"

"The one who you fired just because he was rude to you?"

I considered pointing out that this was a gross misrepresentation. She poked me with one of her long fingers.

"Anyway, he was there and loving every second of it and talking to a man I didn't know who seemed to be equally amused."

"Is it starting again, John?"

"I don't think so, Robbi. What's twenty divided by three?"

"Six and a bit more than a half, why? Are you changing the subject?"

"Tyler's eight-year-old brother, Petie, told me the answer straight out. Six point six six with one left over. Did I mention that he was eight?"

She punched me. But I had changed the subject.

CHAPTER THREE

It was almost a week later – a Sunday. I had still not replied to the Select Committee summons. I had still not made the phone call. Lady Hannay was 'training' the Collies again on the drive. I was perched on the doorstep watching despairingly.

The back door of the newly refurbished lodge house at the top of the drive opened and Paul Browby stepped out. I knew he had already seen me and taken in the whole panorama with one quick glance – once an SAS NCO, always an SAS NCO. Paul had taken to his gamekeeper/assistant estate manager role almost instantly. He even got away with wearing Plus Fours and gaiters; not something I would care – or dare for that matter – to try in front of my spouse.

A movement from the stable block caught my attention. Grace was bringing out the horses. I walked back inside, grabbed Robbi's gilet and shrugged my shoulders into a quilted jacket. In the yard my horse, Jemima, was chewing at her bit and fretting anxiously on the cobblestones. Her ears were moving back and forwards listening for any clue as to what was going to happen next. I spoke her name quietly and her ears flicked back. She turned her head towards me and whinnied, doing a little dance on the cobbles, tugging at her reins.

"Let her go, Grace."

Freed from the constraint, Jemima tossed her head and walked towards me, nuzzling in to my shoulder, pretending deep affection, when all she really wanted was one of the lemon sherbets I carry in my jacket for her. I let her find one and then tormented her with the wrapper for five seconds before giving it to her to crunch in her strong teeth. She blew on me gently while I stroked her velvet muzzle. Grace was watching enviously.

"Grace, I've put the bar up one notch on the jump in the paddock as you asked. Are you sure you're OK with that, because Robbi won't go out until she's convinced Mavis can clear it?"

"No, that's OK, S'John. Honest. Robbi knows Mave can do it."

Why was it that Robbi was Robbi to everyone from the refuse collectors to the Lord Lieutenant of the county, all of whom she knew by first name while I remained stubbornly *Sir* John to all and bloody sundry? A car horn sounded at the gates and Paul admitted the visitor. Robbi was now clucking over Grace who basked in the attention of her adored mother hen as Robbi's brother Dave coasted to a halt in his new Landrover Discovery. Grace hadn't seen him before and I kept my eyes on her as Dave straightened and Robbi jumped up into his arms. Her jaw dropped at his sheer massive bulk and the way he lifted Robbi off the ground with his arms out at full stretch. I saw her note how he and Paul smiled at each other.

Fifteen minutes later I led the way on Jemima up the narrow bridle way, across the pine plantation, through the gate beside the cattle grid and up on to the escarpment and the open down, grazed by Jack Cartwright's sheep, that marked the edge of the Fosse estate. I pulled on Jemima's reins so we could pause in our usual position to look back down at Fosse Manor nestled in the valley below. Grace was jumping Mavis and I could see Margaret, newly returned from America, walking down to the kitchen garden. I glanced across at Robbi. She grinned back at me. I clucked to Jemima. Robbi whispered in Teddy's ear. We galloped.

Eventually we slowed to a canter, to a trot and then a walk, back across the short springy grass that clung to the edge of the Cotswold tops. I undid the gate beside the second cattle grid and we dismounted to lead the horses down the steep, high banked, single–track lane into the beech woods that marked the edge of the manor's land and Jack Cartwright's farm, hooves striking sparks from the stones on the old track. We had re–mounted near the bottom of the hill when Robbi tapped my arm with her crop and pointed. There below, moving towards us at a trot was the Hunt. I pulled Jemima up and stared – the Hunt on Fosse land? What the hell? They weren't going to stop either. I looked round. Robbi nudged her horse up beside me to block the lane.

"Video this on your phone, Robbi. Get photos too."

I held her reins and walked Jemima forward and turned her sideways across the lane. Robbi sighed. "John, please, you know you're not well yet."

I nodded, watching the riders. From this distance I didn't think I knew any of them. My mobile rang. I answered it without taking my eyes off the riders.

"John, it's Nick Maitland. Look, we have a problem."

"You mean you have a problem, Nick. What the hell's the Hunt doing on Fosse land? You know the agreement. You're the Master of Fox Hounds for God's sake."

"John, I'm sorry. It was young Mallin. He brought some new chaps along and, well, frankly they're hooligans."

"You'd better call the police, Nick, before this gets nasty. Robbi, phone Paul."

And they were on us. The hounds surged round us, freed from the ministrations of the whippers–in and huntsman. "Get out of the fucking way. Didn't you hear the View Halloo?"

I was polite. "I didn't, no. In any event, I'm sorry, but you're on Fosse land here and the Hunt is not welcome."

"The Hunt not welcome? Who the fuck do you think you are?"

He was short, burly, mid-fifties, red faced and sat his horse well – an experienced hunter by the look of him. I sighed and continued to temporise. "I'm John Hannay. This is my estate. Look, your MFH, Nick Maitland, just called and told me he'd warned you about this, so if you can let the huntsman through, you can make your way off my land and find whatever it is you hunt these days somewhere else."

A taller, younger rider was pushing his way through on his horse. Now this one did look dangerous. He was shaking with what I guessed was Coked–up rage. "Get out of our fucking way, you fucking little prick."

He raised his whip hand and lashed out at me with his crop, back handed. I tilted my head to take the blow on my helmet and felt a searing pain over my right eye. I whipped up my arm to ward off the next blow and felt the same stinging pain across my wrist. For the first time in my life, I regretted never carrying a riding crop. I stood in my stirrups to get inside the next blow and then there was a thud and his horse jerked and skittered. Jemima danced on her hooves, upset by the noise. Something was obscuring my vision. I put my hand to my eye. It came away covered with warm wetness – blood was pouring down my face from a flap torn in the flesh above my right eye. At least I could see again. Paul was standing behind the rider on the back of his horse. He had one arm under his shoulder, trying to break his hold on the weapon.

"Let go of the crop, please."

He said it quietly and reasonably. He said it again, more loudly this time, to make sure everybody heard him. The rider made the mistake of trying to break the hold. His arm began to bend in a direction to which its joints were not accustomed – back and back. It snapped at the wrist. He screamed and then Dave's enormous parade ground voice broke through the chaos. And all was still. So quiet I could hear the drip of my blood on to the road below. I felt weak now. "Paul, don't let that crop..." and I slid sideways to lean on Robbi. "... no one touch that crop. Fingerprints."

The silence lingered. All the testosterone had bled out of the pumped-up riders. They were worried men... and at least one woman, I noticed. Well, well, well, Mrs Glossy Mathilda Robinson. Dave was beside me in three quick steps. He tore the sleeve of my jacket and whipped a tourniquet round my wrist. "Paul, you got that tape?"

Paul, still balancing on the horse's back, threw a roll of gaffer tape down to him. Dave pushed the flap of flesh up and taped across it, pulling it hard down on to the bone of my forehead.

"Ow," I said. Quite mildly, I thought.

"Blooming baby," came the caring response.

Robbi undid my helmet and lifted it off my head. I straightened in the saddle and saw the blue flashing light at the bottom of the hill. I looked at her, turning my head slowly. She wiped some blood from my cheek and smiled her gentle smile. "I'm not sure if this is going to ruin your beautiful face or make you look dashing and piratical."

I tried not to smile back. "Robbi, I'm sorry..."

"Shhh."

Chief Inspector William Thornton was unamused. Within one minute he had radioed for an ambulance for the rider with the broken wrist and me (against my protests) and had his young constable taking witness statements. So far as I could hear Mrs Glossy was going off on one about my 'naked aggression and violence towards people exercising their inalienable rights'. Robbi had finished on the phone to Margaret requesting Grace's presence to help ride the horses back when he came across and looked up at me. "You ever pick fights when the odds are in your favour, John?"

"Show Billy the riding crop, Paul. No one apart from that idiot has touched it."

The policeman examined it and then looked at me shrugging. "Other end, Billy. He hit me with the other end."

He turned it round, careful not to touch it with his bare fingers, and examined the other end. He lifted the tassel and whistled. "My, my. That's a new one on me."

Beneath the wrist loop, hidden by the tassel was the edge of a Stanley blade, stained red with my blood. He turned to the uniformed policeman behind him. "Constable, the man with the broken wrist – back of the car now! He can have his arm seen to after we've charged him with assault."

The sound of our Landrover chugging up the hill made the horses skitter again. A red faced and furious huntsman and two whippers-in had also arrived and were rounding up the hounds. Grace jumped out of the Landrover, wriggled through the horses and came to stand by us. Jemima snorted at her. Grace took one look at me, put her hand over her mouth and burst into tears. The ambulance arrived. Dave lifted me off Jemima. I pressed his arm to stop him. "Grace, you take good care of Jemima. Paul will take Teddy. They've both been spooked, but I know you can do it. Dave, I am not being carried by you again, it's undignified."

Dave smiled. It wasn't his nice smile. He looked at Paul. "Fiver says he won't make it."

"No takers."

Bastards. Mind you, Paul was right not to have taken the bet. I staggered after ten paces and Dave swung me up and deposited me at the ambulance. Grace's sobs carried through the noise. Robbi climbed in beside me as I was laid on the gurney.

"Are you a relative?"

Dave rested a heavy hand on the ambulance man's shoulder. "She's his wife. And she's going with him."

The ambulance man decided to fuss with the bed straps. The van backed up. I looked up at my wife. "What on earth's the matter with Grace?"

"You may have lost pints and pints of blood, but it certainly hasn't cleared what passes for your brain, you idiot."

I stared at her blankly. "I look that bad?"

"Worse actually, but that's not why she's crying."

I tried to shrug. It hurt. I gave up.

"She has a massive crush on you, you ass."

"Don't be ridiculous."

Robbi gave a deep, exaggerated sigh.

"But she's only sixteen, for God's sake. I mean I'm not exactly old enough to be her father, but..."

"Yes, you are."

"But..."

I tailed off. I had for some time suspected Robbi of saying things like this just to wind me up or maybe it was designed to stop me thinking about the pain. Either way it worked.

And I still hadn't made that call.

CHAPTER FOUR

Monday morning: Robbi tried to pass me the phone. "It's the local paper. They've heard about your run–in with the hunt."

I looked at her. She waggled the phone at me. I sighed and took it with my left hand. The hunter's blade had nearly severed a tendon in my right wrist and, to be frank, it still hurt like hell. "Hello. No, I can't make any comment. Because it's sub–judice. Yes, I could talk off the record. I have to come into Burford tomorrow morning so perhaps I could pop in. Yes? Yes, I know it. At ten then. Goodbye."

She looked at me.

I looked at her. "I'm not well enough."

"Rubbish. You don't need your wrist for sex, well not this kind anyway."

I realised later that all this had probably just been yet another attempt by her to distract me from the pain – not that I was complaining, you understand.

* * *

I was in the study with Paul and Miranda analysing the estate accounts when I received a text instructing me to pick her up from the local Academy School at seven pm. I made arrangements thinking how extraordinary it was that in little more than a couple of months Robbi had become far more part of the community than I had ever managed or wanted to in thirty-six years. My phone bleeped again.

and don't even think of sending Paul.

I groaned. "Cancel that, Paul. I have to go."

Paul and Miranda pressed their thumbs into the desk top in gestures that demonstrated their views on my marital status. The phone bleeped again.

and try and make an effort to look smart for once!!!

I groaned once more and turned to the vexed problem of what on earth to do about Glebe Farm and its appalling tenant farmer.

* * *

At five to seven I parked the Landrover in the school car park and followed the signs to the PTA meeting. I paused in the doorway, hoping to catch sight of Robbi immediately, but as more and more heads turned towards me, I retreated into the entrance and pulled out my phone. I caught the scent of her perfume just before she put her hand over my eyes from behind and then she was round in front of me, touching the stitches over my eye gently and murmuring up at me. "You know it's ever so funny living out here in the wilds. They've already heard about the Hunt and they are all dying to see the fighting baronet and they're probably thinking I'm asking how my brave little soldier boy is feeling, when all I am really doing is sooo enjoying seeing you looking sooo embarrassed."

As smiling still hurt, I tried my best not to.

"Come along now, Sir John. The headmistress wants to meet you."

She took my left hand and led me through the throng, some of whom made not the slightest effort to disguise their fascination. I liked the headmistress – Catherine Simmons. She was self–possessed and had that natural patina of dignity that good teachers acquire over the years. Robbi disappeared into the crowd after the introductions and I took the opportunity to ask my question.

"I have an issue, Catherine, if I may – although I know this isn't the right forum for it."

"An issue, John?"

"Well not an issue as such. It's just that I have been left a somewhat large inheritance by my grandfather and I know he would have wanted me to use for the community. So I wondered if I could talk to you about some kind of charitable set up with the local schools."

Catherine positively beamed. "John, I would love to talk to you about that. To be fair, though, I think you also need to include Janice Scowcroft – she's the head of the primary school."

I smiled back at her forgetting that smiling hurt as much as it did. "Tell you what, Catherine, why don't you and your husband and the Scowcrofts come and have supper next Saturday? I'm pretty sure Robbi's going into the primary school to do some reading with the reception class this week, so she can ask her then."

And then I had to be introduced to (nearly) everybody in the room. By eight p.m. my face was fixed in a rictus grin and even Robbi appeared to have had enough fun at my expense. I threw the Landrover keys at her. She glanced at me as we pulled out of the car park. "So, do you think Catherine has anything to do with the hunt?"

"No. I don't know about the primary school head teacher, of course."

"Good. I like Catherine. I wouldn't have wanted her to be involved in any nastiness. What time are we seeing the newspaper people tomorrow?"

"Ten."

* * *

I had spooned oats into a saucepan, added salt and water and left the porridge bubbling gloopily on the warm plate while I tried to do yesterday's Guardian crossword – the quick not the cryptic one. Robbi bounced in (she has a tendency to bounce before breakfast which, of course, I don't find in any way annoying), complained about the lack of grapefruit, sat on my lap just to try and annoy me, stole the crossword, and brewed coffee. I sighed. The dogs barked and ran to the scullery door.

Robbi smiled. "Morning, Mimi. Porridge on the Aga, but the useless sod forgot to buy any grapefruit."

Our estate manager, Miranda, came in kicking off her Hunters and reprimanding the dogs for jumping up. She placed the post in front of me, kissed Robbi, crouched down to talk to the dogs then ladled out a bowl of porridge. I leafed through the letters – junk mail, junk mail, junk mail. I went to chuck them in the recycling box and almost too late noticed the official brown envelope with the local authority logo in the corner. The murmur of Miranda and Robbi's gossip drifted away. I tore the top off the envelope and studied the formal enclosure. I picked up the house phone to call my childhood guardian and family lawyer, Marcus Wethers. "Uncle Marcus?"

"John, my boy, how are you?"

I heard Aunt Mary in the background proffering love to Robbi as well as me. "Love to Aunt Mary too from both of us, Uncle Marcus. Um, Uncle Marcus, do you know of any good barristers who specialise in planning applications?"

"Tell me the story, John."

I slid the letter across the table to Robbi and continued. "You remember I told you how we had put in an application to turn the old rooms over the stable back into an office and living area following the original nineteenth century plans exactly?"

Miranda read the letter over Robbi's shoulder. Marcus continued. "They've turned you down? On what grounds?"

"Well, none that I can understand. I know you think I am paranoid, but what with the Hunt attacking us..."

'You think someone is getting at you?"

"In a word, yes."

"Very well, John. It might be an idea to take counsel's advice. I'll sniff around for you."

I heard background noise. "Sorry, John, that's my driver. Now you be careful. Do you hear me?"

"I'll be careful, Uncle Marcus. Anyway, Robbi's in charge now."

"That'll please, Mary."

I put the phone down and looked across the table at four worried eyes. "We might need a barrister."

Miranda looked from one of us to the other. "Look I know it isn't any of my business, but are you really trying to say that this planning application refusal and the attack by the Hunt on you are part of the same plot?"

Robbi put her arm round Miranda. "Yes, Mimi. We think it is."

When women start hugging the next stage tends to involve tears. I left.

CHAPTER FIVE

The offices of the North Cotswolds Weekly Gazette were untidy and grubby. I had opened the door quietly. A young couple were hunched over a huge Mac screen, concentrating on page layout. I watched them, trying to get a feel for how the meeting might go. The woman was short, pretty, with a retroussé nose, a gamin haircut and a grand estomac. The man looked up first and glanced at his watch.

"Sir John? Sorry, I hadn't realised what the time was."

I smiled politely and remembered too late that smiling pulled the stitches over my eye. He saw the grimace and straightened up to come round the desk and shake hands. He was also short, stocky with curly red hair, clear blue eyes and a broken nose. It if it weren't for the clear eyes and open smile, he could have looked dangerous. I held out my left hand.

"Oh, I'm sorry I hadn't realised you were injured in the fight."

I put my hand on Robbi's arm before she spoke. "No comment."

"But we're off the record."

"We are now – now that I confirm formally that the conversation we are about to have is off the record, provided you agree to it in writing."

I produced the short agreement I had typed out. He covered his surprise well, passed the paper to the short woman and smiled. "I married a lawyer."

The woman took the paper and stood slowly, putting her hand to the small of her back. Robbi beamed. "How many weeks to go?"

"Three. Can't wait to get him out."

She smiled back at Robbi. I liked the look of these two. The woman glanced at the paper, signed it and passed it back to Robbi.

"So, Sir John, may I introduce..."

"Your wife, Annette, Mr Warburton. You met when you both worked on the Manchester Evening News and when you inherited some money you bought this paper in order to have a 'change of lifestyle'."

Luke Warburton studied me. I rarely gave away anything in first meetings, but I knew that tomorrow was their press day and if anything was going to be printed about me, I had to cut to whatever his chase might be.

"Should I ask you how you found that out, Sir John?"

"Not unless you want to know the rest of what I know about your business. Why don't you tell me what you know about me instead?"

"I er, it's just gossip really."

I was gossiped about? That was interesting. "Go on."

"It, er. Well, it says that you are very reclusive and you retired from the City of London having made a fortune, that you were the most eligible bachelor in the county and that you have married the most beautiful woman in er..."

Robbi grinned. "The world'll do."

"That you had a tragic childhood and are greatly disliked by a large number of 'influential' people in the county."

"Why would that be?"

"Because you won't have anything to do with the pursuits and pastimes of those people."

I glanced at Robbi. "And my wife?"

Annette Warburton took up the story. "Sorry to say, Lady Hannay, but we couldn't find anyone to say a bad word about you."

Robbi laughed. "It's only 'cos they don't know me as well as they know John."

I nodded sagely. "Tomorrow's your press day isn't it?"

He nodded in turn. I raised an encouraging eyebrow. "So, what are you going to write about the unpopular John Hannay then?"

"Well, we were rather hoping you'd be able to give us a quote about the fight."

"What fight?"

"Look, Sir John, we're off the record now."

"I know and I repeat, what fight?"

"Well, how did you get your injuries?"

Robbi decided to be more direct. "Mr Warburton, have you spoken to Billy Thornton?"

"If you mean Chief Inspector William Thornton, he declined to speak to me."

The door opened behind me. I ignored it. "One more question: if I don't give you a quote what are you going to write?"

A newspaper landed on the desk in front of me. "Already written."

The voice was thin, squeaky, South London. I looked round to see a pale, greasy skinned, vastly overweight, bespectacled man in his mid-forties wearing a cheap hacking jacket, blue cord trousers and brown shoes – brown shoes with blue trousers! He shook his head, sneering at me, his jowls wobbling. I sighed. "And you will be the partner that Mr Warburton took on when the paper began to lose money after the change of format to Berliner. You're not a local man either are you, Mr Collier?"

The Collier eyes narrowed to the point where they almost disappeared in the folds of fat on the Collier cheeks. He glared at Luke Warburton. "What have you been telling them about me, then, Warburton?"

I looked back at the North Cotswold Weekly Gazette's editor who had picked up the paper and was staring at it in horror. He looked up at us. "Hunh? What?"

I reached out quickly and pulled the paper from his suddenly lifeless fingers. He reacted too slowly, trying to pull it back. It was a headline worthy of the paper's new tabloid format.

MULTI MILLIONAIRE BARONET
IN
"UNWARRANTED ATTACK"
ON
LOCAL HUNTSMAN

Beneath it was a half-page picture of the man who had attacked me with his arm in plaster and a sling. Robbi leaned over my shoulder reading the smaller type below.

Reclusive local landowner, Sir John Hannay, thirty–seven, is expected to be charged with assault against a member of the North Cotswold Hunt. The alleged assault took place on Sunday 14th October on a public highway. Twenty-nine-year-old hunt member,

Anthony Mallin, had his wrist broken by the Baronet in an attack by him and his employees lasting several minutes, which resulted in local police being called.

Sir John who recently married Essex glamour model, thirty-one-year-old Roberta 'Robbi' Lord, would not comment on the record when approached by the North Cotswold Weekly Gazette...

I stopped reading and stared at Collier in amazement. Robbi had got to the bit about her being a glamour model and was giggling. She took the paper across to show Annette Warburton.

"And you are seriously going to publish that?"

"We have five witnesses who have all made sworn statements."

I gave him the long stare. "I have only read the first two pars and there are four factual errors already."

I turned back to Warburton and raised an eyebrow.

"I er. I er." He was out of his depth.

"I think you need to have a board meeting."

Collier laughed at me. "Maybe you're even more stupid than they tell me. Or maybe..."

"Or maybe you think I don't know what your shareholder agreement and what your far from standard Memorandum and Articles of Association say. You have a choice, Mr Collier – and I am talking just to you, you will note. I am not going to insult you by telling you what the choice is."

I stood up, catching my right wrist on the edge of the chair. I winced again and he laughed. Robbi walked round the desk towards him. I said nothing. I'm quite good at saying nothing. She stopped inches away from him. "Why did you laugh when my husband winced in pain, Mr Collier?"

'My husband', I wondered when I would get over the surprise of hearing that. He sneered at her, breathing out as he did so. She turned away wrinkling her nose in disgust at the smell of his breath. And Collier lost it. "You think we don't know about you, what a common little gold digger you are, showing off round half the county and coming over all Lady Muck when everyone knows what a slut you really are."

He was very nearly frothing at the mouth now, spittle forming on his lips as he shouted. Robbi glanced at me warningly. I was not to intervene. She smiled at him. "There, there, Mr Collier. You'd better calm down before you have a heart attack or a fit. Did you know you were foaming at the mouth?"

He went purple. His fists clenched and unclenched and he lunged at her, arms outstretched. Luke Warburton threw himself over the desk. I tripped him as Robbi took one step to the right, paused and delivered an extraordinarily fast and exquisitely timed knuckle punch to the throat. He crashed forward narrowly missing Annette's desk and hit the stained, nylon carpet with a floor–shaking thud, raising a small cloud of dust. Robbi looked down at Luke Warburton still lying on his back where I had tripped him and then turned to his wife. "Do you know, Annette, I think your husband's looking up my skirt?"

I stepped over the stertorously breathing body and picked up the newspaper. "Are you going to stop this, Mr Warburton?"

"I can't. He has editorial control."

I looked at his wife. She nodded. I spoke to her. "You know what I'll do, don't you?"

She nodded again and sighed. "You'll injunct and if we distribute, you'll sue."

"And if there is a court case, what will the judge do?"

She shook her head, tears running down her cheeks. Robbi rushed round the desk towards her. "Stop it, John. Don't get upset, Annette. We'll sort something out." She turned and glared at me. "Won't we, John?"

She put her arm round Annette and held out her hand to me. I supplied the requisite handkerchief. Annette blew her nose. I controlled my anger and thought, walking slowly up and down the room. From what our private investigator friend, Palmer, had told me on the phone earlier, the North Cotswolds Gazette was not exactly over–funded. I crouched down over the flabby body and looked in its jacket. It had a wallet. I went through the contents: two credit cards, one debit card, two for the price of one voucher for an Indian restaurant. These were not indications of wealth. I dug out my phone. Palmer answered at the second ring. He was intrigued.

"Two calls in one day. Is there are something I should know?"

"Probably. Here's an account number on a debit card."

I read out the sort code as well. He sighed.

"Do you want me to phone you back, Palmer?"

"Yep."

Warburton had got up and was brushing himself off.

"So, what's the story with your man here, Mr Warburton?"

It was a sorry tale. They had bought the newspaper

virtually sight unseen and their inadequate due diligence had missed a ten-thousand-pound debt to the printers. Collier had appeared on the scene as an enthusiastic, volunteer reporter. The day the invoice arrived from the printer Collier had been hanging round the office. He had joined in the general despair and had 'suddenly' had a brainwave. His mother had died two months previously and had left him some money. You may guess the rest. Collier's London lawyer had insisted on the changes to the Mem & Arts and the shareholder agreement. Less than a week later their pet worm was already beginning to turn.

My phone rang – Palmer again. That was quick. I answered it. "I thought I was supposed to be phoning you, Palmer."

"Whatever. He's had three lump sums of twenty k each paid into his account on the fifteenth of each of the last three months. He also gets a one-thousand-pound allowance from his mother each month."

"Didn't that stop when she died?"

"What do you mean, died? I ran a few checks and mummy is alive and well and living in a nursing home in Surbiton."

"So where did the lump sums come from?"

"Trying to track those now, John. Funny thing is that whoever paid them in was trying not to be found. It's going to take a while. So, am I invited to Fosse, pretty please?"

"When can you be here?"

"Day after tomorrow. Love to Robbi."

He rang off. I looked at the Warburtons. They looked

at me. I looked at Robbi. She glowered at me. It was my turn to sigh. What would I do with a local paper? "OK. Mrs Warburton – Annette – can we find some common ground?"

She smiled nervously.

"You will not publish this story."

She nodded her head vigorously. Her husband shook his. "We'll order this edition to be pulped which, by the way, won't stop the story getting out, but at that point we close down and then the story will definitely get out."

"Why will you have to close down?"

"Because Collier didn't pay off the printer."

The man on the floor stirred and snored. I kicked him experimentally. He didn't move. I kicked him again for luck. "How much?"

"The original ten k plus interest, plus the aborted print run."

"Twenty k ish?"

"Probably."

"Due when?"

"Ninety days ago."

He looked at his wife. "I'm so sorry Ann–Ann, I really fucked up."

I sat down on a dusty chair and thought for a while. I hated making decisions on so little information and I was flying blind here. Robbi walked over and crouched in front of me. She pushed her hair back and stared up at me. I sighed and passed her my phone. She flicked through the addresses and dialled the number of Tony McElroy, our broker.

"Karen? Robbi. Yes. How's your new man? Really? Oh blimey. Oh, well, good luck with that then. The dishy husband? He gets dishier every day, but hey, I'm biased. Is Tony there, Karen? Thanks, dear."

A short pause.

"Morning, Tony. Very well thanks, and so's the man."

I looked at the Warburtons. Luke Warburton was stroking his wife's hair and she was looking up at him seemingly oblivious to our phone conversation. I stood up and walked towards them. "Annette, can you show me the latest invoice from the printer?"

Listlessly she passed me a piece of paper. I looked at it and verified the name and address on Robbi's phone. She raised her eyebrows at me, still speaking to Tony McElroy.

"Can you take authority on the phone to do a transfer, Tony?"

I held four fingers up to her. "For forty k. And my part of the password is…" She turned to window and spoke quietly. "Here's John, Tony."

She passed the phone to me.

"Morning, Tony. All well?"

"Morning, John. Yes, thanks. What's your part of the password?"

"No idea, Tony."

I turned to the window and watched the Warburtons in the reflection. If this were a scam…

"You don't improve, John. You know that, don't you?"

"I do know that, Tony, yes."

"By the way, got an interesting prospect. You know the place where Robbi used to work?"

"Continental Atlantic?"

I pressed the speaker button on the phone and held it out for Robbi to hear.

"The very same. Going down the plughole unless someone can rescue it. Capital adequacy issues. I was just thinking. Remember the idea we talked about, John."

"The consultancy?"

"You got it. Well, this could be your ideal vehicle. Needs a chairman though!"

"Not me, thanks, Tony."

Robbi waved her arm and mouthed something at me. I caught on. "Hang on, Tony, we may have a solution for you on this one. What's the timescale?"

"Couple of weeks. OK, now you have both provided total verification of your identity – hah! What's the amount again?"

I glanced at the Warburtons again. They were staring at me intently. I stared back at him.

"Forty k, Tony."

"Where to?"

I kept an eye on Warburton as I read out the bank sort code and account details. He stood up mouthing at me and shaking his head. Annette took his hand and pulled him back. She also was watching me closely. I turned off the phone's speaker.

"Make it a Faster payment if you can, please, Tony. Time is of the essence." I put the phone down and looked at Annette. "So why did I do that, Annette?"

She shook her head. "Either because you can afford forty thousand pounds just to keep your name out of the paper or you're more impulsive than you look."

I nodded. "Or both. Your next problem to solve,

however, is going to be replacing the story. Any ideas?"

Luke Warburton turned to his reporter's notebook, flicking back through the pages of neat shorthand. He shook his head. "Nothing that we can do in the time."

I walked across the obstacle strewn office. I had never got local papers. By all rights they shouldn't be around anymore what with the Internet. They'd only ever been vehicles for advertising anyway, the editorial just filling the gaps between the car and house sales, the small ads and the hatches, matches and dispatches. I stopped walking, took a breath prior to speaking and stopped. I looked at Robbi. She was watching me with a tolerant smile.

"How old did you say Grace was?"

She looked suspicious. "Just sixteen. Why?"

I turned to Luke. "The Comprehensive is running a trial scheme for disruptive pupils. It's equine therapy and the first results have been spectacular. The worst of the girls has stopped offending and her school results have improved exponentially and the school's a pioneer in this field. It'll probably save thousands off the education budget. That's a good story isn't it? Suits bleeding heart liberals and die-hard Tories alike."

He shrugged. "It's OK. How do you know about it?"

"Jooohn!"

It's amazing how many syllables she could get in to a single syllable word. Luke Warburton looked from me to her.

"It's you, Lady Hannay? You're the equine therapist?"

Robbi shook her head. "I'm just teaching her to ride in exchange for mucking out our horses. Horses are good for troubled children. Everyone knows that. And she desperately needed someone to talk to as well, someone who had the time to listen, that's all." She turned in my direction. "John, she's a kid for God's sake."

I opened my mouth to apologise, but she put her hand across it and moulded her body against mine in the way that I do quite like (and she bloody knows it), shook her head at me, smiled at Annette and addressed Luke.

"Do you know Catherine Simmons, the head teacher at...?"

"Yes."

"Then ask her."

"But wouldn't it...?"

"No."

Annette was already on the phone. Robbi moved round in front of me, putting her arms round my neck. "You are a clever little baronet, aren't you?"

"You don't mind?"

"Not at the moment."

"Um, Robbi?"

She looked over her shoulder at Annette who was waving the phone at her.

"Mrs Simmons wants a word."

Robbi let go of me and took the receiver. "Hi, Cath, how you? Yes. No, I don't mind. Can you clear the school governors in time? Well, I suppose so. Which one was that? Oh God. I'm sure he's a perv. All right, all right. What's his number?"

Within two minutes Robbi had the governors' agreement (in return for agreeing to consider becoming a governor herself). I watched the chaos that is a newsroom (however small) descend. Annette stepped over Collier as if he had always been there. I focussed on the body. I phoned Paul. As he was just up the road, I gave him directions. Collier stirred and muttered something – all activity stopped. He breathed again and snored shudderingly. The doorbell rang and Paul was there. He gave the room his normal quick scan and stood by the door, his back to the wall, assessing the situation and the people. Only when he had considered them to be harmless did he move towards the body. He crouched beside it, felt the pulse, sniffed at the breath and winced. "He's dead drunk."

With an effort he pushed the body on to its side and examined the man, going through the pockets I had ignored. He sat back on his heels. "You hit him, Robs?"

She nodded agreement.

"Pull the punch?"

"Of course."

It was his turn to nod. He stood up and studied the desks. An old metal bar used for holding newspaper pages down was half hidden on Luke Warburton's desk. With a handkerchief round his fingers, he picked it up and laid it across the floor beneath the body. My phone rang.

"Hallo?"

"Morning, John. Billy Thornton here."

Now there's a coincidence, Billy. I was just about to phone you."

"And why might that be, John?"

"Well, if by any chance, you were able to come round to the offices of the North Cotswolds Gazette, I could tell you in person."

"Now there's another coincidence, John."

The phone went dead and door buzzer rang again. I picked up the only copy of the newspaper and crossed the room, talking over my shoulder. "Try and get him into a sitting position, Paul."

Chief Inspector Thornton stepped in. I held up the newspaper and pointed to the body. Billy nodded and raised a hand at Paul who had managed to get Collier into a slumped but seated position against Warburton's desk. Billy read the front page. Then he looked at me. I talked for two minutes. He shook his head.

"What was that idiot thinking of, trying to publish a story like that? You'd have sued the arse off the Gazette.... which has no money so would have closed and the bad publicity about you would still be out there. That's what you're thinking isn't it?"

I didn't reply. He looked at the body on the floor. "What's the matter with him, Paul?"

"I don't know, Billy. I thought it was just a drunken stupor, but what with his weight and the smell of his breath I'm beginning to wonder about a diabetic coma. Better get an ambulance I guess."

The policeman nodded, crouched beside him, sniffed, nodded again and radioed. Paul lifted the head and pointed to the bruise on the throat.

"What do you reckon caused that, Billy?"

Thornton glanced round and pointed at the steel rule. I stepped back and watched the chaos begin to resolve itself. An idea crossed my mind. I smiled and dialled Harry Livesey. Harry was a 'friend' who had half helped and half hindered us in our early battle against Medina.

He had, however, one useful and redeeming future – well two actually. He spoke many languages and he was a brilliant horse rider. I mean, I'm good, but Harry, well…

The phone rang. He answered. "What?"

"What do you mean, 'what'? Here's your close friend John Hannay calling you for a catch up and you just say 'what'."

"Sorry, I should have said: 'what the fuck do you want, Hannay, you toe rag?'"

I nudged Robbi. "I just wondered if the great horse rider, Harry Livesey, were in the area and wanted to pop round this arvo and demonstrate his horsey skills?"

"Why?"

"Well, there's this teenage girl."

"On my way…"

The phone went dead. I explained to the Warburtons that one of the country's leading Polo players would be there to show Grace some riding tricks. The ambulance men had arrived and were looking at the body on the floor in horror. Luke Warburton had typed out a statement for Billy and signed it and I promised to report to the Station with mine later. Billy turned to Paul. "Going to be at the Clay shoot on Saturday?"

Paul smiled. "Why?"

"Oh no reason." Billy Thornton laughed. "Just that some people who weren't at the clay shoot last time didn't believe the shooting of two simultaneously fired clays at one hundred and eighty degrees to each other was possible."

He raised a hand at us and left. Warburton looked up at me from his desk, grinning with delighted enthusiasm.

He looked suddenly nervous. "How are we going to repay you, John?"

"Well, you can do me one favour."

Both of them looked at me. They were worried looks. Robbi smiled.

"You can bring us a copy of the new edition of the paper next week when you come round for supper at Fosse? Next Saturday – and please don't bring a bottle or flowers or anything and no dressing up either. Now what's your next move re the Incredible Hulk?"

They looked at each other, before Luke spoke. "Well, we go to the bank and see if they'll extend the overdraft."

"They won't."

"How can you be sure."

I glanced at his wife. "Tell him, Annette."

"We have nothing to secure the overdraft on."

"And, if you'll forgive me for sounding like the Dutch Uncle of myth, you have to get rid of Collier before you do anything else. Annette, I'm not a lawyer, but the revised Mem & Arts looked to be highly suspect to me."

"They're legal, John. We signed them."

"In that case we'll have to make him an offer he can't refuse."

Warburton looked half amused. "Does that involve Robbi going round and beating him up again?"

I thought about this. "Whoever gave Collier the money it didn't come from his dead mother who is currently alive and well and living in a nursing home in Surbiton."

They stared at me.

"And, whoever gave Collier the money, it seems

likely they gave it to him to cause mischief – possibly to you – possibly to me. That story would have been out today and if I hadn't met you, I *would* have sued you and closed the paper."

They were still staring at me.

"So, one of my colleagues will have a look at Collier's computer and see what we can find out. If we find evidence of illegal activity, we can use it either to force him to sell his shareholding back to you for a sensible price or find out who is behind him and have a little talk with him. Either way you get your paper back and I find out who is trying to damage me."

Annette spoke first. "I'm a lawyer, John. I have to be careful."

"You're not in practice. Luke?"

"I don't know, John. I've made up my mind that this is going to be Annette's call. I've made enough cock ups already."

It was my turn to stare at them. "Maybe I have, to quote the forty third president of the USA, misunderestimated you two. So, just to be clear. I operate on the *cet animal est très méchant* principle. I have been attacked. I will defend myself. You guys want out, that's your call. I shall say no more about it."

Robbi was more diplomatic. "What he's trying to say in his inept way is that whether you work with us or not we are going to find out what this was all about and why John was attacked on Sunday. He very nearly lost the use of his right wrist and you know how serious that is to a man."

"So, it was you who was attacked, John? Can you tell

us about it... off the record?"

I told them. Annette asked the first question. "And Chief Inspector Thornton has got this evidence."

"That's why he was coming to talk to you. It seems to be insane."

I regretted that word. Robbi stiffened and looked round at me. I changed the subject. "Robbi, if you take the Landrover, Paul can give me a lift back to Fosse."

Robbi looked at me sharply and I raised my eyebrows at her enquiringly. She narrowed her eyes. "Hannay... I'm warning you. Paul, I hold you responsible."

Paul looked up at her. For what?"

She glared some more and left to pick up Grace. Paul looked at me. "Come on, then."

"How did you know?"

"Because everyone carries their front door key with them and when I frisked that fat bastard just now, he didn't have it so you had to have taken it."

We did go back to Fosse as I had promised Robbi, but only to pick up an external hard drive. Paul disappeared into the lodge house and emerged carrying a cardboard box with an old computer monitor in it. He drove us into Carterton. En route, he gave me the simplest of briefings.

"We're delivery men. Put this baseball cap on and take your jacket off. We look for the house. We park the van. You go and knock on the door and I come in behind you holding the box up high. As soon as I am obscuring you from the road, use the key and we'll go straight in. No looking around, no recce, just in and out, quick as we can."

My phone bleeped. It was a text message from Robbi. *Please, please don't do anything dangerous.* Now I felt like a complete shit. Then I wondered if that was what she had intended. I was still very new to this relationship thing.

It went exactly according to plan. We pushed through the morning's junk mail and were in his living room. The thin curtains were drawn and a pale, crepuscular light illuminated the remains of many days and many pizzas and coke cans and chocolate papers and crisp packets and dirty socks, sweat stained tee shirts, a giant flat screen TV and... aaah. It was a relatively new Mac Book Pro. I looked for somewhere to sit and eventually knelt in front of it promising myself I would wash these trousers tonight. The download was going to take six minutes. I warned Paul. He shrugged and went to the front door shouting something indistinguishable over his shoulder. He returned soon after waving a screwdriver.

"A Ford Mondeo has just stopped up the road. How long?"

"Done." I pocketed the hard drive and picked up the box, grunting at the pain in my right wrist. I held it high in front of me looking down at the step as Paul called a goodbye over his shoulder and slammed the door. He hurried past me, opened the back of the van and I climbed in, putting the computer box on the floor.

He whispered. "Put Radio One on loud."

He picked up a clipboard, seated himself on the floor of the van with one of the rear doors open and started to make notes and yelled at me to turn it down. My phone bleeped. It was Paul: *Send me a text.* I obliged. I could see him in the mirror as he stood up, took his phone out of his pocket, read the text and then shouted to me again. "Last delivery. Turn that bloody radio down."

He stretched, wrote something else on the clipboard, shut the back doors and got into the driver's seat. "OK, let's see if we fooled them."

He drove down the road away from the parked car, backed into a drive and swung the van round to head past the Mondeo, leaning forward to obscure my face from the watchers and laughing loudly as he did so. The car didn't move, but neither of us relaxed until we were out of Carterton. "Glad I changed the number plates now."

"What?"

He grinned. "Robbi called me when you were getting the hard drive at Fosse and told me to do it. I always keep a spare set for emergencies."

CHAPTER SIX

I was staring at my phone again still trying not to make 'that' call when Tony McElroy called at five past nine the next morning. "Just tell me who you've got in mind for the chair, John. I spoke to the administrator last night and I have the feeling they'll bite your hand off."

I was off guard and not concentrating. "Sorry, Tony, I was busy yesterday and I haven't spoken to her yet."

I bit my tongue too late. Before I could say another word, he jumped in. "Hah. Got you. Hah!"

Shit. I yawned ostentatiously.

"It's Emma Fitzgerald, isn't it? Go on, I'm not going to tell anyone..."

"Got to go now, Tony. Speak later."

He was still laughing when I put the phone down. I called my old boss, The Boss – Emma Fitzgerald. "Em?"

"Super Trader! How's Lady Beautiful? What do you bloody want?"

"How bored are you, Em?'

"I'm never bored. I love my job."

The phone went down. My bleeper went off. The dogs started barking. Robbi squeaked. Palmer had arrived. I went out the side door and round to the stable yard where Robbi was hugging Palmer who was looking decidedly embarrassed. He glanced across and I toasted him with my coffee mug. My phone rang.

REVENGE

"John?"

Hmmm, John, not Super Trader. "Yes, Em."

"What's the deal? Are you involved?"

I told her. "Interested?"

"What's your involvement?"

"I don't know yet. I'll invest if you'll be chair."

"Got to be more than that, John, if you want me in. Talk to Robbi."

"OK, Em... Em?"

"Yes?"

"You serious?"

"Yes. Now fuck off while I go and find a kitten to decapitate."

I called Tony. "I need data. All of it. On a hard drive. Today."

The chugging of Miranda's ancient Beetle drowned out conversation. Our Estate Manager jumped out of the car and ran to join the group hug. I perched on the old horse trough clutching my lukewarm coffee mug and watched them. A year ago, and I would have gone back inside just so I could be on my own. Not that I'd ever minded crowds. I had even liked, occasionally, having one or even two friends, but I admit to having preferred my own company and I maintained an active objection to being the centre of attention of any sort or manner. 'Me' was all I had relied on since the age of eight and I had grown very used to me over the years. Odd way to put it really – made me sound smug. Smug – moi?

Breakfast finished, Palmer sat back and rubbed his hands. "Show me the money!"

We went into the study. It took ten minutes to bring him up to speed and show him the hard drive. "All right,

51

John. All right. Understood. Well?"

"Well what, Palmer?"

"Well, is there anything else you want to tell me, Hannay?"

"Er, no."

"Well fuck off, then."

Palmer's social skills had not improved with the passing of time. My bleeper alerted me again just before lunch. The motorcycle courier had arrived with Tony McElroy's figures on a hard drive. I took it into the study and commandeered the second Mac. Continental Atlantic was a dismal story – disciplined twice by the FCA, a series of complaints from disgruntled clients, in breach of their capital adequacy ratio on four occasions in the last twelve months. I turned to the accounts. Not that they would tell me anything if they had a halfway decent accountant. Last year's audited accounts showed that they did, but this year's monthly management accounts told a very different story. Nothing had been manipulated at all. Well, well, well. A hand touched my shoulder. I looked up and smiled at her. "I was just thinking of you in your little pleated skirt when I was in my little glass office."

Robbi peered over my shoulder and came round in front of me to sit on my lap, still staring at the screen. I looked round for Palmer.

"Where's he gone? Has he found out anything?"

"He said to say he had no intention of waiting for you to deign to notice his existence and he's gone for a bike ride. You've missed lunch and tea."

She looked at my spreadsheet. "So, what's the score?"

"It's OK. The fundamentals are sound, but one of the directors, probably the chairman, has been creaming off profits like it's going out of fashion – recently illegally."

How come?"

"You're not allowed to take dividends as a director if your company is loss making. There is no way this company was profitable for the last year."

"So, what's the point of buying it?"

"Client list – massive and probably willing to give it another go under new management especially if the new boss is as famous as Emma Fitzgerald. FCA registered, sales team in place... and if we play it right about a million in cash."

"What?"

I grinned as she stared at the accounts on screen. She saw my reflection, turned round to slap my head and then decided not to, curling her fingers round my neck and kissing me instead. She leaned in and kissed me again, biting and pulling at my bottom lip with her small white teeth as she did so.

Palmer walked in. "Get a room for God's sake you two."

Robbi surreptitiously wiggled her bottom on my lap. "Good bike ride?"

"Mind your own business."

I shook my head at him. "You know I think we had both forgotten what a delight you could be, Palmer. Hadn't we, Robbi? Come on, what's on the hard drive?"

He sat down and tapped the keyboard to reactivate the Mac. "Well, to be honest it was dead easy. Chummy is into BDSM."

We looked blank, well I mean I know I looked blank

and I would like to hope that Lady Hannay did as well.

"Someone hacked his computer – oh for God's sake, bondage, dominance, sadism, masochism – life in the provinces: sheesh!"

Palmer turned the screen round to show us. Collier hadn't deleted the incriminating pictures. He secured them with a password that had taken Palmer only thirty minutes to break. I thought about the sixteen stone of miserable blubber and almost felt sorry him.

"Anyway, he's a sad sack of shit, but the guy who's hit on him is a very different sack of something or other. He's used a Hotmail account and a proxy server and he's pretty much impossible to trace. I thought about pretending to be Sad Sack and sending him a whingeing email, but I thought you would prefer it if they didn't find out that we'd hacked him."

I agreed.

"Now his bank account is a bit more helpful. Would you believe the idiot used the same password?"

There was a momentary hiatus while Robbi and I looked marginally discomfited. Palmer continued obliviously. "He's had those three times twenty k go into his account. It's from an offshore account in Guernsey. But that doesn't mean we can't trace it and when we do, we'll use a little algorithm of my invention to see where else it goes."

"Where it goes?"

Palmer pushed his glasses on to his forehead and rubbed his eyes. "I think 'it' is quite a sophisticated program which means it cost a few bob. You don't spend that kind of money just to pay off some little creep in the wilds of Oxfordshire. This could be something quite big. Oh, and that car registration number you gave me..."

"Yes?"

"It's a fake number."

"You're kidding."

"Nope, good eh?"

He rubbed his hands together gleefully and went to find Paul. Robbi and I headed to the kitchen where I stared at Continental Atlantic's accounts again and wondered why, or indeed if, I was the only one to have seen the mistake. I needed an accountant. Robbi was pondering over some papers across the table. I moved slowly and surreptitiously to sneak the last of the coffee from the Cafetière. She hadn't noticed, she hadn't seen... God, she moved faster than a striking snake. I was in receipt of the basilisk stare.

"Hannay?"

"Yes, dearest."

"Do sod off..."

"Yes, dearest."

She poured the remains of the coffee into her cup and grinned at me over the rim.

"Do we know any accountants, Robbi?"

"What?"

"Do we...?"

"I heard what you said."

"I suppose it was the juxtaposition of you stealing the coffee and me asking about accountants that confused you."

"Hannay?"

"Yes, dearest?"

"If you call me dearest once more, I shall hit you."

"Again."

"That was a slap because you were trying to sneak the last of the coffee."

"It was my bad wrist."

"You lying toad. David Thatcher."

"Who's he?"

"He does Andy Barraclough's accounts for his wine shop in Northleach. Now..."

That sounded ominous.

"The flat."

It was ominous. My flat in Mayfair had not been mentioned before. It was the last direct physical and emotional link I had to my mother, to my family if such it could be called, but it was also unresolved 'stuff' – a place of horrors and twenty–eight years of nightmares. I looked at her. She looked at me. I took a mental deep breath.

"Sell it, Robbi."

Robbi watched me. She stood, swung her long legs across the table and perched, facing me with her feet on the arms of my chair. I sat back and waited for the moment to pass.

"Sell it, Robbi. Really."

She slid down on to my lap, put her arms round me and rested her head on my shoulder.

"Just sell it, Robbi. Just sell it."

And still I hadn't made the call.

CHAPTER SEVEN

She was in fishing mode and there was nothing I could do about it, trapped as I was with / by her on the London train from Swindon the next morning.

"So, do we want a London base, John? And if we do what can we afford? I mean from what the agent at Foxton's said you should get a ridiculously large amount for the flat, but where would you want to have a house in London, John? Westminster?"

Robbi claimed to have fallen in love with Westminster ever since we had first stayed in an hotel there. I claimed it was me she had fallen for and the location was less than wholly relevant. I was regarded with a jaundiced eye, two jaundiced eyes in fact. She tapped her fingers on the table to emphasise her words. "So, if we had met in Scunthorpe, I would want to buy a house in Scunthorpe, would I, John?"

"But I would never have gone to Scunthorpe. In any event you met me in Cannon Street."

"No, I didn't, I met someone called Alex Bruce. Stupid name."

We grinned at each other. She reached into her Tardis of a shoulder bag and shoved some papers across to me. Estate Agent details – I might have guessed. I browsed through them half–heartedly. I had never had to buy or sell a property; you could call that one of the few advantages of having your parents murdered when you were a child. Robbi clambered round to sit beside me.

"I like this one."

This one was a mews house off Jermyn Street.

"But..."

"Joooohn!"

That was a warning. Oh dear. I stared at the grammatically incompetent house descriptions and reached a tentative conclusion. "Look, I'm going to be crap at this. I mean I've never had to do it and the only home I care about is Fosse Manor and you're obviously going to be brilliant at it so why don't you just go ahead and buy a place for us?"

She studied me, looked down at the house details and drummed her fingers. I could see she was planning her next line of attack. I jumped in quickly. "Look, everything that's happened in our relationship has been one way so far. You've had no say in any of it. I'd really, really like this to be your decision, Robbi."

"You do know that you're pathetically transparent, don't you?"

I raised my eyebrows.

"You just can't be arsed to put any effort into this, can you? What happens if I choose a place you hate?" She watched me warily and carried on. "You do know that married couples are supposed to make decisions together, don't you?"

I counter attacked. "You won't choose a place I don't like. I know you won't. You know you won't. Go on, do this for me. Please."

I smiled winningly. She glared at me, then snorted with laughter and leaned in to kiss me. "You are such an upper class tosser. That silly simper of yours is enough to make anyone want to scratch your dreamy, grey eyes out. All right, John Richard, all right. I'll buy our house in London and you'd better bloody like it. But on one condition..."

"What?"

"I want parameters."

Do you know, it's never worth trying to beat a woman. By the time I'd finished 'offering' her parameters I may as well have gone out and bought a bloody house myself. I steeled myself for the meeting with Dave at the flat.

* * *

Dave stepped past me at the front door, placing his stethoscope on the panel. He listened, looked at me, shrugged and held out his hand for the key, indicating that we should stand back. He unlocked the heavy mortise and listened again. He turned the handle and pushed the door gently. It swung open with that familiar soft squeak and bumped gently against the doorstop. Nothing. Dave repeated the process with every door while we waited in the hall corridor, Robbi clutching my hand tightly. It was if I had never been away: it was as if I had never set foot in here before. I opened the drawing room shutters and pushed the upper sash window down letting the noise from the street filter in. The door buzzer rang and I was pleased to notice that even Dave jumped. A wicked little throwing knife appeared in his hand.

"Hello?"

It was the Estate Agent. Robbi took over. I waited until she and the agent had left the room and opened the safe behind the Rex Whistler portrait of my grandfather. I took out all the papers, pushed them into Robbi's bag and walked across to the window. I saw Dave start to move, caught a glimpse of something on the roof of the house opposite and then the wind from the sniper's bullet made me stagger. I hit the floor with Dave on top of me. He looked down at me, put his finger to his lips and pointed. I rolled one way. He rolled the other. When he got to the window, he pushed the shutters back into place and peered through the crack.

"Lights."

I flicked the switch down.

"There a back door?"

"Side. Go right. Along the landing. Door at the end."

"Count thirty and open the shutters again, but stay out of sight."

"OK."

I heard Robbi's laugh and prayed she wouldn't find a reason to come in here for the next twenty-two seconds. I grabbed a make–up mirror out of her bag, pulled my phone out of my pocket and found Dave's number – six, five, four, three, two... here I come, ready or not! Lying on the floor I pulled the shutters back and slowly raised the mirror. It was just big enough. I tilted it left and right, up and further up. Got you. I called Dave.

"He's on the roof directly opposite the entrance."

"I'm there."

I had forgotten the extraordinary speed at which he could cover ground.

"Show him something, John."

He turned his phone off as I raised my arm. Then there were voices in the corridor. Jesus, no, Robbi, no, Robbi, no Robbi, no! I scrambled to my feet and tripped. My leg had gone to sleep. I hopped to the door. Another bullet smacked into the wall. Plaster dust floated to the floor. I whispered a pagan invocation for Dave to make it in time, took a deep breath and opened the door trying to fill it with my body. Robbi's eyes snapped open wide. She knew instantly. Don't say anything. Please don't say anything. My phone rang.

"I got him."

"I'm going to call Alan Cummins, Dave. You OK there for a few minutes?"

"No worries."

The agent put his laser measuring tool away.

"Well, Sir John, I don't think we'll have any problems selling this for you. Lovely property if I may say so. Remarkably big too. With those embassies round the corner, there's always people looking for this kind of thing."

Robbi hurried him. "Thanks very much, then. You'll call me about that other place won't you, but we have to rush now."

He left. I took her across to the wall and showed her the bullet holes and got my phone out. I had been driven into a corner. I made the call I had been trying to avoid for far too long. I called Major Alan Cummins of MI5.

"Morning, John. Long-time no hear. What's up?"

"Someone's just shot at me. In my flat. Dave Lord was with us. He's got the shooter."

"On my way."

As the receiver went down, I heard him say, "shit".

I felt the nausea and the ache in the base of my back again. One of the few times I had felt that adrenaline ache had been the last time I was here – only that time it was me who had instigated the shooting. I called Dave to let him know Alan was on his way and sat down heavily. Robbi took my pulse. I shook my head at her. It would be fast, but not that fast.

"Oh, John."

"I'm so sorry, Robbi."

She hugged me.

We watched the arrival of Alan's team through the window. A black Mercedes People Carrier with tinted windows screeched to a halt. Alan was out of the front door first, looking up at me. I pointed towards the entrance across the road. He flicked his fingers and three men bulked out with Kevlar waistcoats and holding machine pistols slid the rear door back and raced across the pavement. Pedestrians froze or scattered depending on their speed of reaction. Alan walked towards our door. I buzzed him in. He'd changed, I thought.

"How can Medina be orchestrating something like this, Alan? Isn't he supposed to be under some kind of unbreachable security?"

"He is. I'm still managing to get a weekly report and I can tell you he's under medication at an ultra-secure unit. Our friend the army psychiatrist says he's in a state of severe clinical depression and won't or can't face the fact that you beat him. He sees no–one apart from a profoundly deaf male nurse and the doctor."

Robbi had been sitting, head bowed, on the sofa – the sofa behind which I had hidden on the day I had killed a man whose name I still didn't know and whose face with the red hole just above the hairline I still saw in my nightmares. She stood up and stared straight into Alan's eyes. "What aren't you telling us, Alan?"

He shook his head. She narrowed her eyes.

"Even if you're not exactly lying, you're hiding something from us." She paused. "Why did you say you were *'still managing to get'* a report? What's happened, Alan?"

I caught up. That was the change I had noticed as he had come in. He had lost authority somehow. I joined in. "There's been a shake–up at MI5, hasn't there, Alan. Have you been demoted or just side–lined?"

"Side–lined, I think. Nothing I could put my hand on, but I am now seen as a threat to the current incumbent's job. Then there's the Medina effect."

I glanced at the ceiling light. It was still on so I turned it off, pushed the sash window back up and screwed up the old–fashioned sash keys, swung the shutters back into the walls and then walked slowly across the room to peer at the bullet holes again – so little damage to something like a wall. It gave me time to think. Alan and Robbi watched me.

"Was it you or Mr Holroyd who said there was going to be a great closing of ranks around Medina?"

He shrugged, still watching me. I thought through the issues. "But the ranks didn't close in time and we broke through and now... Oh I see. I see. Oh."

Robbi glared. Alan watched.

"They've all lost money, haven't they?"

"Who have? John, make sense!"

"Whoever put the money up for Medina to bet against Sterling back in July. Who were they, Alan?"

"We don't know, John. That's the point."

Robbi stepped back to look at him. She cocked her head and then looked at me with a raised eyebrow. "You want us to find out, don't you? You want to use John as bait for the trap."

He smiled up at us both, unabashed now that the truth was out, now that he no longer had to dissemble. "Think of it as more of a lure than a bait."

I stood still and thought about that. Hmmm.

Dave was watching us from the door. "Either way, Major, you're putting my sister and my brother–in–law in the way of danger again."

"Either way, Mr Lord, yes."

Dave grunted. "Just so long as we know."

I glanced at him. "Aren't you going to tell him that he can't do this to us, that I'm not well yet, that Robbi's life is too valuable?"

"If you wanted to say all that, John, you could have shown Major Cummins the door ten seconds ago, but you didn't, did you?"

Robbi's head was down again, but I could tell she was smiling behind her screen of golden hair. The door buzzer went. I looked at Dave. He picked up the entry phone, grunted and pressed the door release button. He answered Alan's unasked question.

"Sergeant Skinner, sir."

"Didn't he serve with you, Mr Lord?"

"Yes, sir. Good man."

Sergeant Skinner entered, registering the room and its occupants in the way I have come to associate with the SAS.

"Report."

"Small time hoodlum, sir. Ran a PNC check on him. Record as long as your arm, very violent, but this is his first time with a firearm so far as we know, sir."

"Who's he working for?"

Skinner glanced at me in surprise and looked back at Alan who just nodded at him. "He hasn't told us that yet, sir."

Dave growled. "Come on Malc, if you can't do it, give me five minutes with him."

Skinner smiled. "Just let the Major give us the word, Dave, and he's all yours."

I wondered what Alan's resources were now. He had managed, after all, to get a fully armed team round to my place within five minutes of my call – assuming they were from MI5. I studied the three men. They studied me back in turn. "Can we include Sergeant Skinner in our conversation, Alan?"

"That's up to him, John. Sergeant Skinner knows about Medina. Sergeant, do you want to be included in a conversation that may have a deleterious effect on your career."

Skinner straightened to attention. "Sir, I have no idea what deleterious means, sir."

Dave gave him his half smile. "It means you could end up cleaning the bogs at Catterick Camp, son."

"Oh well... sounds cushty then."

I arranged my thoughts in neat soldier like lines so I could share them with some neat soldiers.

One: As I had been attacked, someone in the know must have told the people who had lost their money that it was my fault.

Two: they believed that I should be eliminated which suggested they didn't believe they would get their money back and wanted revenge instead.

Three: if we could convince them that I still had most of the three billion left to me in the strange codicil to my grandfather's will, then they might decide it was worth keeping me alive so they could get their hands on it.

Four: this could be very dangerous as Robbi or any of the Fosse household would be an obvious kidnap and hostage target.

Five: why didn't I just run away and hide somewhere?

Six: because as Angela Arbuthnot had pointed out, Hannays are more than a little mad.

I didn't share 'five' or 'six'.

Alan straightened his legs in the armchair and studied the ceiling.

"Anything in our favour apart from the fact that we've got our hands on one of them – mind you he's a very, very small cog..."

Robbi raised three fingers. "Three, not one."

We looked at her. "You haven't commented on the damage to John's beautiful face, Alan."

"Oh, that. Well, I had heard on the grapevine that John picked a fight with the North Cotswold Hunt. Very in character if I may say so."

Robbi explained while I played down any attempts to make my role sound heroic. The last thing I wanted was for British Intelligence to assume I was up for any piece of lunacy their fevered imaginations might concoct. Alan held up his hand. Robbi smiled at him. "Time to see Mr Holroyd."

"Precisely. I shall brief our Mr Holroyd now. Sergeant Skinner, for your information Mr Holroyd is a very, very senior civil servant with whom I work from time to time. For your further information, Mr Holroyd does not officially exist. I will leave you to puzzle through that conundrum. Shall we say four p.m. in the bar at BAFTA on Piccadilly? Mr Holroyd is a great lover of film and I understand he is at a screening there this afternoon. Sergeant Skinner?"

"Sir."

"I would be grateful if you would keep an eye out for Sir John and Lady Hannay for the rest of the day. Mr Lord will advise you on their situation."

* * *

The bar at BAFTA, the home of The British Academy of Film and Television Arts, was rammed. Mr Holroyd looked both lost and out of place among the poseurs, wannabe filmmakers and job–hunting technicians. We abandoned the idea of talking there and walked out onto Piccadilly. Mr Holroyd was a member (inter alia, as he put it) of Dartmouth House, the club for the English Speaking Union in Charles Street. We sat on sofas in the empty Wedgwood Room while Mr Holroyd rubbed his glasses on his tie absent–mindedly. The tea arrived. He thanked the waitress and Robbi poured without having to be asked. She winked at me. I saw Alan smile. Mr Holroyd looked up.

"I can't see the point in pretending that I am sorry to have you two involved again. Alan had been squirming on a hook of indecision for some days as to when to contact you when your call came in. The issue is very different this time, though, I fear. In many ways it is much more dangerous than dealing with Medina."

The door opened and a tweed-clad old buffer huffed at us, came in, selected a Daily Telegraph from the rack, huffed at us some more and went out.

"We had trouble, as you will remember, in trying to ascertain the source of Medina's wealth but we have an inkling now, no more, wouldn't you agree, Alan, of where the funds came from. Quite a few people were involved, John, and they are very unhappy to have lost so much. They have also now learned about you."

"What have they learned?"

Mr Holroyd removed his glasses and stared at me myopically. "That you were left a huge fortune in gold by your grandfather, that you used some of it to fight Medina Ventures during last year's G7 conference, and that you still have a big chunk of it left."

"Was it that little shit ffitch who told them?"

"We don't know. He was on sick leave for some time after the events of July and August and it is only recently that such events have started to recur. We don't know how 'ill' he was and how much he remembers, but you were never on his Christmas card list at the best of times, were you, John? So please enlighten me as to the current situation."

We talked. Holroyd sipped tea, listened and asked the pertinent question. "Perhaps you can outline your strategic approach to the next stage, Roberta, and then we can see onto which square we should move."

Robbi looked at me. "Sicilian defence."

Mr Holroyd nodded in an annoyingly mandarin manner. "Interesting, interesting. In this case, though, you are Black and it should be White who takes the first pawn and then there is an exchange from which Black tries to draw territorial advantage in the centre of the board. I am not aware that you have any pawns to sacrifice."

Extended metaphors bring me out in a rash. I thought about pawns. "ffitch again."

"Correct me if I am wrong, John, but Mr ffitch is not your pawn to dispose of."

"They don't know that."

He wiped his glasses and held them up to the pale light filtering in from the Mayfair evening. The diesel engine of a Black Cab depositing a passenger in the street outside vibrated the window catch. He sighed. "The problem with chess is that you can't cheat at it."

Robbi shook her head despairingly. "You can if you pinch pieces off the board when your opponent isn't looking."

Alan stood up and tightened the window catch. The vibration stopped. Something niggled at the back of my brain and I tried to think back to the first time we had met Mr Holroyd in his official Jaguar in Clerkenwell. But

I didn't know him then. Maybe I thought I knew him now, but didn't. Whichever – there was still too much talk of pawns. I looked round the table. Robbi was sipping her tea and watching me. Alan was doing the same and Mr Holroyd had fallen into what used to be called a brown study. I clumped my cup down on to my saucer and looked across the low table. Mr Holroyd looked at me. "I wasn't day dreaming, John. I was continuing the chess metaphor in my head." He paused and sunk his chin towards his chest and continued, looking at none of us. "Alan, are we able to put out a sufficiently strong story to convince those we wish to convince that ffitch is working for us and not them?"

"Yes, sir."

"You don't even need to think about it, Alan?"

"No, sir."

"But you do not wish to share your methods with us."

"No, sir."

"In that case, ffitch it is. I take it you will inform us when the disinformation is in the public arena, Alan."

"Yes, sir."

"In that case..."

I decided it was time to drop my little bomb. "I've had a summons to appear before the House of Commons Treasury Committee in a week's time. It's about BTD and Medina trading in the summer, um..."

I trailed off. Mr Holroyd had frozen, cup halfway to his mouth for the last, lukewarm sip of tea. A drip fell, unnoticed on to his tie. Alan sat forward, but my eyes were on Robbi. She stared at me. She glared at me. "When were you going to tell me this?"

"I.…" I shrugged. "There were seven other letters in the same post. They each contained a sheet of paper with just one letter. Together they made the word 'revenge'."

She sat back, looked at Alan out of the corner of her eye, and then addressed Mr Holroyd. "Mr Holroyd, can you brief John on the membership of the Treasury Committee. Someone on it might..."

She looked back across at Alan with her chin up. He smiled at her. Mr Holroyd had noticed the tea stain and was making hapless attempts to wipe it off his tie. It spread. "I think Alan will be able to help you there, Roberta, but I would like to think about the implications of all this if I may."

I nodded. I couldn't blame him for that. I had done nothing but think about it. There was one thing though. "Just one thing, Mr Holroyd..." He watched me. I always had the feeling that he was doing us the compliment of overestimating our abilities. "There was a lot of talk here about pawns. Were pawns on your mind?"

He smiled. Alan didn't move. "No more than normal, John. No more than normal. Don't misunderstand me. It would not be sensible at this stage to open with the Chicago Gambit. I am sure you take my point." He stood before I could answer and held out his hand. We shook all round and walked out and along Charles Street to pick up a taxi in Berkeley Square.

* * *

She sat down immediately in front of the iMac in our hotel suite while I, knowing my place, hung our clothes in the wardrobe. After two minutes she looked up at me.

"Oh dear."

"Oh dear, what?"

She pointed at the screen. I looked over her shoulder at the chessboard on screen and the Wikipedia comment below. She had highlighted the last sixteen words...

The Irish Gambit, Chicago Gambit, or Razzle Dazzle Gambit, is a weak chess opening that begins 1.e4 e5 2.Nf3 Nc6 3.Nxe5, intending 3...Nxe5 4.d4. White's pawns occupy the centre, **but the sacrifice of a knight for a pawn is a very high price to pay.**

* * *

By which time it was seven pm and time to go and meet The Boss. She was in thoughtful mode. We ate dinner at Scott's, which had never been my kind of place although Em appeared to be more than at home there. She watched me over the rim of her glass.

"So, tell me more about this company of yours."

So, I told her. She pushed away her plate. "All right, we have a retail brokerage with a client list of several thousand probably dissatisfied clients and a million in the bank which they don't know about. Yes?"

"Yes."

I waited to see where she would go with this and pinched a potato off Robbi's plate when I thought she wasn't watching. She speared it back off my fork in mid-air and grinned triumphantly.

"When you two have quite finished playing at love's young dream, perhaps you could tell me what the point of buying it would be."

"We set up a consultancy and remain totally independent..."

She interrupted, leaning forward across the table almost aggressively. "What's the fucking point of that?"

I paused and looked at her for a moment, replaying the conversation. "They want you out, don't they?"

She sat back and studied me then turned to Robbi. "That's why I want to work with him again, Robbi. He's a pain in the ass in an office – self-centred beyond all belief, the worst team player in the history of, of, of team playing, obsessive, opinionated, moody, uncommunicative, disruptive, insubordinate, but..."

Robbi was intrigued. "But what?"

"But he has intuition like only a woman should have. Did you realise they wanted me out?"

Robbi shook her head.

"It was the weirdest thing. For a month after our coup, I was the toast of the City. I took a long weekend in New York and they practically gave me a ticker tape parade on Wall Street. Then back in mid-September I began to feel a change. I could tell they wanted Max Jarrod to take over. He's a good man, though, Maxie. He met me off–site and just blurted out that the board thought I was past my sell–by–date and had lost my nerve after the coup. They'd brought in a new non–exec chairman – English and a fucking aristocrat – to try and make BTD part of the City elite and not just an upstart outsider. You know what the City can do."

I nodded my head slowly. I certainly did know. It's an extraordinary thought that in many ways the City of London is no more a part of the UK than Jersey, the Isle of Man or the Cayman Islands. It's a self–serving, money laundering, self–ruling state within a state – with its own representative in Parliament (the City Remembrancer, fyi) who sits just behind the Speaker and lobbies on behalf of the City – and its own revenues and taxes, which no one ever sees or hears about. There are some ten thousand souls who actually live in the City, but they have no power. The power lies with the money. Even the Queen has had to wait when she visited the City – just a little reminder to Buckingham Palace and Westminster of all the times the City has bailed out the monarchy and the government. And the City hadn't liked our coup.

"So, they forced BTD to take on a City chairman as revenge? They'll force you out and they're trying to have me killed."

Emma Fitzgerald didn't choke on her brandy or burst out laughing or swear. She straightened slowly, put her glass down, leaned towards Robbi and put her hand on her wrist. "Robbi. I am sorry."

Robbi shrugged. "Don't worry, Em. I'll protect him and God only knows he needs protecting. Can't shoot for shit and leads with his face."

She pointed at my fresh scars, turning my chin towards Emma with her hand to give her the full frontal of my forehead. I hadn't been going to tell her of our little adventures, but this was an opportunity to compare timings. I briefed her on the Hunt. I briefed her on the local newspaper and I briefed her on ffitch. The timing of her demise at BTD fitted with ffitch's reappearance at the Treasury. Another brandy arrived.

"OK. All right. I think it's time for Emma Fitzgerald to change jobs."

"Continental Atlantic?"

"You mean Fitzgerald–Hannay–McElroy? Too many 'oys' and 'ays', but whatever. We buy it out of administration and just let them trade on for a bit before changing direction."

"After we stop them selling worthless stocks."

I walked outside to call Tony McElroy. He lived in Chelsea. We took a taxi. By midnight we had the outlines of an agreement. Tony looked at his watch, smiled and phoned the Insolvency Practitioner who had, he claimed, told him he could call any time – day or night.

* * *

At seven the next morning we walked into BTD. It had only taken Robbi an hour to make up her mind what to wear. She informed me she had gone for the understated, business like look, although I would have thought by now, she would have learnt what a waste of time it was telling me anything like this – either it looked good on her or it didn't. It always did. The Boss was already in, looking fresh, working hard – how she did it I have no idea as I would have hated to see the state of her liver. I endured the ribald shouts. Robbi perched on Jocasta's desk swinging her long legs. The Children who had caused me so much grief in the trading battle against Medina, now fully fledged junior traders, came across shyly to shake my hand. Max looked at me nervously. I squeezed his shoulder reassuringly and nattered to him about la vie en general – about anything, in fact, that had nothing to do with our presence here today. At seven-thirty The Boss took the floor.

"Morning, children. Nothing much to report on money trading fronts today although if anyone can get advance indication of the US treasury report due at sixteen hundred today, it would be worth sharing with group. A little blip of trading from BTD in advance of that announcement would have an interesting effect tomorrow. OK, matters arising. I'm leaving. Maxie will probably be taking over, so it's goodbye from me and its..."

She picked up her bag and crossed to the lifts. There was silence. I was reminded of the silence after Dave roared at the Hunt members when I could hear my blood dripping on to the road. This time all I could hear was my heart beating – like Robbi said, sixty beats to the minute, regular as a clock. Annabelle laughed uncertainly. Jocasta stared at me.

"This anything to do with you, John?"

I shook my head. "Only in so far as she told us last night when we were having dinner."

"Why then? Why are you here?"

"Why do you think I'm here, Maxie?"

Max sighed deeply. "Because she didn't want us to see her break down and you're her only real friend and she wanted you to explain rather than me."

I took over the story telling. "They wanted her out. The City didn't like our coup. We took them all on and beat them and they don't like that. They're bad losers. I rather think that a lot of money was lost by a lot of very powerful people so getting rid of The Boss is their revenge. From now on BTD is part of the City elite. It's no longer a powerful upstart. It's inside and Em wouldn't fit in well with that. She'd never have let them tell her what to do. So, she's gone in her own time and in her own way, The Boss to the end. And it is the end – the end of an era. There'll never be anyone like her again."

I raised my coffee cup. "So, to The Boss."

The whole floor stood and raised their coffee mugs and teacups and saluted her in silence. The lift door pinged and Sebastian rushed towards the floor. His footsteps slowed. He stopped. He stared. I put my cup down and walked past him with Robbi by my side. At the lifts I turned. "She's gone, Sebastian; the greatest trader of her generation and the best boss in the City. She's gone. I hope they paid you your thirty pieces of silver in advance."

CHAPTER EIGHT

It was now just before eight o'clock and we were back in the glass walled sanctum that was Continental Atlantic. I had slipped in quietly after Robbi and The Boss and no one had even noticed me, so fixated were they on the sight in front of them. The Boss crooked a finger at Keith. He went. Robbi was catching up with Louise, the one-time receptionist, now trainee general manager, and part time girlfriend of Harry – although thinking about it, the 'part-time' bit was irrelevant – they must all have been. The Boss crooked her finger at me. I walked forward to join her. The murmuring started. She put a hand on my shoulder, stepped on to a chair and up on to a desk.

"Listen up!" She looked at them and laughed. "Right, children. Anyone not know who I am?" She looked round from left to right. "Well, I'm your new boss. John here – sorry this is the John you thought was called Alex – and I have bought your little company and we have bought your little lives. Anyone doesn't want to be bought, there's the door."

It was Christmas Eve and all through the house, not a thing stirred, not even a mouse.

"We're going to leave your little lives alone for a little while and then exciting things will happen which will stop your little lives being so, well... little. John?"

She stepped back down off the desk.

"Ladies, Gentlemen." I looked around and nodded at the faces I remembered. "I'm sorry for the previous deception, but needs must and the devil was driving hard at the time. My name is John Hannay and I worked for Miss Fitzgerald for seven years at BTD. You can check me out on Google if you need to."

Out of the corner of my eye I saw that Darren, the trader whose desk was by the window looking on to Cannon Street, was already doing this. His eyes widened; he nudged the new trader next to him, pointed at his screen and sat forward, staring fixedly at me.

"As Miss Fitzgerald said we have a few things to sort out, but there is one thing that is going to change as from now – no more boiler room tactics, no more shorting shitty stocks, no more little old ladies losing their savings. Keith will be sending out letters to all clients telling them that CA is under new management. We've injected enough cash to tide the company over and I'll pass on my thoughts on stocks and trades to Keith. But I'm just a trader like you. Miss Fitzgerald is the Boss... your boss and my boss. If anyone thinks they can try it on with her I would suggest they either forget that thought or leave now. This is a new era at CA and through absolutely no hard work of your own, you have all suddenly stepped up three divisions. Now..."

I looked round at them all staring into their eyes, trying to see if there was any value in any of them. I counted five in silence.

"Don't let Miss Fitzgerald down. You will never get a chance like this again in all your lives."

I glanced back at Darren meaningfully. Good boy, he caught on. He stood up and began to clap. The brighter ones followed suit immediately applauding louder and louder as it sunk in that they had a future again. I knew that Em would also have noted the ones who were slow in joining in, the ones who looked resentful and the ones who appeared to have no clue at all as to what was going on. She stepped down from the table and walked into Keith's office. We followed obediently.

There was a further hour of drafting the letters to clients, writing the press releases, hiring the Boss's favourite Financial PR company, putting out calls to her pet journalists – in short doing everything necessary to make sure the City knew that it was she who had walked out of BTD because she no longer wanted to work for them and not the other way round.

By ten we were in a taxi on our way to collect what Robbi called 'our stuff' from the hotel. She was becoming irritatingly and increasingly mysterious, but by ten-thirty I began to think I knew why. Our bags were left with the concierge and, dressed in hiking clothes and boots that I didn't even know we had with us, we headed not for Paddington Station, but Waterloo. Didn't I know for God's sake, that it was the anniversary of our first trip six months ago when I introduced her to Fosse? No, for God's sake, I didn't know. I'm a man. I'm bad at anniversaries – especially six-month ones.

We changed trains at Salisbury and again at Bath and Swindon and disembarked at Kemble just after two o'clock. This time a bus was there and we sat at the front like children peering out at the countryside and nattering with the driver. We got off at Foss Cross for the five–mile walk back to the Manor on that still October afternoon. It was idyllic. I've always loved being at Fosse at this time of year with the yellowing leaves beginning to droop on the trees, the muted, mauve tints of early evening, breaths drifting behind in the quiet air as the sun drops into a layer of thin reddish cloud clinging to the hill tops. By the time we unlocked the gate beneath the Copse it was dusk and only the Jackdaws were still making their presence felt as they circled above their roosts. I glanced up at them, paused and glanced again. I put my arm out and held Robbi back, staring intently at the birds. "That's not where they roost."

Robbi pulled me down beside her onto the twisted trunks of the old hedge and phoned Paul. I drew my knees up and wrapped my arms round them and we sat quietly for five minutes. Then the rain started. Just a few drops at first followed by the downpour that comes with the edge of a new weather front. This was good. I stopped Robbi from putting on her waterproof jacket. "The rain will make too much noise on it. Best tell Paul what we're doing as I don't particularly wish to get caught in friendly fire."

The leading edge of the front had passed and the rain had settled to a drip and patter on the beech leaves as we crept up the hill. Robbi clutched her phone in her hand watching the screen. It flashed. Paul was across the other side of the clearing on the top of the hill. She held the rain–splashed screen up for me to see:

"WAIT."

We waited. I heard it first. Sobbing: it was a woman sobbing. Robbi stared at me and raised her shoulders. I

81

pointed at the phone. She texted Paul while I crept clumsily forward and upward towards the clearing. I crouched at the edge, peering into the gloom, wishing I had Paul's night vision goggles. I thought I could just make out a figure, upright against the smooth, grey trunk of the oldest of the beeches on the other side of the clearing. I leaned forward. Then Robbi's hand was on my leg holding me back and Paul was beside me, passing me the goggles. I pulled them on as he scanned the area with his sniperscope. Once I had adjusted to the green, grainy image intensifier, I could see the woman clearly. She was standing against the tree, slumped forward. Good God, she was tied to the tree with thick ropes, looped round and round her chest which was naked! I took off the goggles and passed them to Robbi. I put my lips to Paul's ear.

"Is there anyone else around?"

"No."

I looked back across to the lone tree and whispered again. "Do you think she's booby trapped?"

Paul shrugged and mouthed back at me. "Probably."

Then Robbi was tugging my arm and whispering urgently. Paul held up a finger warningly. We both leant in to listen. Even in this weather, I caught the faintest hint of her perfume. "It's that woman."

I raised my eyebrows.

"The woman from Buxton."

"Mrs Glossy, you mean? Mathilda er, Mathilda... Robinson. She was with the Hunt, Paul. She was the one who had a go at Robbi in the Supermarket"

Paul raised a finger to his lips. "Stay here."

He slithered out of the cover of the trees and snaked his way on his belly across the clearing in slow motion, his hands outstretched in front of him, questing like an insect's antennae. He stopped dead and felt for the wire that I could now see at ankle height in front of him. My thoughts coalesced. I reached forward and tapped him on the ankle. He peered back and I beckoned him. We left the clearing in silence and walked back to the road. He looked at me questioningly.

"She's been put there for a reason. What is it?"

Paul looked down at the rain bouncing off the tarmac. "Either so that they would know we had found her, or to punish her or to kill her and at least one of us."

Robbi butted in. "Or just to see how we react."

"Robbi's right, Paul."

Paul looked back over his shoulder and rubbed his hand over his cropped hair sending a spray of water outwards in all directions. He looked at me and nodded.

"So?"

"How long would it take to get back–up from one or two of your erstwhile SAS colleagues?"

"Frank Johnson has a motorbike. He and Gareth Spinetti both live in Worcestershire. They could be here within the hour. What's the plan, John?"

Plan? Ah, well, yes. Plan. Hmmm. Did this woman in the Copse have anything to do with the supper party we were supposed to be hosting the day after tomorrow? Hmmm. Plan.

"Ow, that bloody hurt, Lady Hannay!"

"You have been *concentrating* for a minute. It's raining. I'm wet and you've started shivering."

I sighed. The sigh turned into a shiver. She was right. "Paul, get Spinetti and Johnson here now. Get that woman out of there without anyone knowing a thing about it and get her back into her own bed without anyone knowing a thing about that either. I shall text you her address when I get back to the Manor. Any questions?"

Paul grinned and turned to Robbi. "You know, given another five years and a lot of training it might almost be worth his while applying to Sandhurst again."

He phoned Spinetti. "Gareth, get hold of Frank and get your ass down to Fosse now if not quicker. We have a job to do tonight."

Robbi walked me home fast, rubbing my back hard every few steps, seemingly in the belief that this would stop me from becoming feverish. So far as I could see it just made me stumble. Paul had called ahead and Margaret had already filled our enormous old bath. I left Robbi digging out towels and walked down to the drawing room to pour a whisky and then into the kitchen pulling off my boots and greeting the collies. I sat by the Aga stroking the dogs and letting the warmth from the stove penetrate my damp clothes. My head nodded forwarded and I jumped as Spit licked my fingers. Why would they have put that woman in our wood? Why? I yawned, downed the whisky, pulled off the rest of my clothes, chucked them in the washing basket in the scullery and climbed naked up the stairs, clicking my fingers to let the Collies know they could follow.

I walked into the bathroom and stopped dead, smiling. All that was visible of Robbi was two knees, two nipples and a nose. I climbed in behind her pushing her forward. She blinked, smiled, sniffed then spoke.

"Where's my whisky, you pig?"

I pulled her back so she was lying on me, still covered in the hot, bubble coated water. She sighed contentedly and yawned again. I woke when she sneezed, pulled the plug out with my toes and watched as more and more of her body became visible under the foam. I blew hard on one segment of the foam and a breast emerged. She smacked me on the forehead with the back of her hand. I reached for a towel and wrapped her in it. She murmured happily.

The silent alarm flashed on the wall above the steamed-up mirror. She reacted instantaneously. "I'll call Dave, John. You call Margaret, though she should have seen the alarm."

The intercom buzzed before I reached it. "Margaret? You OK?"

"Yes, John. Someone's just tripped the alarm. Paul had already told me to put the steel shutters up so I'm safe."

"Good. Robbi's tried calling Dave and Paul, but no reply, so could you keep calling them and make sure you stay safe?"

"It's you they're after, John, not me."

Robbi was dressed and unlocking the upstairs gun cabinet. She turned to me. "It was a distraction. Mrs Glossy I mean. It took Paul out of the action. There's just us here now."

She threw tracksuit trousers and a tee shirt at me, placed my shotgun and a packet of cartridges on the bed, grabbed a stack of long magazines for a Glock and followed me to the stairs. I had mocked Palmer when he had insisted on making the study a 'safe' room, but now... My foot was on the top stair when I heard the click of the front door. How the hell had they got through the inner alarm ring?

Robbi grabbed me and thanking the monastic builders of the fourteenth century for building in stone, not creaking wood, we raced back to our room. Spit was alert, growling deep in her throat. I snapped my fingers and she went silent, her nose pointed towards the door. Spot joined her, her hackles up, guarding. I snapped my fingers again. "The cellar."

Two steps and we were in the dressing room. I locked the door from the inside. Robbi rolled the rug back and I lifted the small hatch we had put in place after we had removed the billions of dollars' worth of gold from the cellar my grandfather had excavated in 1937. No torch. Before she could stop me, I had unlocked the door, raced to the bed, grabbed the torch from the drawer and fled back into the little room.

Robbi stepped down into the hole. I pulled Spot towards me, stroking her head to quiet her. When only Robbi's head was in view, I picked up the nervous dog and carried her to the hole where Robbi whispered to her, lowered her down the rungs and dropped her the last few feet to the cellar floor below. I turned to Spit who had been watching intently. I passed her down to Robbi who received a lick on the nose as she was lowered in turn. I threw the torch to her, opened the door to bedroom, left it ajar and stepped back and down into the darkness. I stood for a few seconds with my feet on the fifth rung down, typed one word into my phone and texted it to Dave.

The word was 'gold'. He would know that it referred to the enormous cache of gold that my grandfather had hidden in the secret cellar. I turned the phone off, pulled the trap door over my head, reaching round the side to pull the rug over. God knows what it looked like, but I could do no more.

* * *

I glanced at my watch. We had been here for forty–five minutes in the dark. Spot sat up beside me, growling low. Spit joined her, nose pointing up. Robbi clamped her hands over the dogs' noses. There was the sound of distant voices and then heavy footsteps amplified by the brick lined shaft and then scraping, scratching, dragging. Robbi placed the torch on the floor pointing directly up the shaft and took the safety catch off the Glock. Reluctantly I broke open the Purdey and slotted two cartridges in. I whispered. "Let me shoot first, Robbi. Twelve bore might cut 'em up a bit, but it won't kill them."

"Besides which, you wouldn't hit them if they fell on you."

I smiled, raised my grandfather's shotgun to my shoulder, tucked it to absorb the recoil and wished I'd brought my ear plugs. In this confined space the noise would be shatteringly loud. I spoke over the worn, wooden stock.

"Shut the door on the dogs, the noise will terrify them."

She led the worried animals through the small door. Another scrape and a small shower of dust sprinkled prettily through the torchlight beam; a tiny shaft of light, then another shower of dust and the hatch swung up. "Block your ears. One of us needs to hear."

As a body leaned into the light, I fired both barrels: a scream and another shower – not of dust. The torchlight glowed pink in the haze. I broke open the Purdey again. Smoke roiled around the tops of the barrels. "Fire a burst, Robbi. They mustn't have a chance to shoot or throw anything down."

She tilted the Glock and sprayed. In my half-deafened state, it sounded like a car wheel–nut impact wrench, so fast I couldn't distinguish one round from the rest. It worked. Another cry – no blood shower. I had reloaded now. The dogs were barking. I stepped forward, tucked the stock into my shoulder once more and fired upwards – one barrel. I counted five and fired the other one. Nothing this time. They had learnt a lesson of sorts. I nodded at Robbi. She stepped forward and fired one shorter burst, aiming at the top rung. The bullets hit home, ricocheting off the metal, spiralling into the room above. I had reloaded. I looked up. There was only one thing left to do. I grabbed the Glock from her, threw her the shotgun and ran up the ladder. As my left hand grasped the top rung, I swung the Glock up, fired round in a 360–degree arc and threw myself up and into the room. A hand came through the door with a machine pistol grasped in it and I wasn't going to make it. There was no way I would be able to get the barrel of the Glock back round however fast I swung it.

Then, an explosion in my ear – a squeal from the door – the searing heat of a gun blast by my cheek – Robbi beside me with the Purdey oozing smoke – a huge voice roaring from the landing. And I knew only one man with a parade ground voice that powerful. I slid to the floor. Robbi heaved herself out of the top of the tunnel and sat beside me. She smiled weakly and held her hand up, horizontally. It was shaking. I smiled and raised my own hand. Interesting – rock steady. I took a deep breath and hauled myself to my feet, put my finger to my lips and pointed. We kept to the walls and crept to the door where a rivulet of blood was trickling towards me. No movement. Silence.

I mouthed at Robbi. "All right?"

A reluctant nod – then Dave's voice. "You two OK?"

"Yes, Dave. They alive?"

"Maybe. You can come out."

We walked through the door, stepping over the slumped arm, its owner unconscious, breathing heavily. Robbi pulled a pillowcase off the bed and whipped a tourniquet round his upper arm. Two other men lay watching Dave warily, bleeding from a variety of wounds. Robbi walked towards them and kicked away their weapons.

"Any others, Dave?"

He nodded. "They're under control."

A voice from the floor below: "Dave?"

"John's bedroom, Paul. Send Frank and Gareth out to sort the ones in the drive. Get them into the kitchen."

CHAPTER NINE

Ten minutes later, we were sipping from mugs of strong tea in the kitchen. Dave checked the dressings on the wounded men, stepped back and studied them. "Military – quite well trained. Not British. Good tactics."

I disagreed. "Good strategy, bad tactics. Putting the woman in the clearing was clever. Whatever we did with her it was a distraction. Tactics... You sure they're soldiers. It was pretty inept."

I had their attention now. Esprit de corps, even in a beaten unit. Interesting. Assuming they were beaten that is. I stared at the man I assumed was the leader of the unit. He sneered and spoke.

"One word."

He was Russian?

"And that word is?"

"Revenge."

He sneered some more. Robbi glanced in my direction.

"Jemima's restless, John. Now we've got this lot bagged, I'll go and calm her down."

She shrugged her shoulders into her enormous waterproof coat, pulled on her Dubarries and left. I stared at the scullery door and shrugged. I'd called Alan Cummins, but how long before he got here? Jemima restless? Why? I started running before the others had even absorbed the information. I yelled as I ran. "There are more in the stables!"

I slipped on the wet cobbles outside the scullery door, nearly lost my footing and was round and into the stable yard in seconds. Jemima's door was open and she was in the yard snorting in the damp, cold, early morning darkness. I walked towards her slowly, holding out my hand to lead her back into the stables as the SAS men raced past me, guns in hands. It was too late. I felt it. No, I knew it. I stroked Jemima's muzzle, walked back inside the house, grabbed my wallet, my jacket, lifted the keys to the Landrover off the hook in the scullery, passed Frank Johnson in silence, ran through the hall and out into the front drive. I climbed into the Landrover and left. How far in front of me were they? Five minutes? They could head east towards Oxford or West towards the M5. I thanked God for Palmer's preparations on the Landrover, pulled down the cover over the computer screen he had installed, reached below the dashboard for the switch and waited in the lane, the cold diesel running rough, red vapour curling up from the exhaust pipe into the still, dark air behind the rear lights. What if she wasn't wearing her microchip? The screen bleeped. I peered at it, leaning forward to find the direction. West. They were taking her towards the M5. Which meant they were going North... probably. Probably wasn't good enough, though. Not when her life depended on it. I engaged first gear and drove. The Defender was not the fastest vehicle in the world, but it was stable, solid, and with a full tank should have given me a cruising range of four hundred miles. But the tank wasn't full – nowhere near. The bleep was still ahead of me by about five miles I guessed. I needed more than a guess. I glanced at the clock. It was twenty–nine minutes past four. I called Palmer. After seven rings he answered.

"What, John?"

No irritation. If I was not mistaken, there had even been concern. "They've kidnapped Robbi."

"No, no, no."

"Palmer, listen. I'm in the Landrover. That device you fixed under Robbi's finger nail. What's its range?"

"You mean in relation to the screen in the cab?"

"Yes."

A pause. "Give me a second."

A scrabbling. A curse. A rustle of paper. "John?"

"I'm here."

"OK. The screen is eighteen centimetres diameter. Assume a mile for every centimetre from the edge of the screen to the centre. What do you reckon?"

"Three... four centimetres, maybe."

"OK. Call it six miles."

I groaned, disconnected and turned the phone off. Eight minutes later I was nearing the traffic lights at the junction with the A40. They were red. I didn't brake, straight through – ignoring the bleep heading further and further away from me across the screen – accelerator on the floor, down the hill, past Northleach at seventy-five, past Foss Cross on the A429 at ninety, cutting right on Welsh Way and out on to the A417 northbound with my foot still flat to the floor. The bleeps had disappeared – the screen was empty and silent. I knew it was only to be expected – they were only seven or eight miles away, but I was deep below them off the Cotswold escarpment. I realised I was muttering to myself. I breathed deeply, gripped the wheel hard and hoped, for their sakes, that any roaming badgers had headed back to their setts early tonight.

The A417 joins the A435 below Crickley Hill and heads West towards the M5 at junction 11a. I swung out on to the road and floored it again. An early morning driver in a patched-up Vauxhall Astra flinched as I shot past him, his car jinking towards the kerb. Five minutes later I was over the M5 and braking to a halt on the hard shoulder just beyond the slip road up from the northbound side of the motorway – not a car in sight. I pressed the switch to turn on my hazard warning lights and reversed slowly down the hard shoulder of the slip road to the motorway, pausing twice to let first a car and then a white van come up past me. I kept reversing until I was fifty yards south of the junction. From this vantage point on the hard shoulder, I could pull out on to the M5 northbound or go back up the slip road and work my way back round to be able to head south if they went that way instead. I turned off the headlights and stared hopefully at the screen. Nothing. Nothing at all. I leaned forward, groaning and banged my head on the steering wheel. The pain helped.

My heart missed, then beat faster. I eased back. The screen was still blank. I turned it off and rebooted. Nothing. I peered out of the window. I remembered my days with the school camera club learning the now redundant art of photography on film. The sky above the Cotswolds was maybe a quarter of an f stop lighter. City people, in their neon lighted cocoons, often get dawn wrong. Dawn's not an event; it's a process, a gradual infusion of colour into a monochrome world – black to greys to blues to washed out polychrome. City dwellers often confuse dawn with sunrise. Again, they're wrong. Sunrise is glorious, full of hope. Dawn has little beauty. It's just a step on the way to being able to see. I looked at the dashboard clock. I'd been here four minutes. I calculated that if they had driven at somewhere near the legal speed limit and stayed on the A40 until it joined the A435, they should have been here a minute ago. In despair I reached out to turn on the phone.

The screen bleeped. Then nothing.

I stared at it, willing it to bleep again, counting: seven, eight, nine. A system error? A random event? It bleeped again and then again and again until the pattern was set. They were coming down the A435 just as I had always known they would! I had never doubted it for a second. I hammered the steering wheel and yelled up at the lightening sky. Now the only question was whether they went north or south. I booted up the phone. Twenty seconds later it chirruped at me – messages, messages. I called Dave. He answered immediately. "Tell me you've found her, John."

"She's on the A435 heading towards the M5, Dave. I'm on the M5 northbound below the slip road to Junction 11A. I can follow them if they go in either direction. Wait."

I watched the blips on the screen. So near and so unreachable. I pulled out the binoculars and peered at the bridge over the motorway. A vehicle was crossing towards my side of the road. I engaged first gear.

"Dave. They're going north in a Double Cab four by four pulling a trailer."

I changed up and up again and was just ahead of the Double Cab as it came down the slip road, headlights on full. I couldn't believe they would go straight off again at the next junction and the one after that was southbound access only so I could slow down slightly and let them overtake me before Junction 9, ten miles further north. Watching the blips, I could see they were catching me up quite quickly. They must be doing eighty or more. I speeded up to eighty-one and switched on my front fog lamps in order to give the Landrover a different and easily changeable look to someone watching their rear-view mirror for followers – at least until it was fully daylight.

The mobile phone rang.

"Yes, Dave?"

"Robbi has her mobile with her. They'll check it soon so turn your phone off now. Palmer says there's a spare one in the glove compartment. Frank Johnson is on his bike fifteen minutes behind you. Stay in touch."

I gave him the Double Cab's registration number.

CHAPTER TEN

The endless hours that followed were the most stressful of my endlessly stress filled life. I was too wired to feel any need for rest and too on edge to be able to contemplate anything but the three-lane strip of black tarmac ahead and the Double Cab pulling its trailer four hundred yards in front, heading further and further north.

Frank Johnson passed me on his enormous Ducati Monster with a wave of his hand just before the Frankley Services south of Birmingham and I let my speed drop to seventy-five as I knew we would be approaching the log jam where the M5 joins the M6 and I had no desire to be sitting in a stationery queue directly behind the Double Cab. I lost sight of both bike and Double Cab altogether until just before Stoke when Frank's taillight reappeared. I settled in two hundred yards behind him and worried about fuel. They would have to stop sometime.

They didn't stop before Manchester. They didn't stop at Lancaster or Burton in Kendall either. The fuel gauge showed a smidge over empty. Either I stopped on the hard shoulder and used the Gerry can or risked it to the next services wherever the hell they were. The answer was over fifteen miles, over twenty miles. I couldn't afford to drop my speed too much either. Frank was out of sight now and the smidge was non–existent. Then finally the sign to Tebay services and thank God – a motorbike on the hard shoulder just before the hundred–yard marker. I followed the bike up the slip road into the far corner of the service station's car park. It was starting to snow.

Frank came towards me flexing his fingers to get some warmth back into them. He pointed at the ranks of petrol pumps. The Double Cab was on the rank furthest from where we stood. I reached into the Landrover for my binoculars – three heads silhouetted against the lights from the shop. A fourth was filling the tank. One of the silhouettes climbed out of the cab and checked the buttons on the trailer cover – quite big, that trailer, one metre high and about two metres long. The trailer checker and the petrol filler walked towards the shop, the trailer checker waiting halfway, out of the snow, under the edge of the roof beyond the pumps, looking back at the Double Cab. I opened the door of the Landrover again, pulled out the phone, the Glock, spare clips, the torch, my gloves, the hand mirror and the fourteen–inch Bowie knife. I passed the keys to Frank and spoke to him. My voice sounded cracked and harsh. "I need a diversion directly between the shop and that van."

He opened his mouth.

"Just do it, Frank."

"Sir!"

I walked forward cautiously to the rank of pumps. Frank revved his bike, drove too fast towards the shop, slowed too late, skidded on the slush as he stopped, the bike sliding away beneath him as he tumbled back, his helmet banging on the kerb. He staggered to his feet shouting:

"Fuck!" He heaved and pulled at it. "Give us a hand, mate."

The trailer checker stepped forward reluctantly and as Frank let the bike nearly topple over on top of him, I unbuttoned the corner of the trailer cover and squeezed into the gap. It was packed with soft stuff. I wriggled and pushed and squirmed and finally managed to pinch the buttons down on the corner from the inside. A minute later the trailer jerked and bounced forward. I hit the underside of the cover nose first – virtually no suspension. I hadn't thought of that. My arm smacked against the side and then the surface beneath the trailer changed and we were on the motorway and the bouncing settled to a bearable rhythm. So, what was in my little abode? I shone the torch round – sleeping bags, kitbags, plastic boxes full of food and on the floor beneath the bags, a long, flat wooden box. I knew what was in it. I pulled the Bowie knife out of its sheath and levered up the edge. As I thought – semi–automatic assault rifles. I'm sure Dave, or even Robbi, could have told me exactly what model they were and their rate of fire, but I didn't care. I just needed to work out how to immobilise them. I rested my head on my hands and stared at them...

I woke as the trailer bumped over something in the road and slowed. I peered at my watch. I had been asleep for over two hours. I took a risk, turned on my phone to check the compass bearing. Heading North West still and at Latitude: 55° 52' 42" N, Longitude: 4° 15' 29" W. I checked the internet – Glasgow. The trailer bounced and twisted its way through and out of the city

– I felt sick. I tried to picture the route – up past Loch Lomond towards Fort William and then either left past Loch Eil on the road to the Isles past Arisaig of the white sands, or right and up the long road beside Loch Ness towards Inverness. I pulled out one of the semi–automatic rifles and worked on dismantling any moving bits... *'And today we have naming of parts'*. I had been a pretty poor excuse for an army officer, but it didn't take even me long to remove the bolt head from the bolt assembly and turn the locking piece. I raised the trailer cover by half an inch and as no one was in sight behind I dropped pieces from the three rifles out on to the road and watched them roll away into the snow-coated distance.

The last time I had done this journey had been on the way to a wedding on the Isle of Skye. If I remembered correctly that had been about a five–hour run – but it hadn't been in driving snow. I slept again. I came to the surface as my head was banged once more against the trailer cover above me. The trailer rattled and bumped over some rough ground and stopped with a jerk. I clutched the Glock and slowly, slowly, lifted a corner of the cover. Snow whipped in against my hand. I eased a corner of the hand mirror out and peered into it. She was there. She was alive. She was walking. One man stood behind her with a hand gun. Another was leaning out of the cab door also armed. I could have shot one (just about) but not a chance with the others. They forced her to squat by the road in front of them to pee – and they laughed. I caught a glimpse of her face as she walked back to the cab – pale, withdrawn, scornful.

I didn't sleep again. I looked at the compass bearing on the phone, shut it down and texted Dave the Latitude and Longitude on the phone that Palmer had left in the Landrover. I had no idea how far behind us they were. All I knew was that we had passed Fort William. I was positive now that Skye was our destination. Surely, they would be getting tired soon. They had carried out a night exercise and had been driving since four thirty in the morning. Time? Twenty–seven minutes past twelve so getting on for eight hours now. It was somewhere in the region of five hundred miles from Gloucester to Skye so allowing for the stops they should be on the Skye bridge within half an hour.

I shivered, wriggled down between two sleeping bags in a feeble attempt to get warm and waited. The road noise changed. We must be on the Skye bridge – finally! I slid the sheathed Bowie knife down the side of my trousers, shoved the Glock into my pocket, pressed the top of the wooden box down and tried to make it look as though a six-foot two-inch man had not been hiding in the trailer since Lancashire. I texted Dave the word 'Skye', turned the iPhone back on and alternated between the compass and the map – so long as we weren't heading up into the Black Cuillins – the mountains had looked threatening enough in mid–Summer so God knows how they would look in Winter. No – we turned left down what I guessed was the A851 south, away from Portree. I turned on to my stomach and began to open the cover. I had to be ready to move in an instant.

The van braked, swung right, lurched and the trailer bounced horribly. I braced myself as best as I could against the sides as the vehicle slowed to a halt. A door opened. I used the mirror again, but through the falling snow I could see virtually nothing. We lurched forward again, the van now moving at little more than a walking pace. They must have stopped to open a gate. They had to be near their final destination. I slithered out through the gap at the end and crouched over the rear light bracket, pulling the cover back taut, pressing the buttons down, peering round the side of the van. I made out the shape of a small house up to the left. The trailer bounced over a rut, I lost my grip and fell clumsily into the snow, smacking my ankle against a hidden stone. I was on my feet and racing to the side of the house as the headlights of the Double Cab described a slow circle on the turning area in front of the building. There was a window on the side of the house nearest to me. I peered in as the headlights played over the front door – a living room of some sort with a glass door on the far side. I turned to go round the back and winced at the sudden pain in my ankle. This was no time to be feeling pain. I ran on in a half crouch – no windows, just the chimney breast at the back; but on the far side – a single storey outbuilding with a half–glazed door. I turned the handle – locked. I stared around wildly – a flowerpot all but buried in snow. I kicked it and there was the key. I scrabbled with numb and clumsy fingers and turned it in the lock. The engine of the Double Cab was still running. I put two fingers over the torch and allowed the small beam of light play across the mouse dropping strewn, grubby little room – ancient gas cooker, big red gas cylinder, prehistoric paraffin convector heater, a box of matches and dirt, lots of dirt. I grabbed the box of matches, twisted the connector of the gas cylinder, turned the lever, throttled it back so the hiss couldn't be heard, then slipped through the connecting door into the living room, shutting the door behind me. It was marginally cleaner. From the noises outside I guessed the men were unhooking the trailer. A quick glance round showed only one hiding place of any merit – a Victorian linen press. It had an empty cupboard at the bottom just large enough to hold a six-foot two-inch man if he crouched down with his spine crushed against the back of the cupboard and his bottom squashed on to his ankles – one of which felt as if it had swollen to twice its normal size. I pulled the cupboard doors shut as the key turned in the lock of the front door. I think two of the men came in. A chair was dragged across the floor.

"Sit down here, girl. Tape her. I'll get the food."

Footsteps fading – the teeth grating tear of parcel tape coming off a roll.

"Alright, pretty one. Just stay still. Mmmmh, sweet! Going to have fun with you and when we get the money, you know what we do? More fun before we get rid of you once and for all."

He laughed. I forced myself to stay still. Grunting and then steps and muttering in what sounded like Russian to my untutored ear – raking at clinker in the fireplace and then steps drawing nearer to my hiding place. I daren't use the Glock. The men outside might see the flash even if they didn't hear the cough. I slid the Bowie knife out of its sheath and held its five–inch handle with both hands, the base resting on my groin, the nine–inch blade pointing up. My heart raced. He opened the drawer above my cupboard and the floorboards squeaked as he bent and pulled both doors open wide. I caught a momentary glimpse of a shocked face as I came off the floor of the cupboard with my whole body behind the thrust of the knife into his stomach and up into his rib cage, knocking him backwards, clamping my hand over his mouth as I twisted and pushed and watched the light die from his eyes as life left him. I had the briefest of moments to reflect on my second killing – it didn't get any easier – then raced across the floor to where she sat waiting. I cut the tape with the bloody knife blade and dragged her towards the kitchen. She stumbled and half tripped, but we made it. I pushed a handkerchief over her face against the gas, pointed to the back door and left her to make her own way there as I turned the gas cylinder lever to full on. She hissed from the door and waved a bottle at me. Paraffin. Excellent. I grabbed a rag from one of the filthy work surfaces, pushed it into the bottle and upended it, watching the liquid fill the fabric. I motioned her out of the door and followed, leaving a trail of paraffin behind me, then waited, the door pushed almost closed, listening for the arrival of the other kidnappers, the hiss of the escaping gas loud against the stillness of the empty room. I heard the front door open and a yell. I lit three matches together, held them to the soaked handkerchief, rolled the bottle into the room, eased the door to quietly behind me. I grabbed Robbi's hand and sprinted for the corner of the house. She was ahead of me by one pace and just round the corner when the blast hit, hurling me five foot forward and three foot high into the snowdrift-covered log pile. It hurt. I heard her giggle. She could giggle at a time like this? Madness!

"You call this a rescue, Sir John?"

I brushed snow out of my eyes and stared over her shoulder at the blaze. The kitchen had gone and it looked as though the living room was following. She pulled me to my feet and we crept round the side of the house. I passed her the Glock.

"Can you take out a tyre on their van from here?"

She peered through the snow.

"Might take two or three shots. They've got semi–automatics, John."

They've got semi–automatics that won't work."

She nodded her appreciation. "Watch the front door, then."

I watched and waited. I heard her breathe in and then the sharp cough on the outward breath. And there was a movement. Not by the blazing house, but beyond and above the van. I pulled her down beside me.

"Did you get it?"

"Of course. Did you see anyone?"

"Yes. Behind the van."

"You really call this a rescue, Sir John?"

I straightened and pulled her to her feet. "Lady Hannay?"

She curtsied. I bowed. "Run!"

We ran – slipping and sliding over the snow – keeping her in front of me, shielding her from the threat. A crack from behind. Robbi yelled over her shoulder. "That's only a hand gun. Not a chance he can hit us with that."

A bullet whipped through a branch over my head – the next caught me in my left shoulder, flinging me forward as she threw herself over the lip of the bank down towards the road, laughing, picking herself up and running on, shouting over her shoulder. "John Hannay, I love you!"

Oh well, perhaps she wasn't completely mad and perhaps it didn't hurt quite that badly.

"Quick, John. There are headlights down the road."

Ignoring the stabbing pain in my ankle and the throbbing pain in my shoulder I raced after her, trying not to get left too far behind and, oh Glory, it was a little bus. Robbi danced up and down beside the road waving frantically and the driver slowed to a halt. He studied us through the open door as did the passengers, correction, the school children. I gabbled at him chaotically.

"I'm so sorry, but we've just been driven off the road by a maniac in a van towing a trailer. Our car is back down there in a ditch. We were on our way to Portree. Do you go that far? Is there any way you could drop us there? I've twisted my ankle and hurt my shoulder."

"And I've hurt my hand"

Robbi held up a blood stained, rag covered finger.

"Get in now and warm yourselves. The children will make room for you."

And they did, welcoming us in soft Highland voices, helping us to seats and offering us sweets. I sucked an extra strong mint gratefully, realising it was my first food since leaving the Cartwright's farm yesterday afternoon. Despite the pain and the blood seeping through my quilted jacket I could feel sleep washing over me. I forced myself awake and looked blankly out of the window. The snow was turning to rain. I pulled my phone out.

"John?"

"I've got her. She's safe."

I heard him breathe out slowly. "Good boy."

"I've texted you the details of where it happened. There's some tidying up to be done and one still at large... and Dave?"

"Yes, John."

"Can you get a team in and clean up the mess now and re-paint our bedroom and dressing room so it looks as though nothing has happened?"

A pause.

"I can, John, yes. Going to tell me why?"

"I can't say too much, but I have a plan."

He groaned, but I could hear the amusement in his voice.

"And, Dave make sure they use Vinyl Silk paint on the woodwork, not gloss because of the smell, and chuck heaters in the rooms so they dry off fast. We don't want anyone thinking there's been some decorating going on, do we? Now, has Major Cummins arrived there?"

He grunted and I heard the rustle of a phone being passed from hand to hand.

"John? What can I do?"

"I'm on the Isle of Skye, Alan. I need a hire car in Portree I can drive to Inverness airport and at Inverness airport I need a private jet to fly me to whatever the nearest airfield to Fosse is and I need a nurse on board.

I know you're not a travel agent, Alan, but I'll call Tony McElroy and he'll authorise the use of funds and..."

"I can do all that, John. John? Are you all right?"

I yawned. "Sorry, Alan. Yes, I'm fine, thanks."

"And Robbi?"

"You can speak to her yourself. Here she is."

I passed her the phone. "Hello, Alan. Yes... yes. No. I'm with John now and that's all that matters. OK. OK. Bye."

She passed the phone back. "He says he'll call you back."

Ten minutes later he called with directions to a taxi company that would drive us to Inverness and five minutes after that, he called again with the name of the Private Jet company at the airport. I begged a strip of cloth from the driver and pushed it over the hole in my shoulder. By seven p.m. we were in the air. The cabin attendant was some kind of military nurse and Robbi's shredded fingernail was bandaged, she was injected with a variety of antibiotics and painkillers and something heavy duty to make her sleep. Once she was dozing, I removed my coat and tee shirt and see what the damage was to my shoulder. I was lucky. Straight through the fleshy part, no bone or tendon damage. The nurse cleaned the wound, stitched the hole, shot me full of God knows what stuff, strapped my upper arm to my side, wrapped my ankle in ice and then I was fed and pampered.

The nearest airfield that was open at that time of night was Bristol. Paul had been allowed to bring the Bentley right up to the steps and we were out of the airport in five minutes. By eleven we were back at Fosse Manor to be greeted by cheers from Dave's cleaning crew who had already finished the bullet hole repairs and painting, but had insisted on staying there to welcome us. Five minutes of back slapping and toasts and then Margaret ordered Robbi into the bath. Madness, I thought once more – twenty–four hours ago she was in exactly this same position only then Lady Hannay had slept on my chest as the water cooled. I showered, trying to keep the water off my bandages, pulled the bath plug out of her bath, reached for a towel and wrapped her in it. She murmured happily – and this time the silent alarm did not flash above the steamed-up mirror.

CHAPTER ELEVEN

It was the next morning. It was the day of the supper party for the owners of the local paper, the local head mistresses and their spouses. Today was a day when if anyone was watching – and I was damn sure they were – I had to be seen in all my normal places in all my normal activities.

I wanted to know if Dave's team had found the man who had shot me on the Isle of Skye. I wanted to know if Major Alan Cummins' interrogators had squeezed any drops of information from the squad that had broken into Fosse Manor. I dragged myself out of bed at seven leaving Robbi still deeply asleep. My shoulder hurt more than my ankle. I swallowed Paracetamols, pulled on a pair of much too large Hunter boots – belonging to my father I think – to cover my bruised foot and left a note on my side of the bed – 'Riding. Paul watching'. I saddled Jemima, texted Grace to get a taxi over on the Fosse account to muck out and to bring her manicure kit. Then I rode up onto the hills. It was only just full daylight when I reached the top and I was able to gallop away the awful memory of the fading light in the eyes of the dying man with my Bowie knife deep in his rib cage. At eight forty-five I drove the Landrover into Northleach to collect some wine from Andy Barraclough, buy milk, to limp and let people know that my horse had crushed my ankle and bruised my shoulder against a gate this morning, but mainly just to have my face seen.

Back at Fosse, Grace had arrived and was mucking out. I limped back up the stairs with the dogs to find Robbi still deeply asleep. The dogs lay by the bed while I showered and dressed and then I joined them and we all sat silently and waited. At three minutes past ten her eyelids flickered, her eyes half opened, she blinked and burst out laughing as the dogs ran round and round in manic circles on the bed. She held out her hand to me.

"Hello, John Richard."

I took her hand and felt the bandage, looked down at the finger and up at her face. She was still smiling.

"May I?"

"If you must."

I undid the bandage and sighed with relief when I saw how much better it was. "Tonight, Lady Hannay, we have guests and one of those guests will know your finger nail was torn off."

She nodded slowly.

"So?"

I walked to the door and shouted. Grace trotted upstairs obediently and peered round the door. "Robbi, show Grace your finger. Grace, you need to put a false nail on top of that and then you need to paint all Robbi's nails. Nothing too fancy, just varnish like she normally wears. No one must know the nails are false. I'll bring some breakfast up."

I left them to their hugging and crying, went to the kitchen and started in on the cassoulet.

* * *

Robbi slept most of the day for which I was thankful –
mainly for her, but also because she still hadn't seen the
bandaging round my shoulder. At seven fifteen that
evening Annette Warburton, the heavily pregnant co–
owner of the local newspaper, phoned in a panic to let
me know she was a vegetarian. I had already gone for a
Gruyere soufflé with anchovy sauce and baked a couple
of loaves of bread so I prepared a Stilton sauce for her
soufflé and was quickly throwing together a Tuoni y
Lampo. I sniffed at the cassoulet.

Seven forty-five p.m. – Robbi strolled into the
kitchen. She looked now like a sixties model, flat pumps,
tight, ankle–length slacks, a sloppy pullover and no
make–up apart from black, black eyeliner. She saw the
look in my eye and backed away laughing, scribbled a
note for our visitors which she stuck on the front door,
telling them to let themselves in and selected some
tracks on the music system. The macaroni came to the
boil as Leonard Cohen came up on the speakers. She
stepped into my arms and we waltzed round and round
the old kitchen table as Cohen's magical, harsh bass
voice filled the room:

Take this waltz, take this waltz
It's yours now, it's all that there is

I turned off the macaroni and drained it just as the
next track started:

You shake my nerves and you rattle my brain
Too much love drives a man insane

I defy anyone not to dance to Jerry Lee.

You broke my will
But what a thrill
Goodness gracious great balls of fire!

She high stepped towards me finger jiving. God, could I do this with a damaged left ankle and a bullet hole in my left shoulder? I tapped my right foot and swung her. She laughed and the Collies slunk into their basket by the scullery door appalled at this exhibition of human insanity. I spun her, swung her into my arms and we jived and jived as if our lives depended on it. I spun her faster and faster until she collapsed into my arms laughing as the music ended. There was cheering and clapping from the doorway. Our visitors had all arrived together and were standing in the doorway applauding. We took a bow and I wondered if the stitches round the bullet hole had burst. Robbi studied me and went to prod my arm. I moved away quickly. She studied me harder.

I dived into introductions. Catherine Simmons' husband was 'nice'. Stubble bearded, rangy, gentle, worked in IT. Janice's husband, Miles Scowcroft was a dick – no inverted commas required. He was wearing a cardigan and a cravat and had brought a not very good bottle of Merlot. Robbi effected introductions. Miles was unimpressed. "I was not aware that the press had been invited to this gathering."

Luke Warburton grinned, approached the table and laid down the new edition of the Gazette. "Evening, Councillor."

I poured large Manzanillas all round and a glass of water for Annette and joined Catherine and Robbi peering at the page – pages rather. Luke had inserted a four-page centre spread of colour photos of Harry's riding tricks, of Robbi cheering on Grace and Grace herself, laughing and hugging Robbi and Harry. I turned back to page two to the interview with Catherine. She had sung Robbi's praises, sung the school's praises and managed to shoehorn in a reference to their greatly improved standing in the Ofsted ratings. I toasted Catherine and looked at Luke. "Do you ever get any reaction to stories?"

"Yes. We sometimes get the odd call." He laughed as Annette smacked his arm.

"Stop it, Luke. Tell them."

"We've never had as many calls. 'Could we do more stories like this?' 'Who is the gorgeous Polo player and would he give private riding lessons?' 'Did we think Lady Hannay would open the Flower Show?' 'Why do we waste time on young wastrels like that? 'Children like that should go to prison.' And on and on. With a bit of luck, the ad sales should be right up."

A shadow crossed the door. I looked up quickly and then stared. "Uncle Ludo?"

The shadow smiled slyly. "Good Lord, Angela, we've finally got one back on him. Never seen the boy look startled before."

He turned to Catherine Simmons who was standing nearest the door. "Nothing like shockin' a chap to get a good reaction. He hasn't called me 'uncle' since he was seven, you know. Haven't seen him wearing his chef's outfit since he owned that restaurant either."

I looked down at myself realising I forgotten to remove my Chef's whites – one of my cooking habits that I stuck to more out of superstition than anything else. Robbi raced round the table to hug and kiss the elegant, elderly couple and I effected further introductions.

"I'm so sorry... this is Ludo and Angela Arbuthnot and I thought at this time of year they buried themselves in the Borders and never came further south than Roxburgh. What's happened, Ludo?"

A funeral, followed by a fuel pipe issue is what had happened – that, and the fact that their butler and general factotum, Lockhart, had been unable to mend it and that Paul and he were now working on it together. Robbi was still hugging Angela Arbuthnot. "But you must positively stay the night and Angela can come out riding with me tomorrow morning. Please say you'll stay. John always makes far too much food and you can advise on our new plan."

There was a discreet cough at the door. I knew that cough. Robbi managed to stop herself from hugging the latest arrival. "Lockhart, you're all staying the night. We've just turned a couple of the attic rooms into a suite and we've got lots of room for you too."

"That's extremely kind of you m'lady, and I had in fact come to tell his Lordship that Sergeant Browby says the repair cannot be made until tomorrow morning and he has already offered me a room for the night in the lodge house."

Miles Scowcroft's reaction to 'his Lordship' was a pleasure to behold – not just a dick but a snob to boot.

"Lord Arbuthnot, I..."

Ludo laid his hand on his arm, smiling. "Ah, well now. It's not Arbuthnot d'you see. It's Clanroyden. I mean the family name is Arbuthnot and the family home is Laverlaw in the borders, but the name comes from Clenry Den in Fife which is down the road aways. Silly really, but there it is."

I took Miles away from any further gaffes by asking him if he would help bring some more wine up from the cellar. His eyes lit up. Robbi started on the guided tour of the manor with the others as I unlocked the ancient door at the top of the cellar steps. He positively prowled round the extremities of the ancient cellars and when he started tapping the walls, I realised he actually thought he might find some of the Hannay family secrets. "Is this as far as they go, Hannay?"

I reached for another couple of bottles of Mussantino and stepped back from the racks. "Yes, Miles. The kitchen and the dining hall are the original 14th century monastery, but there's nothing under the dining hall, we had the floor scanned a few years ago and it's solid rock. If you go and find the others, I'll finish off the cooking and lay an extra couple of places. The soufflé will be ready in five minutes."

I left him to join the guided tour, grated the pastry on to the apples for the Tarte Tatin, retrieved the bread from the warm oven, re–laid the table, changed out of my whites and counted down the soufflé.

I liked the Simmonses and the Warburtons more and more as the evening progressed, Miles less and less as he drank more and more and about Janice, I remained neutral. Eventually I shoved stuff into the industrial size dishwasher in the scullery and followed the others into the small drawing room. Robbi had adjusted the dampers on the wood burner and it was blazing up against the winter chill. I decided the time was about right.

"You see Ludo, we were thinking that I had all that inheritance and that I should be using it for a charitable use so..."

He caught on immediately. "How much was it again, John?"

"About one point three billion give or take." I kept my gaze on Ludo.

"And it was left to you by your grandfather on condition that it was put to good use."

"Correct."

I turned to Catherine Simmons. "I just thought we should try and develop what Robbi's done with Grace a bit more. But we don't want to get into paying consultants and having a professional management team in until we know it's going to work. So, it would be down to you and Janice and the PTAs..."

Miles butted in. "And the governors and local authority, of course."

"Possibly Miles, possibly."

I might have guessed the little shit could see a role for himself in there. I turned away and out of the corner of my eye I saw Janice dig him hard in the ribs with her elbow. I warmed towards her. Catherine had missed the byplay.

"But, John, I know a little about charities. You're going to need some staff and an office of some sort."

"Well, I did have that covered. I had put in for planning permission to redo the old offices over the stables, but..."

Luke Warburton snorted. I paused and raised my eyebrows at him? He pointed towards Miles who rose to his feet his face mottled with anger. "I have had just about enough of this farce! I am not going to sit here and be insulted and mocked by a third-rate hack and an over privileged brat who doesn't know the meaning of a single day's hard work let alone a lifetime of commitment to the community. Janice, come along. We will call for a taxi outside."

He stormed out of the door. Janice started after him. Angela Arbuthnot spoke quickly. "Janice you really do not have follow him, you know. It may be rather bad form to say so, but your husband has been behaving odiously all evening."

Janice sat back down uncertainly. I used the intercom. "Paul, one of the guests is leaving. Can you call George to arrange a taxi?"

I walked out to the front door where Miles Scowcroft was standing trying not to look uncertain. His face mottled again as I approached him. I held up a hand. "Mr Scowcroft, I have absolutely no idea what your problem is. However, I intend to be charitable and put it down to an excessive fondness for alcohol. Janice is staying here. A taxi will arrive at the gates shortly. Goodbye."

I held the front door open. A voice spoke from the drive and I jumped.

"Sorry, John. Just wanted to accompany the gentleman to the gates. The drive can be a bit bumpy in the dark so I brought a torch."

"Thank you, Paul. Mr Scowcroft, I suggest you have no more to drink tonight so you can reflect on your disgraceful behaviour this evening."

I limped back into the silent drawing room. Ludo regarded me with a wry smile, raised his right hand and opened it. A small electronic device was resting in his palm.

"He put this one on the mantel shelf and I'm pretty sure he stuck another one to the bottom of the kitchen table."

I kept up the act. "Luke, what was so funny and what on earth is going on with Scowcroft?"

Luke took his eyes of the electronic device and eyed me suspiciously. "Miles Scowcroft is the chairman of the planning committee that rejected your application. It was the biggest farce I had ever seen. He just railroaded them into rejection and now he thinks he was invited here so you could have a go at him."

I reached for the intercom which flashed before I picked it up.

"Yes, Paul?"

"He's gone, John. Not a happy camper. Any problems?"

"Yes, 'fraid so. Could you pop down to the house? There's something here that requires your professional expertise."

Janice let out a strangled sob. Robbi jumped up and ran across to her. "Don't cry, Janice. I have no idea what's going on, but I'm sure we can sort it out."

She caught the box of tissues that I threw. Janice blew her nose. "I am so sorry, John, Robbi. I have no idea what is going on either."

"Don't worry, dear. He probably had too much to drink."

Luke was kneeling over the device on the floor. He looked up at me. "You know you're a right bastard, John, don't you?"

I raised my eyebrows, but did not disagree. How could I?

"Well, here I am in the middle of a great story and you made me sign an agreement that it was all off the record. I should have known better."

I half smiled. Janice was watching me from behind the handkerchief. I shook a rueful head at her. "How long have you known that you were married to a complete arse, Janice?"

She managed a wan smile. "I never wanted to admit it, but probably since the beginning. And recently he's just got worse and worse and he's started drinking heavily too."

Angela moved across to sit the other side of Janice. "Is that very recently, my dear? Exactly when?"

"I don't know. Is it important?"

"I think it might be. Was it before or after John's planning application?"

"I don't know when that was."

I leaned back to think. The architect had adapted the old plans in October and I had sent them in... "It would be about the beginning of November, Janice."

She nodded and blew her nose again. "That might be right, yes."

Catherine's husband joined Luke on the floor as Paul came in the door. I pointed. Paul crouched down beside them. "It's a Q bug or something very like it. Extremely sensitive to sounds, but before you use it the first time you need to programme the unit to let it know to report to you."

Catherine's husband looked at him curiously. "And how do you do that?"

"You just send a text message to the Sim card number in the unit plus your mobile phone number and then it recognises you."

"So, it could be monitored from anywhere."

"Yep, anywhere in the world."

"There's another one under the kitchen table, Paul."

He nodded at me and left. Catherine cleared her throat and looked very headmistressy. "It would seem, John, that there are a lot of people hereabouts who are after your blood. What have you done to deserve this?"

I shrugged at her. I had no idea where to begin or even whether to begin. Ludo smiled and intervened. "I don't think, for once, that John is to blame, Catherine. Have you heard about his grandfather?"

Luke perked up. Careful, Ludo. He smiled at me reassuringly. "Well now, perhaps this bit can be on the record, eh, John?"

"That rather depends..."

He waved an arm at me dismissively. "John's grandfather was a First World War hero who was involved in all sorts of, shall we say, unconventional activities as well as the more straightforward ones like exhorting his men to follow him over the top and attack the machine gun emplacements of the Boche with little more than bayonets. And after the war he carried on working for the government in more of these, ah, unconventional activities and it is my view, and by the way the view of my grandfather who was a very close friend of his, that he made a number of extremely serious enemies."

Luke nodded slowly. "And these enemies are now getting their revenge on John – his grandson?"

"I did not say that and this is now off the record. Is that clear young man?

Luke blinked at the steel in the voice of this hitherto amiable, elderly man. Ludo sat forward, holding his hands out to the blaze behind the glass doors of the wood burner. "John is very highly thought of in certain circles. You may know that he is a financial genius."

I shook my head. No, no, no.

"You can deny it 'til the cows come home, young man. You forget that I've seen you in action. Roberta can attest to this as well, can't you?"

"I wouldn't say 'genius', Ludo. I mean he's terribly big headed at the best of times."

Luke looked from one to the other as they both smiled at me. I stayed quiet.

"So, John was of enormous help to the government last year and some rather greedy City types are out for revenge because he scotched their greedy little scheme. Why 'scotched', Angela, is it just another example of English racism?"

Angela smiled. "Probably, dear."

I interjected – mainly because it would annoy Robbi. "I think you'll find it's from late Middle English, Ludo – scocche. Possibly from the Norman French éscocher."

Robbi groaned. It had annoyed her.

Angela looked directly at Luke. "You seem to be a very pleasant young man, Mr Warburton, and your wife is positively charming. However, John has suffered greatly over the years and I would be unhappy in the extreme if you were to be the cause of any more suffering. Do I make myself clear?"

I closed my eyes for a second. I never used to get this tired. I opened my eyes. Paul had come back in and was standing in the doorway, with a total of four bugs resting on a handkerchief in his hand. Four bugs, the bastard had planted four bugs! I pointed at them and made steering wheel signs. Paul nodded and went to put them in the Landrover. Luke looked round.

"I would never do anything to hurt John, Lady Angela. He rescued the paper, didn't he Ann–Ann?"

Annette smiled at Angela. I closed my eyes again. Too much information. Too much information. Far too many people knowing far, far too much about me.

"Lady Angela, I can assure you that John is a personal hero of ours. If there's a John and Robbi Hannay protection society, just show us where and we'll sign up right now."

I opened my eyes and looked at Catherine and then at Janice. They had joined in the general smiley atmosphere. "So, there you have it, ladies. I am some kind of a mystic saint who is adored by the few and misunderstood by the many. When I die there will be miracles at my shrine and my dried blood will liquefy once a year on the anniversary of my martyrdom. Or, on the other hand, Janice, your husband really is an arse and he appears to be working for some people who lost a lot of money because they weren't as good at money trading as they thought they were – and they think their stupidity was my fault. Now before we all nod off in front of Robbi's attempt to melt the wood burner, are we on for this charity or are we off?"

Catherine clapped her hands in delight and turned to Janice. "Janice I'm terribly sorry about Miles, but this is too good an opportunity to turn down. I think it's wonderful. Thank you, John, and thank you, Robbi."

Janice emerged from behind a tissue. "Yes, I'm all for it. I'm just so embarrassed by what John rightly calls my arse of a husband and I just hope you think I can be trusted."

Annette turned to Robbi. "I don't suppose you have a template for an NDA, do you?"

They headed to the study. Janice looked a question at me.

"NDA – non disclosure, or confidentiality agreement if you prefer. Annette's a lawyer."

Within ten minutes all parties had signed the NDA and the taxi had been called, Janice opting to spend the night at the Simmons' house. We went back into the drawing room where Paul was on the phone questioning Palmer about the bug. He hung up and looked up at me shaking his head. "Another one was in your bedroom, John and one in the study."

I sat down heavily. "Do we have them all?"

He nodded silently, staring at them. "Palmer says to put them back and carry on as normal. He'll fix up enough electrical disturbance to render them useless."

"Don't put one back in the study. Put it in the library. I need the study to think in and I just need to talk to Ludo and Angela for a few mins before that one goes back in here."

Paul nodded agreement. "Do you want me to get Major Cummins on to the bugs John?"

"Yes, please, Paul, but first there is the matter of Miles Scowcroft."

"He's being taken care of, John."

He left. I picked up the decanter and refilled glasses. Angela patted the sofa beside her and Robbi plumped down. I pushed a final log into the wood burner and sat beside Ludo. Angela sipped her single malt.

"Well, before we let you exhausted looking things go to bed, I want a summary of why John is looking like death warmed up again, what's wrong with his shoulder and what happened to your finger, Roberta."

"How did you know about my finger?"

"You've been clutching my hand ever since you sat down, dear, and even an old fogey like me can recognise a false fingernail when she feels it."

Robbi narrowed her eyes in my direction. "Yes, and what is wrong with your shoulder, John?"

I launched into the story of the last forty–eight hours. I finished and topped up the glasses. Robbi shivered. Angela put her arm round her and pulled her into her shoulder. "My poor dear."

* * *

Overnight my left foot swelled back up to double its normal size again so I was banned from the morning ride. I hobbled into the kitchen and was banned from cooking. Lockhart was preparing breakfast. I found one of my grandfather's walking sticks, hobbled to the study, woke up the iMac and looked for my notes – planning: not my strongest suit, according to my wife.

I stared at the map of the estate on the wall of my study. Six hundred and twenty three hectares, one manor house with outbuildings which, thanks to Miles I couldn't improve; two farms, one of which, in the hands of an incompetent crook, was going to wrack and ruin; three horses, one pony, two dogs currently all out together, (God, it must be chaos if Robbi was in charge of the dogs); an estate manager who had never managed an estate before; a gamekeeper who was, for want of a better description, a professional killer and a bank account that may have been extremely big, but was definitely getting smaller day by day. I opened the Power Point presentation I had made in an idle moment and studied my rogues' gallery of suspects. I created an arrow and then another and began to make tentative connections. I added text boxes with dates. I gazed at the screen. I added more arrows. I smelled coffee and drank from the mug. I changed some of the text boxes. I smelled bacon and eggs and ate from the plate. Interesting, the beginnings of a pattern were emerging. I sat back... to a round of ironic applause. I turned on my seat to see Ludo handing a ten pound note across to Robbi. Lockhart had brought me breakfast and the others had been sitting in the study behind me and I hadn't even noticed.

"You know you talk to yourself when you're concentrating?"

"He did it as a child, Roberta. His mother sometimes thought it was deliberate rudeness."

I searched my memory for this, but it was too long ago, too remote, too distant. Any remembrance I could dredge up would be false, I was sure. My mother was lost to me forever. Robbi understood. She looked over her shoulder at Ludo and Angela. "It's about the only thing we had in common when we met, you know. We had no memory of our parents. None at all. Silly really. She sat down on my lap.

"So, husband, what's going on in that upper class head of yours?"

"Well..."

I stared at my Power Point again. "Watch."

I traced the arrows with my finger, tapped the text boxes and explained the key agents and what I thought were their roles. Medina was now out of it. ffitch was off limits. However and whenever Alan Cummins set him up as the pawn, my presence would not be welcomed; which left three names – Collier, Scowcroft and Artinswell. Artinswell was the sole name that had been lodged in my head from before the beginning of what may laughingly be called my first adventure. I had approached this grandson of my grandfather's mentor in a half–baked manner and had been scared off immediately by his unsettling response to my advances. Soon it would be time to look into Artinswell, but first we needed to understand how to take full advantage of the chaos we must have sown in the enemy camp.

"The point is we have yet to get beneath the outside layer. The only people we've managed to stop are the ones taking the orders, not the ones giving them." I stared at the screen again. "Ludo, do you know Artinswell?"

"Yes, I do and I last spoke to him a few years ago in a debate in the Lords, but I can't say I know him at all well. However, right now I intend to exercise surrogate rights of parenting. I have informed Sergeant Browby that you two are to be confined to barracks for the remainder of the day. There is to be no more planning or plotting. He will walk the dogs and attend to the various livestock members of the household. Bed now, children, and no hanky panky."

So, like the good children we were we went to bed without even the remotest hint of hanky or indeed of panky. But even as I slept, the planning still went on in my overtaxed brain.

CHAPTER TWELVE

I woke up on the Monday morning with the word 'overtaxed' in the front of my mind. I swung my legs over the side of the bed and discovered that my ankle was mending. I showered and thought about overtaxing again. As it was seven thirty by now, I considered that it would be in order to text my wealth manager. He called back immediately. "Tell me Robbi's all right, John!"

"What about me?"

"Oh, you'll live. You've got at least seven of your nine lives to go."

"Well, thanks. Robbi's fine now, Tony, although it wasn't a lot of fun at the time. Now I'm sorry for the early text this morning, but I want to pay some tax."

There was a long pause. He cleared his throat and spoke tentatively. "You sure you're all right, John?"

I wasn't, but I told him about the select committee, the probability that a member of the committee would know about the money in the Swiss bank and my desire to remain above and beyond any kind of criticism. He listened disapprovingly.

I wandered outside to see Dave's Discovery parked in the stable yard. No sign of them above ground so I peered into the cellar from the top of the steps. Miles Scowcroft was sagging on ropes, his arms secured to a beam above his head, with Dave standing in front of him in full army combats. As I watched, he threw a bucket of water at Miles. His head snapped up and he groaned. Dave saw me and raised a hand in my direction. I sat on the top step and thought. Dave and Paul watched me. Scowcroft's head slumped forward again. I walked briskly down the steps. "Sarn't Major."

Dave snapped to attention. Scowcroft's head came up, scenting a rescue. He saw my face and the hope faded.

"Sah."

"Any progress?"

"None, sir. The prisoner has declined to co–operate."

"And how persuasive have you been, Sarn't Major?"

"No persuasion, sir. Just asked him for his co–operation as this was a matter of national importance."

"Very well, Sarn't Major, time is of the essence. Persuade him, if you please."

"Sir."

Dave flexed his shoulders, turned to face the sagging body, cracked his knuckles and raised his fist slowly. Scowcroft broke. "No, no. What do you want to know? Who the hell do you work for, Hannay? Who are these men? You cannot do this."

Couldn't I? I remembered all too clearly Robbi's finger and the four bugs in my house. "Carry on, Sarn't Major."

Dave hit him once – tapped would be a more accurate word. Scowcroft squealed with fear and pain and the story came tumbling out. It was pathetically predictable. A small-time property developer, he had over–reached himself before the last recession and been left with one development too many and no one buying. The bank threatened foreclosure. Bankruptcy loomed and then had come the call.

"Let him down."

He slumped to the floor rubbing his wrists and whimpering. I waited until he looked up at me then held his gaze. He looked down. I kept staring at him. He looked up again and swallowed. "I could kill you, Miles. I could kill you now and no one would ever know and I wouldn't even have the faintest hint of regret."

He started to stammer. I waited in silence until the stammering stuttered to a close. "They sent men armed with semi–automatic rifles, Miles. They kidnapped Robbi. They were getting ready to rape her when I found them. I killed one of them, Miles. And I would kill you too or anyone who threatens her in any way. You see..." I paused and stood, moving my ankle experimentally. It hardly hurt. "Before I met Robbi I didn't much care whether I lived or died. The men behind the men who bought your miserable, worthless, withered soul had killed my mother and father when I was a child and since then life hasn't really meant a lot to me – but then I met her, Miles."

He was watching me in horror.

"They kidnapped Robbi, Miles. And you... you, with your pathetic greed and your even more pathetic inability to face the fact you had failed in a business venture. You didn't give a tuppenny damn what anyone did to her did you, just so long as you got your money?"

A shadow half blocked the sunlight. I looked up and nodded at Palmer as he came down the steps. "Who's this?"

"No one now. His name was Miles Scowcroft. He set them up to kidnap and kill Robbi."

Miles was shaking his head desperately. Palmer held out a hand to Dave. "Did he now? Give me a gun, Dave. I'll top him."

Miles had all but lost the power of speech. He was a rag doll, the head lolling and rocking on his neck as he backed towards the wall. He hyperventilated for a while, then managed to speak. "There were three of them. They came to my office in a car at the end of October."

Paul held up a finger. "What kind of car?"

"I don't know. Is it important?"

No one spoke. He stared round wild eyed.

"I don't know. No. Wait. Yes, it was a Ford Mondeo."

"A new one."

"Yes. Black.

"Describe the men."

It took a long time, mainly because he was close to breaking. The three men said they were from Special Branch – SO15. No, he didn't know all their names. Yes, they had shown him their warrant cards. No, he didn't contact them. They phoned him and the number they phoned from was different each time. They said it was for security. One of them had left a business card. It was in his wallet. Palmer browsed through the contents, scattering credit cards and cash on the floor. He held the card up to the light and tapped the number into his mobile. He pressed the speaker button and held it towards Miles. There was a moment of tense silence and then an anti–climactic 'number unobtainable' message. Palmer walked to the bottom of the cellar steps and held the card up to the morning sunlight. "It's a fake. The logo has been scanned – not even hi res. I'm going to call Alan and give him Scowcroft's mobile number."

He walked up three steps and made the call. I watched Miles, gauging his reaction. He was stunned. He slumped to the floor. Palmer walked back down. "Alan's going to eavesdrop on chummy's phone."

Miles raised his head and looked at me. "They said you were a traitor. That you were planning something with a foreign power; that you had to be stopped. They made me... they made feel proud to... to help."

Dave nodded his head. "Standard technique. Make the asset think he's invaluable and doing it for patriotic reasons."

We watched him in silence. His phone rang. Palmer scrabbled for it, hissed at me to call Alan, pushed a mini–jack plug with two earpieces into the socket, passed one to Miles and pressed green. I raised Alan, then listened in on the other ear piece. Dave lifted his Glock and pressed it against Miles' forehead. Miles spoke. I held my phone up to his mouth. If Alan couldn't hear both ends at least he could hear ours.

"Hello. Who is this?"

"Detective Sergeant Crowley, Mr Scowcroft. You didn't answer your phone earlier."

"I'm sorry, no. I was er..." He grimaced pathetically. "... tied up."

"Did you manage to plant the bugs?"

"Yes, all four. Er, are they working?"

"Not very well."

"Is there anything else you need from me?"

"You said she didn't have a torn finger nail?"

"No. I told you. I looked carefully. All her finger nails were fine."

A pause... "Are you sure?"

"Yes, like I said they weren't varnished either, just neatly cut and... and... Do you need me to go back there again?"

There was a distant murmuring. I pressed the ear piece harder into my ear. The voice sounded loud again.

"Not for the moment, Mr Scowcroft. But we haven't finished with you yet."

Miles was gaining confidence. "And my money? Have you paid it in yet?"

A snort. "What do you think?"

The phone went dead. Miles looked round at us nervously. I thought about loyalty. He was too easily bought. I heard Alan's faint voice. "Sorry, Alan. Did you hear the other end?"

"Not all of it, but we're tracing it now. Update me when you can, John. We need to talk."

I looked at the wreck on the floor. "Who do you bank with, Miles?"

"Coutts."

I pulled my phone out and span through the contacts. It would be the same regional manager as mine. I stared at the number. He could, of course, be in on this plot too, but I doubted it. He was almost at retirement age now and remembered my father – not that it in any way endeared the pompous old shit to me. I looked at Scowcroft again. His head was down. I could see he was crying. Another shadow crossed the head of the stairs. Her perfume wafted down the steps in front of her.

She sat down on the step beside me and looked across at the hunched figure. "Did you know they were going to kill me, Miles? Or did you just think they were going to take me to tea at Fortnum and Mason? Can you imagine what it was like to be driven five hundred miles with three men groping at you and telling you how they were going to enjoy themselves on you before they killed you – slowly?"

She slipped her arm through mine and leaned against me. I felt her trembling. Scowcroft looked up at her, full in the face, not a glance and away. Tears were pouring down his cheeks. "Lady Hannay, I am sorry. I am so sorry. I didn't know, but I know that's no excuse. I just thought all the rumours about you and Sir John were... and I just thought... I didn't think. I just wanted to survive. I didn't want to..."

He looked back down. I raised an eyebrow at Robbi. She shrugged and nodded. I dialled the bank. At this rate I would end up owning half of Oxfordshire's most useless assets. "Peter Dale, please. Sir John Hannay."

"Good morning, Peter. I am an early bird, yes, and you are my worm. Listen, Peter, I am sitting with Miles Scowcroft. You can speak to him in a minute. Miles has been telling me of his financial problems, Peter, and how you are being as much help to him as you bankers are to all your other customers who have problems. You can take this as an instruction from me that I will pay the loans that you have called in and guarantee his mortgages. I will come in and sign whatever you want and after that I shall also be closing all my accounts with your bank."

I passed the phone to Miles. He wiped his hand across his eyes and spoke in subdued tones.

I walked back to the stable yard and was ordered to the kitchen by Paul. There I was stripped to the waist by Robbi and Margaret. My bandages were cut off and I looked away while they soaked the gauze pad and eased it off. I risked a glance. Robbi choked back a sob.

"Uh, is it that bad?"

Margaret glared. "For God's sake, John! Robbi's told me how you made sure you were behind her when you ran away from that place on Skye. How do you think she feels? You could have been killed."

Robbi shook her head. "He won't understand, Margaret."

But I did. Six months ago, I wouldn't have, but now I did. Six months ago, I wouldn't have cared if I had been killed. But now I did. I just didn't know how to tell her. Margaret left. I held out my hand to Robbi and led her to the stairs.

CHAPTER THIRTEEN

I spent the next week acting – Member of Parliament, Committee Interviewee, Political Journalist. Each day I selected a role and thought my way through its ramifications and its implications. Each day the dining hall at Fosse became the Treasury Select Committee room. Each morning I walked into the hall, took my seat and studied the photos of each member blue–tacked to the backs of the chairs. Each morning I waited for the information from Alan Cummins and by each afternoon I was disappointed. 'Know your enemy', Field Marshall Rommel had said. I knew their Photoshopped publicity photographs and bland CVs inside out. By the day before the hearing even Robbi was beginning to lose patience with me. I prowled, fretted, bitched, moaned, muttered and whined. It was not a pretty sight.

"Just bloody phone Alan, for God's sake, John."

I shook my head, walked out to the stable block and saddled Jemima in a thoroughly foul mood. I trotted her down the drive, out into the lane and cantered to Jack Cartwright's farm. Fortunately for Jack and Joan they were both out so I took my bad temper up the steep path on to the downs where once again I was able to gallop away my frustration. I trotted Jemima back down the slope through the woods to the lodge house where Paul and Robbi were talking while the three dogs romped round and round in manic circles. I dismounted, but as I started to apologise, I noticed a certain froideur. Robbi had turned her back on me. Paul grinned and tilted his head in her direction. She was waving something at me over her shoulder. An envelope... an envelope, by God. She ran for the manor house with the Collies barking excitedly behind her. I was up on Jemima's back in a second and trotting after her. In the stable yard, I forced myself to slow down and calmly, gently, unsaddled Jemima, wiped her, brushed her, found her feed until she stopped watching me nervously and relaxed into her stall. The house intercom buzzed.

"If you hadn't been behaving like such a shit I would have come out and helped."

It went dead before I could reply. This was not going to go easily. I walked in through the scullery, tugged off my boots and washed my hands. A piece of paper fluttered in the door onto the floor. I picked it up. It was what the Americans call a résumé – a curriculum vitae of the Rt Hon Nigel Kinns, chairman of the Treasury Committee. I stared at it and put bread in the toaster. Spot slunk in followed by an angry whisper.

"Traitor."

I grinned, stroked the dog's head and read. Robbi's voice came through from behind the door. "You know you're no bloody fun at all."

I kept reading.

"I've got the best one in here though."

I poured a cup of tea and buttered another slice of toast. She muttered some more from behind the door. "Sod."

I finished the toast, picked up my cup and walked through into the dining hall. Beneath each photo was a sheet of typewritten A4 paper. I smiled again and waited – not for long.

"Want to know the weakest link?"

I sipped my tea and replied. "Grahame Jackson, Conservative MP for Sittingbourne."

I am sure her heard her stamp her foot. "How the hell, John Hannay, did you know that?"

I held out my hand. She slapped some pages into it. I read. My tea cooled. I smiled. She leaned against my chair from behind.

"Happy now?"

"Yes, Roberta Jane. I'm happy now."

"So how did you know it was him?" I looked superior and declined to tell her about the text I had received from Alan Cummins.

* * *

At twelve minutes past nine the next morning I was standing on the up–escalator of the brutalist concrete statement that is Westminster tube station. I turned left out of the exit onto the embankment and held up my invitation to the security guard at the entrance of Portcullis House, was ushered through the futuristic security tubes and led into a modern, functional committee room. By nine forty-five the room was less than half full of less than half–interested financial correspondents from various newspapers. From my seat in the corner of the room I had vetted all arrivals. I recognised no one. At ten my name was called – I was first to the slaughter. I walked down to the table at the front, swore to tell the truth and laid out my folders in front of me. I looked across at the committee. The committee looked across at me.

They started in gently. The chairman greeted me – then... "Sir John, am I right in understanding that you were central to the activities of BTD during the battle for Sterling, as the newspapers have dubbed it, of July of this year?"

I bent forward to speak into the microphone. "I was at BTD then, sir, yes."

The microphone squealed. I didn't need to lean into it.

"In what role were you there, Sir John?"

"As a trader, sir."

He looked at his notes. "But I understood that you had retired from trading some years ago, Sir John."

"Yes, sir."

"So, what made you return to BTD on this occasion?"

"I had been following the market and I had realised that someone was attacking Sterling and I felt that this attack was wrong... ethically wrong, I mean."

He decided to show his political colours. "Correct me if I am wrong, but I thought that, er, 'ethics' were not something that troubled the City overmuch."

This was predictable. "I cannot disagree with that, sir."

"Can you describe for us what was 'wrong' with this attack."

"The research we had from our analysts led us to believe that the British economy was not doing anything like so badly as to warrant an attack that was putting Sterling at below par to the Euro and at par to the dollar."

The member for Sittingbourne sat forward. He sneered. "Mr Hannay, you are an economist, are you?"

"No, sir."

"Oh, you're not?"

I waited for him to 'put it to me'.

"I put it to you, Mr Hannay that your actions during the period 20th to 22nd July were motivated purely and solely by greed."

I sat and watched him.

"Well, Mr Hannay? I am waiting for an answer."

"I have already answered that, sir."

He sneered at me some more and looked across at his colleagues. Well, if that was his worst, I was home and dry. The member for Bedford East sat up. I shuffled my files... Peter Bibby, LibDem, decent, hardworking constituency MP with a background as an analyst for Kleinwort Benson.

"Sir John, you may not know that I have spent some time in the City..."

"Yes, sir. I remember you were an analyst at KB. Euro dollars, I believe."

He smiled. "You have a good memory, but perhaps that's what we should expect from the Super Trader?"

That was annoying.

"Would I be right in thinking, Sir John, that you made a great deal of money as a trader?"

"You would be right, sir."

"So why, after then going on to become a hugely successful restaurateur, would you return to money trading?"

I looked at each of them in turn. "I believe I have already answered that question, sir."

The Labour member for somewhere in Essex joined in. "Sir John, I understand you were working under the auspices of Emma Fitzgerald."

"Yes sir, Miss Fitzgerald was the senior trader."

"And what, Sir John, was the nature of your relationship with Miss Fitzgerald?"

I allowed my surprise to show. "Miss Fitzgerald was the senior trader – my boss, sir. In my view she is the greatest trader of her generation. It was a privilege to work for her."

He didn't back down. "And where is Miss Fitzgerald now, Sir John?"

I didn't even have to pretend now. I was angry. "I'm sorry? I assume she is at her home. Why?"

The chairman leaned forward to emphasise his control.

"Sir John, may I remind you that you are here to answer our questions."

Fucking idiot. "Oh, you mean, as in 've ask ze qvestions.'"

He glared at me.

"Just one moment, sir. I have been summoned to attend this committee to answer questions about the activities at BTD in July and it sounded to me as if the member for South Somerset has just implied that I was having an affair with my boss. For the record, no I was not. It would have been the height of unprofessional behaviour. But what, sir, has this got to do with the activities of the twenty second of July?"

I looked at them all in turn. Fuck you.

"I take your point, Sir John. Now, please, can you throw any light on the activities with which you were directly involved."

"Yes sir. It had come to my attention that someone was putting a huge amount of pressure on the Pound. As I have said I felt that this was wrong and I went to BTD and told Miss Fitzgerald that I was willing to put my entire personal fortune at BTD's services to stop this threat to my country."

There was silence and then a turning of pages as notes were read. I felt the interest begin in the cheap seats behind me.

The Committee member third from the left spoke up. Again, I checked my files. Matthew Bolton, Conservative MP for Leicester South East. "And, er how much would that have been, Sir John?"

"In the region of three point four billion pounds, sir."

A further, longer silence – no shuffling of papers. Interesting, this, they hadn't been briefed at all. What was going on here? He continued. "And was there any direct interaction between the Treasury or the Bank of England during this period."

Time for a small bombshell... "Not to my knowledge, sir, and I'm afraid to say that I was asked to sign a statement to the effect that I would agree to abide by the restrictions of the Official Secrets Acts. There are, therefore, certain areas on which I cannot comment."

That produced a snort of derision from the member for Sittingbourne. Matthew Bolton continued. "Very well, Sir John. Perhaps you could tell us how much money you made during this period?"

This was more than odd. They didn't know... or someone had given them a stinking brief. Why? What if

I told the truth? Who? What? A penny began to drop. Alan Cummins was behind this... This was him putting out the disinformation he had declined to tell Mr Holroyd about at our last meeting. This was why he was so late getting me my briefings on the MPs. I trod the narrow path. "I provided BTD with an inheritance from my grandfather of three point five billion pounds to BTD for the trades. I recouped this money during the trading, but all profits went to BTD and not to me.

Utter silence. I wish I had brought a pin with me.

"So, you are in possession of three point five billion pounds, Sir John?"

I shook my head.

"No, sir. Approximately a billion is currently held in an escrow account awaiting confirmation of how much tax I have to pay to HMRC while we establish a charitable foundation in which the balance of the money will be controlled neither by me nor my wife. Within a month I will have no control over any of it."

So, there we were. The world now knew that I was in possession of three point five billion quid for the next thirty days. I continued. "My grandfather left the fortune to me in order for it to be used for a good purpose. I intend to continue to carry out my grandfather's wishes."

I looked along the horseshoe of faces. They had no idea what I was talking about. The man on the far left spoke. I checked my files – Labour, Stockport. "In that case, who did make money from the events of July 22nd and 23rd, Sir John?"

"I imagine BTD made a great deal of money, sir, as did any other fund which decided to take the huge risk of going long on Sterling."

The member for Sittingbourne sat forward again. I had the feeling he was about to make his move. "Mr Hannay, these outlandish claims about official secrets and financial sainthood would be laughable if they weren't so transparently false and repellent. You appear to be claiming that you have no use for large amounts of money, but from what I have learnt of your lifestyle, that is precisely what you do need. You live a life of luxury in a mansion on a neglected and run-down estate, you have had to sell your London apartment to finance a marriage to a former glamour model and common prostitute, no less..."

I raised my right forefinger and looked enquiringly towards the chairman. He nodded at me, neutrally. Ever since the News of the World affair way back in 2012 the Select Committees had been enjoying their moments in the sun. I let my gaze wander round the seven members. They were not amused by their colleague's insults, they did not enjoy them, but they were very interested in my response. So far as I could tell the member for Bedford East was the only one to look uncomfortable. I held his gaze for a moment and then with no display of anger shuffled through my files. I opened the one I wanted and looked down at the photo of the puffy face of the member for Sittingbourne. I looked up. He was no prettier in real life. Why on earth did people vote for such monsters?

"Mr Jackson, my wife's background is a matter of public record. When I met her, she was the general manager of a retail brokerage in the City and had been there for seven years. Prior to that she was studying French at a college in Marseilles and prior to that she was a legal secretary at one of the biggest law firms in the City of London. She comes from a family which has served this country in the army for four generations. Perhaps you would like to retract that disgraceful slur on her good character?"

I waited. He sneered again. OK, he'd had his chance and he was pathetically easy to read. He'd made the move he'd been told to make by whoever was trying to damage me and he believed that whatever happened from now on the newspaper headlines would scream variations on the theme of 'wastrel billionaire baronet marries common prostitute'. I was glad he didn't apologise. I sat back for a moment and listened for the noises behind me among the spectators – utter silence again. I felt their expectation. I leaned forward and looked at my file again.

"Perhaps, Mr Jackson, the issue here is that you have an unhealthy obsession with prostitutes. Perhaps this is what led you to insult my wife. Perhaps your regular visits to an apartment in Connaught Street which I understand is known as The House of Sin, have left you with a feeling that all women are prostitutes or can be referred to or treated as such."

I looked him straight in the eye and held his gaze. He turned red. He turned white. He was terrified. I picked up the photos from his file and thanks to yesterday's practice at Fosse was able to allow one of them to swing artlessly over the back of my fingers so that it could be seen by the now expectant crowd behind me.

"Perhaps you would like to deny that these are photos of you with a specialist in what is known by the acronym of BDSM. Perhaps you would describe her as a common prostitute, although I have to say that sex workers deserve much more respect than you would appear to offer them."

The murmuring had started. The chairman leaned across the desk with his hand up. You don't shut me up yet, you bastard, not yet. "Mr Kinns, you allowed Mr Jackson to insult and slander my wife knowing that he was protected by parliamentary privilege. Please have the decency to allow me to correct his error and point out issues which may have led to his disgraceful statement."

I turned back to the beaten MP. I felt nothing but a burning hatred for him and all his kind. "Well, Mr Jackson? Do you have an answer for me? Do you have an apology for me to take to my wife? Do you have anything to say at all? Can you even tell the difference between the lies you tell in private to your wife, family and friends and the lies you peddle in public in your disgusting attempts to destroy other people's reputations and their lives? And you had the crass audacity to call my actions repellent."

The volume of the muttering behind me ratcheted up... and up again. I breathed out and forced my knotted muscles to relax, blotting out the noise and just listening to the pounding of my heart. I poured a glass of water watching my hand – still steady as a rock. An insistent voice broke through my reverie. The chairman had made a clever political decision, but hey, that's why he was the chairman. "Sir John, I think that we should now return to the events of the twenty second of July."

I nodded. Quite right. Slow it all down for an hour or so and just get through some boring financial detail and hope against all hope that the press hadn't picked up the scandal – some hope.

The next hour and a half was indeed very straightforward. I explained the mechanisms of the money markets. I explained the risks that BTD had dared to take. I expressed my 'admiration' for Sebastian Damon (its short, angry, stupid, arrogant, American C.E.O.) and the team that had done so much to defend Sterling. I even digressed into a few well–chosen comments about how I believed that the economy had improved significantly as a result of our defence of the currency. I had some interesting technical exchanges with the member for Bedford East. I knew that he knew that we both knew our stuff. At one o'clock the chairman thanked me for my contribution and asked me to make sure I was available for further consultation if required. I thanked him and concurred without taking my eyes off Grahame Jackson, the soon not to be, (I sincerely hoped), member for Sittingbourne. I sat still in my seat. I didn't turn round. Eventually I leaned forward and closed the files up and went to stand, bracing myself for the press mobbing I knew I could no longer avoid. Then a figure approached my table.

"Why don't you come with me, Sir John? I have the feeling it might be a quieter way out for you."

It was the member for Bedford East. I smiled at him gratefully, but he was looking beyond me at the still half full committee room. "You know, Sir John, we have very good cleaners here. You don't need to pick up all your rubbish."

He looked straight at me. I nodded slowly as the implication sunk in and carefully picked up the file containing the photos of the member for Sittingbourne out of my briefcase allowing three to slide down on to the floor. Without looking round, I followed my rescuer across the floor, round the horseshoe of chairs towards the rear exit. I could hear the scrabble of feet through the chairs as we left and the clamour of journalists... "Sir John? Sir John?"

The door swung to and for once I was on the inside. I hadn't realised how many underground tunnels there were around the Westminster complex. I followed my guide along the corridor, down stairs and through the doors where it changed from bland modernity to worn Victorian. He looked at me.

"Stairs or lift, Sir John?"

I smiled and held out my hand. "How many floors, Mr Bibby?"

"Three, and it's Peter."

"John. I hate lifts, but I'm not sure I can make three floors after that.'"

We shook. He waved his other hand around in a circular gesture. "Norman Shaw North."

I looked suitably blank.

"It's the original New Scotland Yard building. Part of the parliamentary estate."

Oh. Another MP joined us in the lift. I hate lifts at the best of times and this one was getting way to crowded for my comfort zone. The MPs nodded at each other. The newcomer was fat, bloated, smug, like that bastard Jackson. I felt the anger rise again. The unknown MP got out on the next floor and I realised Bibby was watching me.

"You're an angry man, John."

I nodded. "I have a lot to be angry about, Peter."

He gestured towards the lift door and I walked out ahead of him.

"First door on the right."

I pushed the door open and the figure sitting on the windowsill cried out my name, jumped up and ran into my arms... and nothing mattered any more. I buried my head in her hair, breathed in her scent deeply and let the breath and the tension seep away. I felt her body quiver and raised my head from her shoulder to see Peter Bibby smiling at someone in the mirror over the mantelpiece. I turned my head slightly and saw the reflection of his secretary discreetly wiping a tear from her eye. How embarrassing. I stepped back smiling politely, pulled out my phone and dialled. Alan answered.

"Don't use my name, John. Saw the performance. You are an angry little baronet aren't you."

I sighed. "Yes, well... Listen, thanks for the briefing. Er, I'm in the office of Peter Bibby. What may I tell him?'

"Everything you like, but keep me and my superiors out of it. He'll know from this call that there is some official sanction for your actions."

I put the phone back into my pocket and took the proffered chair. The secretary put a cup and saucer in my hands and smiled at me. I could sense some mothering coming on. I glanced at Bibby nervously, but he was simply smiling at my predicament.

"I'm Andrea Bibby, Sir John, Peter's wife. I thought at one moment that I would have to stop Robbi from running down to the committee room to take care of you. She says that you are far from well.'

I smiled at her in the most reassuring manner I could dredge up. "Robbi worries too much, Andrea, and thank you."

Robbi turned to Peter Bibby. "You know he hates lifts, Peter? He's claustrophobic. So I hope the three flights of stairs didn't tire you out too much."

Bibby tried hard not to look at me. "No, no, not at all, Robbi, not at all."

She raised her eyebrows and looked towards Andrea Bibby, shaking her head in disgust, then turned back to me. "You're an idiot, John."

I hung my head. "I know, Robbi, I know."

She did sound genuinely exasperated, but then I did sound genuinely contrite.

"Go on then, tell Peter all about it."

As I opened my mouth the phone rang. Andrea answered it and immediately looked at me. "Just one moment."

She glanced at her husband and then back at me. "John, it's Channel 4 News, they want you to go on tonight and do the main interview."

I shook my head and appealed to Peter. He pointed at the phone on his desk. The call was transferred.

"Peter Bibby here. May I help? Yes, I did. Yes, he is. No, I do not believe it would be proper for him to give any interviews yet. I will tell him that. Yes, of course. Cheerio."

He turned back to me. I shrugged an apology and began to brief him while Andrea took shorthand notes. After two minutes he held up his hand. "John, you may not like this, but the chairman of the Finance Committee needs to hear this."

Robbi nodded vigorously. I shook my head. "I'm sorry, Peter, but no. It's simple really. I have no bias towards any political party, but I trust you. I don't trust him."

I looked straight at Robbi and noticed out of the corner of my eye that Andrea was mouthing agreement to her husband. Robbi's phone rang. She apologised to the room and pressed green. "Hello fatso, not squirted it out yet?"

She listened, glancing at me and then at Peter. "OK, Netty, I'll get back to you asap. Take care of yourself and stay away from trampolines. Bye now."

She spoke to Andrea. "That was the wife of the editor of the North Cotswold Gazette – our local weekly. The Fleet Street vultures have already been on to them trying to find out what they know about us. Poor thing's forty weeks gone and as huge as a house. Dreadful oedema in her ankles too. They missed the one o'clock news so she wants to know what's going on. What shall we tell her, John, Peter?"

Peter Bibby stood, stretched and smiled. "It's such a pity you two aren't in my constituency. I could really do with a 'good cause' right now. First things first: Andrea, you said that Robbi's brother was outside. Robbi, call him and tell him to go to the Norman Shaw North entrance and you two can get him in."

CHAPTER FOURTEEN

It was the next day. It was still early. I was still tired. We were in Dave's Discovery, heading for the hills above Fosse to rendezvous with Grace and Paul who had been sent out with the horses.

I called Luke Warburton and by eight thirty that morning a little party foregathered on the treeless grazing land of the Cotswold tops and huddled together in the lee of one of our recently repaired, dry stone walls. I had already decided the angle I would be happiest that Luke took in the paper. He took photos of us on our horses, told us of the quotes he had invented for us and left to steer his muddy course back to Burford. Dave drove the excited Grace home while Robbi and I cantered the horses across the open grassland, walked them down the steep path, trotted across the lane at Home farm, up through the beech Copse and across the paddock to the gate in the wall at the back of the stable yard. Grace was ordered on pain of Robbi's deepest displeasure to tend to the horses and not, repeat not, to call her friend Jasmine or the boys to tell them we were home. I could have told her she was wasting her time, but such is not my role. She left for the kitchen while I was unsaddling Jemima. I looked at Grace. "When you text them, tell them to keep out of the way and wait for me here after breakfast tomorrow."

She stared at me like I was a magician. I shrugged. "Robbi is a lot nicer person than me. It wouldn't occur to her that you would disobey her or that you would argue that she only said not to 'call' them and of course texting isn't 'calling'."

The kitchen was warm and half–full of ex–SAS soldiers. Margaret had a pile of bacon sandwiches stacked on the warm plate and Robbi was stirring tea bags round inside the enormous old pot. Paul reported. "We caught twelve reporters during the course of the night. Well, four of them were actually photographers so we confiscated their cameras and told them to come back at one pm today and we would return them. There are eight reporters in the dining hall. They slept in the cellar and they're not too happy."

This amused the SAS.

"They were beginning to get a bit uppity so Dave went in a few minutes ago."

I absorbed the information. "Who's watching the grounds?"

It transpired that Frank Johnson was leading a three–man patrol in the woods and Gareth Spinetti was at the gates. I followed Robbi to the dining hall and peeped through the door crack to gauge the reaction. The muttering died the instant she entered. She offered food in silence, smiling shyly. Only one of the eight spoke. "Fucking disgrace it is, kidnapping people in the middle of the night. Who the fuck do you think you are?"

Robbi managed to look both nervous and apologetic. "I'm ever so sorry. John and I were in London yesterday and we've only just got back."

"My arse."

Dave pulled himself upright and leaned towards the aggressor. "Please moderate your language in the presence of a lady, sir."

Robbi turned in my direction. I grinned. Little genius that she was – tears were running down her cheeks. She carried on serving sandwiches in a sniff filled silence. Seven of the eight journalists looked distinctly uncomfortable. I beckoned Paul and Margaret past me and as teas were dispensed, I padded into the room in my stockinged feet and took my place beside Robbi sitting on the ancient hall table, putting my arm round her shoulder and watching our guests. I cleared my throat. "This is a bit of a mess."

I looked round. Robbi blew her nose. "Would you mind telling us which newspapers you work for?"

Seven of the eight complied. I studied the eighth. Dave leaned forward again and murmured in his ear.

"I'm not frightened of you or any of your thugs so you can fuck off."

I looked round at the others. "Any of you know him?"

They shook their heads.

"Paul, could you phone Chief Inspector Thornton, please and ask him which is the best police station to take a trespasser to?"

There was the briefest of struggles – and then there were seven. "I take it you are here because of my treasury committee appearance."

They agreed. "Do you want to ask questions one at a time?"

They started in – and it had worked. Not one of the questions related to Robbi's background at all. All they were interested in was how I knew so much about Grahame Jackson MP and how much more I could tell them about his private activities. I discovered that they had drawn the short straw; the lucky reporters were the ones door–stepping The House of Sin on Connaught Street. Our lot had come to Fosse hoping for a bit of background, a possible interview with a member of staff and a shot of Robbi. Dave came back in. He cocked an eyebrow in my direction.

"Yes, Dave?"

"That er gentlemen, John. He's not a reporter. He won't say who he is, but he is very worried about seeing the police. He just tried to bribe me."

I turned back to the journalists. "Complicated story isn't it?"

They were silent, absorbing the information, the older ones among them writing their Shorthand notes. "Gentlemen, may I ask you one question, please?"

They waited.

"Why do you think it was me at the committee? Why not the Chief Exec of BTD? Why not the Senior Trader? Why me?"

They waited.

"I'm not trying to be clever. No one outside a handful of people at BTD knew anything about it being my money. And before you ask, no, I do not know the answer to this question, but I would like to know who does and who it was who had passed on to the member for Sittingbourne such a pack of obvious lies about my wife. I know it's a typical politician's ploy. Put out some dirt on someone and when it's denied say: 'well of course they would deny it' and then by the time it is found out to be a pack of lies no one's interested and the dirt has stuck. But really – how on earth did he think he would get away with that?"

The younger reporters held their iPhones even closer to me, recording every word. Robbi wasn't keen on the idea of being photographed, but I had already concluded that the more her face was in the public domain the safer she would be. The paps were summoned to collect their cameras and as we posed in front of the Aga in the kitchen the remaining photos of Grahame Jackson in flagrante delicto unaccountably fell from my file to the stone slabbed floor to be picked up by the helpful and tidy minded journalists and removed from the premises.

* * *

Lunch time. Paul was staring at paperwork on the kitchen table. He glanced up at me. "You know how Miranda discovered that Harker's a crook. He's been fiddling the books for years. Well two years ago he started selling off your land with false title."

I looked at him.

"Yep, and guess who to?"

I stared at him.

"Your land agent, Mallin."

I gazed at him.

"So, we did a little raid this morning as soon as I had seen he'd gone into Cirencester. Miranda's got a spare set of keys, obviously, and we found these."

Paul tipped the contents of a foolscap envelope onto the table. Robbi moved the butter dish and started to look through the papers. I pulled pasta out from under the grill and served up. Robbi passed me one of the documents and carved bread – badly. She held up the ketchup bottle questioningly to Margaret and Miranda and didn't even bother to ask Paul as she sloshed great squirts of the thick red liquid onto his food. As chef I could have been insulted by this slight on my culinary abilities, but I had long been aware that I travelled among the cuisinally challenged. I saw Margaret write the word 'ketchup' on the never–ending shopping list. I started to read. I suppose I was accustomed to legal documents, but even a child should have been able to tell that these weren't real. I glanced at Miranda. "Do you remember anything about this when you were there?"

She shook her head, mouth full of pasta. I studied the agreements again. "Is this Alexander's signature?"

Margaret passed her some kitchen paper; she wiped her fingers and leafed through three of the documents. "Yes, John."

"Very well, can you get these photocopied ASAP and, Paul, can you whip back over to Glebe Farm and put the originals back in the safe?"

The remains of the day were spent dozing in front of the wood burner. The SAS boys had refused to leave and were patrolling the grounds and preparing for a night's surveillance. At seven that evening Alan Cummins called to let us know he would be with us tomorrow at ten. At eight, Palmer called to say he wanted a bed for a few nights. At nine we headed to bed and this time I confess that there was an element of hanky and even a certain degree of panky.

CHAPTER FIFTEEN

Alan Cummins was early. Robbi was still in the stable yard mucking out when he arrived. Dave brought him into the kitchen and I cooked breakfast while she showered and then we sat at the table and exchanged information. Robbi, being female and therefore more direct than mere males like Dave and me, asked the questions with her mouth half full of porridge. "My kidnappers?"

"Well, after your husband's display of wounded masculinity there was only one left by the time Mr Lord got there. He appeared to be one of the leaders though and a very tough nut to crack indeed."

Dave growled.

"No, seriously, Mr Lord. We've given him the full treatment."

Did I object to this? After all it had been Robbi they were going to rape and kill. Well actually yes – in spite of this I did object.

"John."

She wasn't smiling. I tried to explain. "I went round to Artinswell's house when I was on the run, Alan – this is before I came to be dominated and bullied by the Lord family, of course. I don't know why I went there. It was just a name that had stuck in my memory for some reason – from when I was a child I mean. And he wasn't there and then I spoke to him on the phone and he said, 'stay there, we need to see you.' Do you see what I mean?"

Alan looked at Robbi, then shook his head. Dave was nodding. "He said "*we*" want to see you, not "*I*" want to see you, don't you?"

"Yes, Dave, I do. But also, Alan, why... why?"

Robbi clapped her hands and drummed them on the table, turning to Alan triumphantly. "Yes, yes, yes. Why was Artinswell's name in John's mind? Who put it there, Alan?"

"Medina you mean?"

I thought about this. Why was I so slow? I should have thought this through months ago. I put my head in my hands and stared at the patina of the ancient kitchen table, recalling something of my scrambled thoughts on the day we beat Medina – the day I collapsed at BTD. I'd remembered all the leads I had missed, all the people who would survive to exact revenge. Even in the extremity of my sickness I had been right about that, if nothing else. "What exactly does he do, Alan? How come he's so wealthy?"

"He's one of the Tory whips in the Lords. But I didn't know he was rich."

I nodded slowly remembering the hall of the house on Queen Anne's Gate.

Robbi patted the back of my hand. "Come along, John dear, share with group. You know how hard we've been working on your social skills."

"Well..."

"Oh, good boy. Isn't he a good boy, Dave?"

160

She clapped her hands. Dave was grinning – Alan too I noticed.

"I used to be very happy on my own, you know. Didn't have to explain anything to anyone or *share* anything either. Right, this will be difficult to explain to you lot as you appear to believe a drawing room is called a lounge and I think I have even heard Alan asking to use a toilet not a lavatory. So, when I went there – Artinswell's I mean – there was a maid and the entrance hall had enough art in it to be at provincial museum level. I say that advisedly because it was the most eclectic collection I have ever seen."

I glanced round. Robbi yawned ostentatiously. Dave shook his head at me and Alan shrugged. "Cultural pygmies. Look, most collectors collect one thing – impressionists, Ming vases, in–cun–ab–ul–a."

"Aaah. That was the word I had to look up after I'd seen Medina's library wasn't it?"

"Yes, Alan."

I looked at Robbi. She had stopped patronising me. She smiled mischievously and nudged her brother. "He's going to say something clever in a minute."

Dave gave one of his half laughs. "Cut to the chase, John."

"Well… in Medina's library, there was a Sheraton break–front glass cabinet full of Ming vases. There was a wall with at least three small, but very nice Monets and one which I would swear was a Sisley and the books…"

Alan stared at me. I raised my eyebrows encouragingly.

"Incunabula?"

"Correct. And in James Artinswell's entrance hall there was one exquisite piece of each one of those very collectible items."

"Jesus!"

"Indeed, Major Cummins. You may well blaspheme."

I pushed a paper copy of my Rogues' Gallery across the table. "Lord Artinswell has to be someone important in this set up. Remember Medina's enormous vanity – his vast ego. Remember the way he looked at his trading floor, his greatest creation."

Alan peered at the paper. "You quoted from the Bible."

Robbi nodded. "You said, er: And God saw every thing that he had made, and, behold, it was very good."

"Well done, little Robbi. Genesis Chapter One."

Revenge never hurt in a relationship. She laughed at me. I smiled back. I was so proud that she was mine, and so arrogant to think I could call her mine... but she was! I lifted the laptop off the dresser, booted it up and found the Power Point presentation. I dragged the text box with Artinswell's name in it from the edge into the centre of the page below Medina's. The linking arrows moved with it. I tapped the screen. "I'd linked Artinswell to ffitch because they had both been in the Civil Service. Artinswell had gone to Eton too."

Alan was tracing some of the links with his finger on the screen. "Tenuous, John. Tenuous. I'll get the boys on to it."

"Alan. Do you mind if we don't do that?"

He glanced up from his perusal of the linking arrows, raised an eyebrow and sat back and waited.

"I just have the feeling that there are more people involved in this than we will ever know about and what with your problems at MI5 which, of course, were caused by us in the first place..."

Alan looked down at the table. "You know, sadly, I think you may be right. Get Palmer on it."

"Get Palmer on to what and where's my breakfast?"

Palmer the charmer had arrived. As statistical analysis like this was what floated his little coracle, I briefed him and left him stocked up with food and coffee. Five minutes later he came back in to the kitchen and co–opted Robbi as his researcher. She hit the Internet. She hit the phones. The whiteboard began to fill. I made lunch and talked to Alan. "On a scale of one to ten, how important am I in this whole thing?"

I waved a fish slice in a vague approximation of two axes of a graph. He smiled blandly.

"On a scale of one to ten, John, how important do you think you are?"

"To me, ten. To you less than five and after you can get to the ones behind all the little people, less than zero."

He traced one of the links on the lap top screen and looked to me very much as though he was hesitating.

"Come on, Alan."

"Well, for reasons I am not entirely clear about, you would appear – on a scale of one to ten – to be ten to everybody."

"What do you mean, 'for reasons I am not entirely clear about'?"

He held up his hands. "Look, my new boss hates me, mainly because I was Sir Ian's man – but I'm still here.

The Home Secretary has a conniption fit every time my name is mentioned, mainly because of your behaviour at the Treasury Committee – but I'm still here. I don't know, John. It's just very odd."

"And what about the future career of Major Alan Cummins?"

"I don't even know about that. A month ago, I wouldn't have given myself until Christmas, but winds are changing, John. Winds are changing."

Before I could pursue this, Palmer entered grinning cockily. "What, Palmer? You can't have cracked it already."

He gave me the finger. "Could've, but no, nothing to do with that. Remember that fat bastard Collier who tried to get you on the front page of your local rag?"

"Obviously, why?"

He grinned in his maddening way. I thought for a second. "You've traced the lump sums that went into his account."

"Yep. Now guess where they came from."

I looked at Alan. He shrugged.

"Jersey?"

"Close, Major, but no coconut."

"Palmer..."

He grinned at me even more maddeningly and rubbed his hands together. "All right, all right, all right. No need to lose your upper-class rag. Guernsey. Now, tell me who sent them."

"Collier's mother – the Prime Minister – the Archbishop of Canterbury. I have no idea, Palmer, for fuck's sake."

"You did."

That shut me up. I stared at him. I stared at Alan. The onions turned brown. I lifted the pan off the hot plate and sat down. Palmer was delighted.

"Explain."

"Well, I told you it would take a bit of time to crack the bank's encryption... You're not hearing this, Alan."

Alan made 'see no evil, hear no evil, speak no evil' gestures.

"So, when I did, I found it originated back on September the nineteenth at a very posh little private bank in St Peter Port which means, John, that..."

"That I must have been there in person. Bloody hell! I wonder what I was actually doing on September 19th."

"Probably shagging that dumb blonde wife of yours who thinks she can creep up on me from behind without me hearing."

Robbi kicked him in the back of his left knee making his leg buckle. He sat down still grinning and explained again, very happy to have the chance to show off once more. Robbi looked round the table. "Would banks like that have surveillance cameras, Alan?"

"Bound to."

Robbi phoned the private jet company that had brought me home from Inverness. Alan made mysterious, muttered calls to his friends at SO15.

CHAPTER SIXTEEN

At six fifteen in the morning, we were waved off by Robbi. By eight we were airborne. The plane was booked in Tony McElroy's name and I paid cash for the taxi to take us into St Peter Port. There would be no record of John Hannay ever having come to Guernsey. For that matter there would be no record of Major Alan Cummins being there either. I was accompanied by a man whose warrant card declared him to be Superintendent Walker of SO15.

At police headquarters in Hospital Lane, I was left in reception while Alan went into a conflab outside in the rain with a burly uniformed man with silver bands on the peak of his cap and a nervous, younger, plain–clothes officer who said not a word, but nodded a lot and kept peering in the door at me. Alan beckoned me out and an unmarked police car took us to the discreet entrance of Bank Lerner close to the harbour. I pulled my Trilby down over my eyes and led the way, leaning on my stick. An elegant receptionist hurried forward, fluttering her eyelashes, and led me to a chair. The young officer stood in front of me, shielding me from the security camera while Alan asked for the manager. There was a brief hiatus. The manager was busy. Could we give our names and return in half an hour? We could not. But the manager was in meetings. We would wait. The elegant receptionist tried to appeal to me. I shook my head. Alan's voice became louder. The elegant receptionist retreated and minutes later we were in front of an irritated manager. Warrant cards were produced. Irritation turned to trepidation. I sat with my back to yet another security camera and waited. Trepidation became ingratiation. My moment had come. "Mr Kenton, do you know who I am?"

"Er no. Should I?"

I pulled my passport out of my coat pocket, a water bill for Fosse Manor and an outpatient's appointment letter for the John Radcliffe Hospital in Oxford. He stared at them. He stared at me and shook his head, smiling uncertainly. "I understand that I am one of your clients, Mr Kenton."

He shook his head again. Alan intervened. "Perhaps you would like to check your account list, sir."

"I don't need to, Superintendent. I meet all my clients face to face and I know that I haven't met this gentleman."

"Check your account list, Mr Kenton."

The irritation was back. We sat and stared at him until with considerable reluctance he complied. He turned to his computer, tapped the keys, stared at the screen and went very still. He grabbed my passport and compared it with the image on his screen. "Um, there seems to be some kind of mistake here."

Alan walked round the desk and looked at the screen. He turned the screen in my direction and I leaned forward. The passport image was too blurred to see, the date of birth was wrong by some twenty years, the address was slightly wrong and the scan of the utility bill bore no resemblance to mine. Kenton stared uncertainly at the outpatient's appointment.

"Look at the date, Mr Kenton. Unless you wish to accuse a consultant at a major hospital of being a liar, you will note that on the very day I was supposed to be here opening an account, I was in Oxford."

Alan glanced at the young policeman who joined in. "I take it you have security camera records of the day in question."

The manager was now so seriously worried that he didn't even think to argue. We were led through to the security room where the young officer came into his own, spinning back through the records to 19th September. He stopped, stared, looked at the manager and pointed at the screen. The 19th September disc was blank. Alan took control. No, Mr Kenton could not talk to his superiors in London. His communications would now be monitored and he needed to sign certain official documents that the young officer placed in front of him. I walked to the window.

"The shop opposite. It has a security camera."

The young officer was dispatched. He returned two minutes later. There had been a break–in in October and the security camera records had been deleted. I went to talk to the receptionist. It transpired that when clients stayed over in Guernsey, she always recommended the Duke Hotel, just off the High Street. I smiled my thanks and declined her kind offer to show me the way. Alan and the by now completely overawed young officer were deciding which shops to check for further security cameras. I told them I would go for a wander and made my way up to the High Street. The Duke hotel was set back in a small, pleasant, early Victorian courtyard. I stood for a moment in the rain, rubbed the scar on my face hard to emphasise its raw newness and entered, leaning on my walking stick once more. I was confronted by yet another attractive young receptionist with a breast badge indicating that her parents had encumbered her with the name of Taylor. I gave her my best smile and started in on my story.

"I'm terribly sorry to bother you, but I have a bit of a problem that I wondered if you could help me with."

She leaned across the reception desk and looked up at me soulfully. I touched the scar on my face self–consciously. "You see I was in a car crash a couple of months ago and I have memory gaps – amnesia kind of thing. The week leading up to the crash is a complete blank and I'm trying to reconstruct it."

"Oh, you poor thing. How terrible."

I gave her a 'mummy's brave little soldier' look and continued. "From what I can work out I came over here to a bank and then I think I may have stayed here for one night on the nineteenth of September. Are you allowed to confirm this?"

I smiled at her in my most winning manner (the one Robbi said made her want to barf) and put my passport on the reception desk. Taylor's eyes widened as she saw my title and she positively drooled at me.

"Well, I'm sure it won't hurt, Sir John."

"Oh, just John, please."

The eyelids fluttered. She checked the computer. "September the nineteenth, you said?"

I concurred and she moved the mouse about for a few seconds, then smiled. "Yes, you were here on the night of the nineteenth. I looked delighted, then concerned.

"Um, the thing is, er, Taylor..."

She positively glowed.

"I'm not sure who I was here with and I er."

I tried my best to look embarrassed. She touched the back of my hand. "That's OK, John. I'm used to keeping secrets."

"Thank you so much, Taylor. You see there's this woman who is claiming I was here with her and I have no memory of ever meeting her at all – ever. From what it says in my diary I was just here on business, but I have no way of knowing."

She looked at the screen and passed me the print out of the check in. "You did check in on your own, John, but of course that doesn't prove anything."

I smiled ruefully. "It's a pity hotels don't take videos or photos of people when they check in isn't it."

My hand was grabbed.

"But they do, John. They do."

"Since when?"

"Since security cameras were put in."

"Oh yes, but I wouldn't be able to see those. Your head of security would go ape."

She giggled. "Oh, you don't have to worry about our head of security, we're BFFs."

She made a call. Another pretty young woman replaced her on reception duty and I was beckoned through the door to follow my new friend, who picked up two mugs of coffee from the dining room en route.

She knocked at a door marked, unsurprisingly, 'Security', and entered. I followed cautiously expecting to be bounced out by a tattooed, beer gutted fascist. Sitting in an office chair in front of a semi–circular desk with a range of monitors above it, however, was another attractive young woman whose face was surprisingly familiar.

Taylor smirked at me. "My sister, Claudia. Claudia, John."

I smiled politely as Taylor passed a cup of coffee across to her sister and explained why we were here. Claudia showed me the monitors and the video records, told me that there had been an outage on 20th September and some records had been lost, but that she kept a separate back up on DVDs. She pushed a box of them across, dismissed me with a casual "help yourself" and listened to Taylor's fascinating and lurid explanation of her last night's exploits with Jersey's young men. I thought for a moment, slid my phone out of my pocket and texted Robbi. A minute later the phone rang and I was able to remove the DVDs of the relevant day while Claudia did her best to get rid of the annoying call from someone called Robbi who wished to sell her some new security software.

Fifteen minutes later I was back outside Bank Lerner wondering where Alan had gone. A car horn sounded and I crossed to the waiting police car. "Sorry. I got lost. Such a pretty harbour. Any luck?"

Two heads were shaken. We returned to the airport. The jet was cleared for take-off and we headed back to Bristol.

* * *

Our taxi was waiting on the approach road outside Bristol airport on a double yellow line with the old driver loudly arguing the toss with airport security about why a taxi driver should be allowed to pick up a disabled passenger closer than half a mile away and why some airports who would remain nameless had done some dirty deal involving back handers he was sure with a big hire car firm that did honest men like him out of a job. I limped heavily and used the walking stick. The security guard showed no signs of embarrassment. We drove away trailing clouds of disgruntlement. I patted the old shoulder in front of me.

"Afternoon, Arthur. George not on this run?"

"Afternoon, Master John. No, old George likes to take it easy these days. An early start like this morning and he needs his afternoon nap."

He laughed and I smiled. 'Old George' was all of twelve months older than Arthur and I was Master John to both of them. They'd driven taxis for my father and my grandfather so to them I was still very much the baby of the family.

"I met someone this morning who mentioned your name, Master John."

"You did, Arthur? Who was that?"

"Ooh, there. Can't recall the name right now. Picked the party up from Oxford and drove him to Burford. What was that name now? Sounded like an animal."

"Poodle? Cat? Chihuahua?"

"Don't be silly, Master John. Anyway, it were like an African animal."

Alan joined in. "Lion? Antelope? Zebra?"

"Hippopotamus?"

"There you go again."

"Never mind, Arthur. If you do remember could you let me know, please."

"I will."

Alan's phone rang. It was the young policeman from Guernsey. He was excited. He had found a shop up the street with full security camera records. I kept quiet while Arthur took us through the gates and deposited us by the front door. He drove off and as I turned to open the front door there was a screech of brakes and spurt of gravel. Arthur leaned out of the car window.

"Master John, it were elephant. The name – it sounded like elephant."

I raised a hand and followed Alan inside. He snorted. "Elephant."

I stopped dead. Alan banged into me. I stared at him, thinking of the man I had spoken to on the phone in his very posh house in St Anne's Gate, the man whose grandfather had been my grandfather's mentor. The man I didn't think I could trust. "Elephant, Alan. It must be Bullivant! You know, Lord Artinswell's family name. No, he'd have said Artinswell, surely."

Robbi opened the door of the study and scrutinised us. "So good news, bad news, no news?"

Alan shrugged. "Not as much as I'd hoped. No visual evidence. Security camera evidence has been removed which says a great deal. Local plods not happy with me, so pain in the bum really."

Robbi stepped back and I got the once over. She raised a cynical eyebrow. I widened my eyes.

She turned away. "You know, Alan, for a secret service person you are amazingly useless at telling when people are lying and John's pretty nearly the worst liar in the world. He got on to something out there. Come along, husband, what have you got?"

I reached into my pocket. "Such a smart ass, ain't she? Sorry, Alan, I didn't want anyone to see I had these."

I produced the DVDs and the printout of the hotel check–in and, while I made tea, filled them in on my adventure. Alan then explained the Bullivant / Artinswell connection. Palmer asked the obvious question. "So, what's he doing down here?"

I shrugged. I needed to let this ramble around in my head. Robbi recognised the signs and herded us into the study. She grabbed the security DVDs, pinched the best chair and pushed the first disc in. The time code clicked along at the bottom of the screen and I clicked my fingers when it reached the time at which I was supposed to have checked in. *I* was a tall, smooth, somewhat jowly man – early sixties, well-manicured and expensively suited. Five other people checked in within a few minutes.

"Lot of people all at once. No one before for ten minutes." Palmer was noting time codes.

"Nor after." So was Robbi.

I plugged in the external hard drive and we looked at the other cameras in the hotel over the next hour.

Nothing, nothing, nothing, until... "Look. There they are. Where's that, John?"

"No idea. Looks like it could be a meeting room."

The five people we had seen in Reception entered the room one after another. Robbi gasped and stopped the drive, then slowly worked back frame by frame. She stopped.

"Look, it's John's Mrs Glossy – Mathilda Robinson. The woman who was tied up in our wood, Alan – the one who shouted at me in the supermarket."

I nodded. This was a breakthrough. She ran the drive forward again. It was my turn this time. "Stop. Back, back. That man there. He was the one in the supermarket when that woman had a go at you, Robbi. I'm sure of it. He was the one talking to Alexander Mallin, our one-time land agent. Wish the other two would turn round. That's never Miles Scowcroft is it? Hang on, someone else has just come in. He's only in profile. Bugger. Anything you can do with that Palmer?"

"Maybe. It's going to take a lot of render time though – overnight at least."

"If this lot..." I indicated the gathering on the screen. "... had a meeting back in September, do you think they are having a new meeting, here, today?"

They stared at me. I carried on. "I mean we've been trying to confuse them – throw them off the track. They keep thinking they have got us – got me exposed in front of a select committee, kidnapped Robbi, planted bugs on us and what happens? We keep springing up again like one of those ducks on a shooting range at a fair."

I paused. "I think..."

Robbi interrupted. "You think that they might be starting to think that one of their group is a traitor."

Alan nodded agreement. I continued. "Robbi and I can't do the rounds of the hotels to find them without being recognised..."

Palmer grinned at Alan. "Well, if you sub us for all the eating and drinking, we will have to do in the course of our research we can start straight away."

Alan glanced up. "Who's this 'we', Palmer?"

"You and me, Alan. No one knows your face round here."

Robbi reached into my jacket pocket, pulled three £20 notes out of my wallet and handed them to Alan. "You'll need a taxi back if you're drinking. Hurry up. It's almost four already."

She chivvied. I passed the Landrover keys across. Alan groaned. He walked to the door as my phone bleeped at me. I stared at it and sighed. It was Liam, Grace's now very ex-boyfriend. God, it seemed an age ago I had asked him and his partner in crime, Tyler, to find out anything they could about the planning committee and especially its chairman, the man I now knew as Miles Scowcroft. They wanted to meet. They had information. Robbi was fixated in front of the screen so I walked out to the drive, realising only when I got there that the only transport was the Bentley. I groaned again and drove to my appointment with the lads. They were in school uniform and looked nearly human. They were more embarrassed than impressed by the Bentley.

"We've been following the planning committee people for you and..."

"And a right boring bunch of twazzocks they are too."

"Thank you, Liam – and?"

Well, we found out the chairman was called Scowcroft and he lived in Burford..."

"So, we staked him out."

"And, four days he ago he disappears. No sign of 'im."

"But we carried on with the stakeout, 'cos we thought you'd want us to and frankly it was the only interesting thing that had happened to any of them committee members."

"So, we was getting a bit bored of it."

Were getting a bit bored *by* it. Did they teach them no grammar in school?

"And we decided that today was going to be our last day and guess what?"

I raised an eyebrow.

"Your man walked round the corner there at ten to five. We was just about to give up and go home. He went down the side path to the back door of his house and he looked a right mess too."

Still a mess. Still here. Why? "When you say mess, what do you mean?"

"Looked like he'd been sleeping rough for a few days. Lot of stubble – nearly a beard. Clothes all crumpled and dirty. Shoes covered in mud. Didn't see him come out, 'cept Ty thinks he got a sight of him climbin' over the fence at the back. Anyways ten minutes later, just as we was walking away, a car come round the corner, real fast and stops outside. Screech of brakes and all. Bloke jumps out and hammers on the front door. Doesn't get no response so goes round the back as far as we could see and then comes running back out – on his own – not your man with him – jumps back in the car and off they goes."

Well, well, well. "What kind of car?"

"Ford Mondeo. Black."

They recited the number plate.

"Thanks, lads. Um, I would like to apologise to you too. I never thought you'd stick it out. What you've just found out – that's really useful. No, more than useful, that's excellent. Thanks. Listen I'll tell Robbi I bumped into you and you were wearing school uniform. She'll be pleased."

They grinned and made strange wrist and finger flipping gestures and four £20 notes changed hands – cheap at twice the price if you think about the minimum hourly wage.

"Well sweet, man! Got to get home now. Laters, S'John."

My phone rang. It was Robbi.

"Just on my way home. I met the lads. They saw Miles Scowcroft an hour ago. Fancy a little drive in the country? Oh, and Robbi, pack some sarnies, it could be a long, little drive."

CHAPTER SEVENTEEN

She climbed into the passenger seat holding a plastic bag which I hoped contained the sarnies and, having waited all of ten seconds for me to explain myself, poked me in the upper arm.

"Well?"

I explained.

"And they were really wearing school uniform?"

I nodded. We drove through the lanes towards the A40. She waved a hand round in a descriptive manner. "There's no way you could track that Mondeo in this thing."

I shook my head and smiled in what I hoped was an infuriating manner. She studied me briefly, turned away, put her feet up on the dashboard, opened the bag and started on the sandwiches. I cleared my throat and held out a hand. She looked at the hand, took another bite and shook her head. Aaah, an impasse. "Artinswell's house."

A sandwich was placed on my left thigh. I looked at it. "Would you like me to buy you an electric bread slicer?"

She shrugged. "It's bread, butter, cheese, tomatoes and black pepper. That means it's a sandwich."

I stared at the unsightly hunk. "I'll take your word for it."

"So Artinswell is in Burford and you're going to try and do what?" She paused. "You said there was a maid."

I nodded, mouth full of an inch of bread and a quarter inch of cheese. The tomato dribbled down my chin. I wiped myself.

"And what did she look like?"

"Filipina. Young. Pretty."

The chewing became more aggressive and there was silence for a while, but I was not fooled. The storm had not passed; it just had yet to break over me. I finished my sandwich and kept my peace. She finished her sandwich, rummaged in the carrier bag and pulled out two chocolate biscuits. I held a hand out. She ate them both, sucked chocolate off her fingers, took her feet off the now slightly grubby, walnut dashboard and turned sideways to launch her offensive.

"So, while you are getting your jollies with some sexy, little maid – in a uniform?"

I nodded.

"Men! What is it about women in uniforms? Give a man a girl in a uniform and he just dribbles. Saw it all the time in the army. So, while you're getting your jollies with a maid in a uniform, exactly what am I supposed to do?"

"Are jollies what I think they are?"

"You know exactly what jollies are."

"The thought of jollies had not even crossed my mind, Robbi."

"Oh, piss off, for God's sake."

I saw a pull–in ahead and took evasive action. As she turned her back on me, I jerked the wheel and swore.

"What?"

"We've got a flat or something. Steering's playing up."

I jerked the wheel again and pulled off the road. As she undid her seat belt, I grabbed her, pulled her back onto the seat, threw myself on top of her and held her down – took some doing I can tell you. I gritted out a sentence.

"You are told by one and all, me especially, that you are the most beautiful woman in the world. I cannot believe my luck that you should have chosen me and not some film star or something and..." I stared down at her. She had stopped struggling. "... and you really think I would go off and shag some maid? Do you think I'm mad?"

She bucked again and shouted. "You know fucking well you're mad. And I saw you looking at Margaret's bum this morning when she bent over in that denim mini skirt she wears."

I realised suddenly that there was only one way this row was going to end. Maybe I was getting better at this relationship thing. Maybe. Maybe this was the first time a newly married couple had had make–up sex on the front seat of a 1958 Bentley Continental in the entrance to a field on the road between Windrush and Great Barrington. Maybe.

She zipped up her jeans and curled her feet up underneath her on the seat. We drove on in a silence that was noticeably more companionable than before.

"Re the jollies, by the way, I really have no idea how to handle an approach to the maid. Which is why you're here. Any clever ideas?"

"Nope, you're just going to have to shag her senseless and then ransack the house."

"My thoughts exactly."

She ignored me.

"Actually, to be honest, all I had thought was that with Artinswell away she might go out for the evening and we could see if we could bump into her if you know what I mean."

She shrugged. "No, it's best if you do it without me. Would she remember you?"

"I think she would because she probably got a bollocking for letting me leave before Artinswell got back."

"OK, well all we can do is get there as fast as poss, hang around outside and play it by ear."

It was my turn to shrug.

It was nearly seven by the time we got to Queen Anne's Gate. By this time Robbi had refined the plan a bit. I was to wait in the pub on Dartmouth Street and she was to wait in the Bentley outside Artinswell's house, on the grounds that, if the maid came out, she would almost certainly have to go in my direction and Robbi would cue me to come out so as to bump into her. I sat musing and nursing a white wine spritzer. My phone rang. I jumped, dropped it, scrabbled under the table and pressed the button to hear Robbi in mid-sentence.

"... left the house. Trim little thing too. Just your type, Hannay. She's walking towards you. Get ready to come out."

I abandoned the drink and hurried to the door. The phone still glued to my ear.

"Shit! Shit! She's coming into the pub. Get back inside."

I turned abruptly back to my table and picked up the half-drunk spritzer and kept the phone to my ear. The door swung open and the maid came in.

"Damn."

"Damn what, John? What's the matter?"

"She's not wearing a uniform."

She disconnected. I grinned to myself, swigged my drink back and walked to the bar in time to hear the barman speak to her.

"Evening, Sam. G&T?"

I stood beside her at the bar, humming, while she was served. As she turned to go, I glanced at her, paused, glanced back and looked amazed.

"Um, I'm terribly sorry, but don't you work for Lord Artinswell?"

She stared and then recognised me. "You came to see him early this year and then ran away before he got home. He was very angry."

"I'm terribly sorry. Did I get you into trouble?"

She laughed. "No. No. I can take care of myself with the Lord."

"I hope I'm not being rude, but could I join you for a few minutes? I'm sure you're meeting someone. It's just that I was thinking of going to see James again, but I hadn't made up my mind."

She positively beamed at me. What a pretty young thing she was to be sure. And how pissed off Robbi would be if she saw me now. The door swung open and a woman in a headscarf and dark glasses came in. Dark glasses on a mid-winter's night – who did she think she was, Jackie O? I just managed to stop what would have been my second double take in as many minutes as Robbi walked past me to the bar. I turned my chair so my back was presented to her and carried on.

"Your name's Sam?"

"It's short for Sampaguita."

"Sampaguita? Pretty name." I smiled at her and spoke loudly enough for my audience of one to hear. "For a very pretty girl."

I heard a snort behind me. The woman wearing the dark glasses at the bar appeared to be having a choking fit. Glad she had such good hearing.

"And I remember your name is Sir John."

"Just John, please. Can I get you another drink?"

"Gin and tonic, please?"

She downed her drink in one. This might be easier than I had thought. I crossed to the bar trying to separate myself from Jackie O. I attracted the barman's attention away from The Racing Post and ordered a large G&T and another spritzer. The dark glasses turned towards me. I turned away. My phone buzzed – a text!

you couldn't chat up a hooker. pretty name. pretty girl. tosser.

Actually, despite Robbi's baleful presence, chatting to Sampaguita was fun. She was amusingly indiscreet about his Lordship although it took me two more large G&Ts for me to catch on to the fact that he was gay. By now she was slurring slightly. She peered at her wristwatch. "Oh dear. I only came out for half an hour and you keep me talking for nearly one hour. I have to be back in before eight."

Such a pretty way of speaking English too. "Why? Does he check up on you?"

"Not always, but it is best to be careful."

"I'll walk you home, then. Like you say, it's best to be careful."

She giggled and took my arm. By the time we approached the Artinswell front door she had stumbled twice and I'd had to put my arm round her – to hold her up, you understand. She dropped her keys. I picked them up, helped her find the lock and then half carried her in. She leaned in to me. "You are very handsome man."

I thought of England. Her mouth half opened, her tongue touched my lips, her head slumped backwards, she snored. I sighed with relief, swung her up into my arms trying hard not to notice how her skirt slid up her brown thighs. As I laid her on a sofa in the drawing room my phone buzzed again.

you in yet? the house, not the maid!!! 💀

I called her.

"You are crude and vulgar. Come round now. She's out like a light."

"Not surprised. The thought of sex with you does exactly the same for me."

I let her in the front door, showed her the snoring body and we hurried round the enormous house looking for God knows what. Nothing of much interest on the ground floor: scarcely lived-in formal rooms and a large immaculate kitchen. First floor revealed signs of character – very large drawing room in which the furniture showed the patina of use, smaller study. I pointed to it, she nodded and we carried on up to the sleeping areas. Sam's room was on the top floor, neat and very feminine, pictures of an extended family back in Manila and a large display of soft toys. Sam was lonely. Poor Sam. Maybe we needed a maid. Robbi sneered at the teddy bears.

"We'd better put her to bed before we go. Don't want Artinswell coming back early and finding her flat out on his sofa."

"You just want to get her undressed."

I sighed and explained.

"If we can put her to bed and I leave a nice note for her, the chances are she won't mention anything to Artinswell. If we leave her splayed out down there, she might say that a man called Sir John Hannay got her drunk and got access to the house."

I stiffened my resolve. "And, Robbi, seriously – if you look around you instead of having evil thoughts about me – you will see the room of a lonely and rather sad child, not a dangerous nymphomaniac intent on breaking up our marriage."

She kicked the side of the bed and muttered something. I tilted my head. "Sorry?"

She grinned. "I forgive you."

I put my arms round her from behind and kissed her neck. She kissed the side of my face. "Told you I could be a bitch."

"You did, too. Come on let's get little Sam up here and tucked up in bed then we can explore that study."

It was hard work. Dead weights are always a struggle to lift and under Lady Hannay's forensic gaze I had to ensure I avoided touching any part of Sam's body that could remotely be construed as having sexual significance. That was not easy with four foot eleven inches of shapely youthfulness. Eventually I laid her on the bed and indicated to Robbi that she should undress her. "I'll leave the room if you want. And only down to her bra and knickers. She needs to think I was a gentleman."

"Ha bloody ha!"

I sat at Sam's tiny desk and composed a note which I passed to Robbi for approval while I went in search of soluble aspirin and a glass of water. I had a feeling she was going to need them when she woke up. I put the note on the bedside table propped up against the glass of water and found a soft toy to tuck up beside her. Robbi started to sneer again, paused, grabbed the toy off me and replaced it with a large, furry pink cat, tucking it up against the girl's chin under the bed clothes and stroking her hair as she did. Sam whimpered in her sleep and Robbi's face softened. "Poor little soul. What's going to happen to her after this is all over, John?"

"She can be my personal valet. Come on, let's get in that study."

It was a big study, not as big as mine at Fosse, but big enough, with nine, four drawer filing cabinets and two walls of shelves. His Lordship was a methodical man. We checked the desk drawers then started at either end of the cabinets and worked towards each other. He had files – whole drawers even – on wine vintages, a drawer devoted to grouse shooting accessories, endless cuttings on holiday resorts, holiday snaps by the thousand, but nothing of any relevance to us at all. We arrived at the centre cabinet and I made way for her to finish the job, pushing the blotter back on the desk top and moving Artinswell's diary so I could perch on the desk. His diary? His diary! I tapped Robbi on the shoulder and pointed. "His diary? God and there was I telling Alan he was crap as a spy."

She read much quicker than I did so I let her spin through it. "What was the date when they were all in Guernsey, John?"

"Nineteenth of September."

"Well according to this, the next day he was having lunch with someone called NR at the Athenaeum. That's a posh club isn't it?"

"Politicians, mainly. At least it wasn't the Turf Club. Full of country types – worst cheddar I ever ate."

"I thought posh people like you were born to be members of clubs like these."

"Not me. I have an aversion for men only habitats."

"Yes, I suppose you would. You'd want little Filipino maids on call, wouldn't you?"

"Filipina – female not male."

I mooched back the final filing cabinet. More holiday snaps of more supposedly cultural locations. And here was one with a middle aged, florid, well-groomed man, standing beside a pretty young lad. I paused and peered at it closer. I looked up. Robbi was watching me.

"What?"

"Seen this man before?"

She took the proffered photo and stared at it for a moment, then smiled the slow smile.

"That's the man who was at the hotel in Guernsey on the nineteenth of September. So, if that's Artinswell, he was there and..."

She looked at the diary again.

"... he must have got back in time the next day to have lunch with N R whatever or whoever N R may be."

I turned over a couple of pages and pointed and turned more pages.

"He met an E L in August and a P O in the first week of July and back in June..."

She grabbed the diary back and flicked back through the pages.

"... there was an S H meeting."

There appeared to be no meeting before June. Robbi went forward into September, licking her finger and turning the pages more slowly.

"On the fourth of September there was an N R meeting, a C O meeting on the twentieth and nothing else in September. The last month there was only one meeting with an E Y and then nothing until... Nothing until today, John when he is meeting an R D. And the only location mentioned is for the first one at that posh club."

"That is, assuming he did meet someone called S H and it's not a code name for something else."

We took photos of his diary pages and photos of his photos. Back in Sam's bedroom I found her mobile and entered her number on my phone. Robbi knelt by the bed and stroked her cheek. "Sam? Sampaguita? Can you hear me?"

I walked across the room. Sam murmured in her sleep. Her eyes flickered open. Robbi smiled at her. "Hello, Sam. I'm Robbi. John called me and asked me to come and help."

Sam reached out and touched her cheek. "Oh! Oh! The room is spinning. Is John yours?"

"'Fraid so, Sam. I saw him first. Now drink this. You'll feel better tomorrow. And we'll call for you soon, Sam. We'll call for you and you can come and live with us. And we'll get you a real cat, Sam. A real cat, not just a cuddly toy."

She lifted Sam's head and helped her drink some water and swallow the aspirin and left her smiling in her sleep.

CHAPTER EIGHTEEN

After eating a late meal, we opted to drive back to Fosse on the grounds that we'd miss the Saturday morning shopping traffic in Knightsbridge.

I swung the car's long bonnet round the corner beyond Home Farm at ten past three on that black morning and hit the brakes hard. The big car rocked, the tyres squealed and I stopped dead, inches in front of a white transit van that was at the head of a small convoy of other vans towing big, expensive caravans. I glanced across at Robbi who was still clinging to the dashboard, her face lit up white in the dim light of the 1960s dials. A burly man, with grey crinkly hair and an earring in his left ear stepped out of the van. I climbed out of the Bentley as doors opened and slammed down the convoy and men of all ages ran forward. The burly man held up a hand and the runners stopped. I smiled in the headlights and bowed.

"Latcho dives, Mr Baptista."

The man shook his head smiling and I heard laughter from the others crowding behind him. He spoke in the rapid, half incomprehensible patois of the Romany. I heard Robbi's car door close softly and felt her behind me.

"Well now, Master John, your memory for your old friends might be as good as ever, but you've forgotten your accent."

"Sorry, Mr Baptista. I've had no reason to speak Romany for a good few years. Were you leaving without even saying hello?"

I walked towards him, hand outstretched, and peered over his shoulder to see if I recognised any of the faces of my boyhood Gypsy friends. They were a tough looking bunch and no one whose face meant anything, except maybe... "Would that be Jacobo Wanne behind you, Mr Baptista? He seems to have put on a bit of weight since he was twelve."

This brought a buzz of amusement from the assembled men – Jaco had always been overweight and lazy. He stepped forward to shake my hand, bobbing his head and grinning – the others followed, Jehan Hearnes, Antoni Buckland, Caspar Smith. Their names came back to me from twenty–five years ago, the last time I had seen Mr Baptista's tribe when they had stayed for the harvest. They'd been magical people to the twelve–year–old boy from the manor then and I confess they still held some of their glamour for me now. I half turned to bring Robbi forward.

"My wife, Robbi, Mr Baptista, gentlemen."

"M'Lady. You're every bit as beautiful as they said, then."

I knew Robbi would be blushing in the light of the headlamps so I butted in. "You know you can't believe a word a Romany says on a full moon, Robbi."

"It's not a full moon, John, so thank you and it's very nice to meet you, Mr Baptista. How do you know John?"

"Ah, we've known the family for generations. I knew John's grandfather when I was a lad and my father knew his grandmother's family, the Lamingtons, for over four generations before that, m'Lady."

"I'm just Robbi, really, Mr Baptista."

He turned as an imperious voice came from inside the van.

"Is that Granny Baptista? May I take Robbi to say hello?"

Mr Baptista led us to the side door of the van where a thin, old woman was hunched over a stick and staring at us with the fixed concentration of the truly blind. Her voice was harsh, but strong. She'd terrified me as a boy. "Come close, John Hannay."

I stepped up to her and she ran her fingers over my face, pausing at the scar, feeling the cheekbones, touching my throat. "They said you'd been hurt, young John, but I didn't realise it was that bad. You nearly died then."

I nodded between her hands. There was never any point in asking how they got their information. The question would be ducked with some meaningless mumbo jumbo and an apology. She released my face and reached for Robbi who tilted her head up nervously. The old woman ran her fingers over Robbi's face, through her hair and down to her neck.

"Humph, very beautiful. You take good care of John Hannay, m'lady. He is special to us."

A baby cried behind her and Robbi leaned past to where a young mother was lifting a tiny child off her breast. Robbi smiled at her. "May I?"

The young woman passed the child forward and slithered out of the van to look up at me. I racked my brain. "Polly, how are you? What's the name of your beautiful baby?"

The young woman answered me with a smile and went to stand beside Robbi who was rocking the baby in her arms with a look of deep contentment. "Her name is Taleatha, m'Lady."

"What a beautiful name, Polly."

I fell back on the elaborate courtesy that I remembered had characterised my father's dealings with these people. "May I please ask you to accept our hospitality, Mr Baptista? It's been many years and I wouldn't want you to think that we had forgotten our friends."

The men behind Mr Baptista nodded their approval. I had managed to find the right words. Robbi rocked Taleatha and watched.

"It occurs to me that we have a place in the mill wood which you might find suitable if you would be willing to consider it."

Mr Baptista nodded and bowed formally. I was relieved that I had managed not to offend him. "Do you mind if I call my gamekeeper. Please be assured that he is not the usual type of gamekeeper. He is er... more military."

Mr Baptista smiled. "Would that be the giant, m'Lady's brother, or the other one – the sergeant with the scar on his jaw who never misses with his rifle."

"It would be the latter, Mr Baptista. I hesitate to say this, but I suspect he's somewhere near already. You there, Paul?"

A grunt came from above my head and Paul dropped into the road behind me raising his arms above his head to show he meant no harm. The Gypsy knives went back into their sheaths. I made the introductions.

"You talking about the clearing in the lower Copse, John?"

"Yes. We can connect water from the field tap and run in a cable from the old barn. I'll let Jack Carter know you're here, Mr Baptista."

"I said hello to Mr Carter first, Master John, before I went to the Manor."

He would have too. I wondered what would happen when leaders of his generation were gone. The younger lads were wilder, more bitter. Robbi looked at the Gypsy leader.

"Mr Baptista, would Granny, Polly and Taleatha like to come up to the kitchen in the manor and keep warm while you're setting up camp?"

He nodded and bowed, stepping back to speak in rapid Romany to the old woman who clambered down out of the van to let Polly lead her to the Bentley. Robbi backed the old car out of the way while the convoy turned at the corner of the lane and headed back down past the manor gates. On the way to the mill wood, I brought Mr Baptista up to speed on the tenant at Glebe Farm and the advisability of keeping his lads away from there.

* * *

"Shut the door, John. Quick. Taleatha's got no clothes on."

I shoved the dogs out of the Manor's kitchen, closed the door and pulled off as many layers of clothes as I could while remaining decent. The tiny, black–eyed creature was squealing and kicking its little legs and arms on a towel on the kitchen table. Polly and Robbi were laughing down at her while Granny Baptista sat by the Aga, clutching a huge mug of dark tea and smiling quietly to herself, absorbing the heat like an ageing reptile. Robbi held out her hand and I allowed myself to be pulled into the magic circle by the table. I put out a tentative finger and tickled the baby's belly button. She jerked, squealed, chuckled and grabbed my finger in her tiny, perfect clutch. By the time we had returned the three of them to the encampment, introduced the Collies to the Lurchers, stopped the dog fight, watched Paul handle the testosterone of the young men and got back to the Manor, it was past seven and I was more than ready for bed.

"Why have you taken to wearing nappies and where's my breakfast?"

I had forgotten about Palmer and Alan. I produced the frying pan – at least no effort was required in satisfying their culinary requirements – while Robbi filled them in on the events of last night in London and the arrival of the gypsies.

"So how was your evening? Do I get any change?"

"You have to be kidding – in fact you owe us another tenner."

"Dream on. So, come on out with it."

"Not too much sadly. Yes, Artinswell was meeting people at the Bull Hotel. It seemed to be six other people – so two less than was at the meeting in Guernsey."

"One of the absentees would be Miles Scowcroft, right?"

We adjourned to the study where Palmer laid out the photos he had sneaked on his iPhone and we loaded up the stills from Artinswell's house. After an hour we had learnt nothing.

And time dragged on.

I fell asleep on a sofa.

CHAPTER NINETEEN

The bulk of the morning's post slithered out of Miranda's grasp on to the floor where Spot sniffed at it, detected nothing edible so started to scratch at envelopes with her claws in a desultory fashion. I pushed her away, gathered up the letters nearest to me and waved away Miranda's apologies. Bloody Christmas – it seemed to start earlier every year – cards, cards, cards, charity requests, more cards! I didn't even know this many people! I slid one envelope addressed to Lady Hannay across the table, picked at the remaining pile, gave up, shoved the whole lot towards Robbi and sulked into my coffee cup. She flicked me a glance and started opening letters, making excited oohs and aahs at each card. Miranda tried not to giggle and eventually I conceded and grinned.

"Anyway, the one addressed to me isn't a card. Looks like an invite to some charity ball or other. Who's the Marquess of Cheltenham? Why's it addressed to me? He a friend of yours from school or is a Marquess female?"

I held out my hand and she skimmed it across. The Marquess of Cheltenham was inviting Sir John and Lady Hannay to a charity Christmas ball at a frightfully expensive hotel in the Cotswolds.

"Marquess is male and properly brought up persons of rank address invitations to the lady of the house on the envelope. Lady – ha!"

I ignored the sarcastic OoooOoooh noise and walked through to the library to dig out an old Debrett's. So... Marquess of Cheltenham in the County of Gloucester... a title in the Peerage of Great Britain held by the head of the Alain–Despenser family since 1791. The title was real then. I booted up the iMac to learn about the present incumbent. He was sixty–seven, no sixty–eight, had been to Harrow, member of Brooks, blah and blah. What about the charity? The invitation said it was in aid of a local children's home. It checked out. I leaned back and sighed. Robbi was bound to want to go. Why had we only just been invited though with a fortnight to go? I peered in the envelope and turned it upside down. A small piece of paper dropped out. It was a note from the Marquess' private secretary to me.

His Lordship has only just realised that you had not been invited to his annual ball before and he wished me to say he would be honoured if you would attend despite the late nature of the invitation.

Hmmm. The phone rang and I picked it up absently.

"May I speak with Sir John Hannay, please?"

"Speaking."

"Ah, Sir John, this is Hugh Digby, the Marquess of Cheltenham's private secretary. I'm not sure if you have received the invitation, but his Lordship..."

"Yes, Mr Digby, I've just seen your note."

"Ah, very good. So, may I add your names to the guest list? His Lordship would be most gratified. There would be no need to reply in writing if you can confirm with me now."

"I'll have to go and check with her Ladyship, Mr Digby, if you would be so kind as to hold on."

God, he had me sounding like something out of a Trollope novel now. I hurried into the kitchen where Robbi was still opening cards. I tossed the note on to the table.

"The Marquess' private secretary is on the phone now. Apparently, we are terribly in demand this year, but it's next weekend."

"We're only in demand 'cos of me being so gorgeous. Why not? What do you reckon, John? Hang on, though. What can I wear to a ball? And my hair?"

"I take it that's a yes then."

I walked back into the study ignoring the continuing, plaintive cries and picked up the phone wondering if Hugh Digby had a sense of humour.

"Her Ladyship says that so long as she can find a dress to wear, we would be delighted to attend. Please thank his Lordship on her behalf."

He chuckled in an oily manner – olive oily though and probably cold pressed from a single estate in Tuscany. "I'm sure Lady Hannay will have time to buy a new dress, Sir John, and we look forward to seeing you at the hotel ballroom at seven thirty next Saturday evening."

"Oh, and Mr Digby, I'd be very grateful if I could park the car near to the hotel. I am, ah, disabled – I have a problem walking long distances."

There was the slightest of pauses. "Mr Digby?"

"No, no, that would be absolutely fine, Sir John. I was just making a note to ensure you are allowed through. Thank you, Sir John. Goodbye to you."

I went back to tell Cinderella that she was going to the ball, but the kitchen was empty. The dogs were still there though, so she wasn't outside. I heard voices and followed the Collies upstairs to the source of the noise. Miranda peered out of the bedroom and wagged a finger in my direction. "Robbi says you can't come in, but that you will be..." She poked her head back into the bedroom. "Will be what, Robbi? Oh, OK." She laughed at me. "You will be delighted with her choice of evening wear and is your dinner jacket clean?"

Not caring whether it was or not I took the collies out in the Landrover to reacquaint them with the Gypsy Lurchers. There was no fight this time – they appeared to have learnt one lesson at least – so I left them sniffing at each other and knocked on Mr Baptista's caravan door. It took me ten seconds on the step outside the caravan to ask him what he knew about the Marquess of Cheltenham. The heads of the other families were summoned immediately and I was listened to in silence. I made a couple of proposals which were listened to in more silence and then after Spit had licked one of the Lurchers on the nose and had not been bitten, I left.

* * *

The ball was a long time coming, but its threat hung over my head during every waking hour. My wife disappeared for unconscionable periods of time either with Grace or Miranda. Three times to Oxford. Granny Baptista's visit to the Bristol Eye Hospital had been initially inconclusive. I'd had one more meeting with the gypsies at which Paul introduced Dave to them. The gypsies watched them both, looked at each other, looked at Mr Baptista and nodded. Mid-morning on Thursday I had a long discussion with Alan Cummins. Afterwards I told Lady Hannay of my concerns. She asked who else I had told and disappeared again.

And at last, it was the day of the ball and I discovered that my dress shirt had a wine stain on it and my dinner jacket was, indeed, creased and grubby. I sneaked round to Home Farm to plead with Joan Cartwright to help with the cleaning while I mucked out the horses and exercised the dogs. It was after six by the time I had collected my now immaculate evening garb from Joan and returned to the Manor where Grace was on watch for me. I was informed that I was banned from my own bedroom so after taking a bundle of clothes in a bag up to Paul at the Lodge House and letting him know that we would be leaving at seven, I showered, shaved and dressed in the cloakroom off the entrance hall and then waited to learn my fate.

At seven minutes to seven Grace came running down the stairs and physically turned me round so I was facing the front door. I heard Miranda giggling on the stairs and then, with my eyes closed, I was turned through one hundred and eighty degrees.

"OK, you can look now, John."

I opened my eyes slowly and looked up at the half landing on which Robbi was now standing, half posing, half smiling nervously. I stared and then realised my mouth was hanging open. I shut it and carried on staring.

"Well? John?"

"Robbi..." I remembered to breathe. "Robbi... Robbi, you take my breath away!"

She put her hand up to her neck, tears filling her eyes. "You're not supposed to make me cry."

The dress was a ball gown of my grandmother's – delicate, pale golden, clinging satin, backless, with a short train on the landing floor behind her. Her hair was swept up in an Edwardian pile above the back of her neck and she wore no jewellery, nothing at all. Just her and the dress. I managed to tear my eyes away from her to see Miranda blowing her nose above her on the staircase. Grace's voice echoed through from the kitchen. "Come on, Auntie Margaret, come on. John just told her she took his breath away. You've got to see them. It's so romantic."

I turned my head to see the normally unemotional Margaret's reaction when she saw Robbi. She came to a halt, her hands coming up to her mouth as she murmured. "Oh Robbi. So beautiful. So beautiful."

Grace was pulling out her iPhone. "We have to have photos. Come along, John."

I let myself be pushed and pulled into position. I really didn't mind at all so long as they would let me keep on staring at her. Paul honked the Bentley's horn outside on the drive as we posed for picture after picture.

CHAPTER TWENTY

There was a queue of cars waiting in the long drive up to the hotel ballroom. Paul mentioned my name and the Bentley was directed to a parking area near the door. "You're such a bullshit artist, John."

"She taught me all I know, Paul. See you in a while. Be careful."

"You're the one who should be taking care. Keep him under control, Robbi."

I stepped out of the car, shivered, leaned on my stick, offered Lady Hannay my other arm and limped towards the main entrance. Once inside, in the light and warmth I could sink happily into obscurity while the world ogled my wife. She kept her hand resting lightly on my arm and smiled her innocent smile. I led her through the reception crowd towards the receiving line, proffered my card to the Master of Ceremonies, noted out of the corner of my eye that he was smiling at me and did a double take. "Charlie? How are you, Charlie? How's Norma? This is Robbi, Charlie, my wife."

I smiled back at him delighted to have found an ally so early in the evening. Charlie had been a tractor driver for Jack Cartwright in the old days and a part time pub singer and compere at any village event.

"Evening, Master John. The missus is very well, thank you, she'll be dead chuffed you remembered me."

"Come off it, Charlie, why on earth would I forget? I'll tell Jack I saw you. You working full time for his Lordship?"

"No, no, Master John, his regular MC went down with the flu and I was first reserve... I'd better get back to the line now or I'll be getting a right bol… telling off."

I led Robbi into the line, nodding to our near neighbours in the queue and listening to their sotto voce comments about my beautiful wife and her beautiful dress. The line was moving at a snail's pace, but it wasn't until we got through the inner doors that I realised why. Each guest had to go through a body scanner of the type normally found at airports, manned by some pretty heavy–duty security guards. I let Robbi go through first and watched the eyes of the guards stay on her – amateurs, Dave would have said. I passed the walking stick to one of the guards, placed my phone on the tray beside the scanner and stepped through. No alarms. I turned to retrieve my stick and realised that the guards were struggling to break the top off. This would not do. "What the devil do you think you're doing with my walking stick? Give it back to me immediately."

I leaned against the scanner and held out my hand. Robbi stepped forward, tapped one of the guards on the shoulder, pointed at the stick and removed it from his hand. They stared at each other, lost for words, still obstructing our progress. A slim, smooth, bespectacled, dinner jacketed man in his early thirties emerged from a side room and hurried towards us. "Sir John? Hugh Digby. How nice to meet you."

I ignored him, took Robbi's arm and turned towards the exit.

"Sir John?" He was pleading. "I am most sorry for the behaviour of the security guards. We have a couple of senior politicians here tonight and this is all for their benefit, I'm afraid."

"It may be, Digby, but having to use a walking stick is enough of an embarrassment without having my disability abused by some of his Lordship's hired bullies. Lady Hannay and I will be leaving now. Good evening to you. I wish you good fortune with your charity."

There I was again, back sounding like an escapee from a Trollope novel. Digby wrung his hands. The little fellow was desperate for us not to leave. Robbi took my arm and her eyelid dropped for a fraction of a second over her right eye. "John, darling, do let's stay for a few minutes to see if it improves. It's taken all week to sort this dress out and you did say you rather liked seeing me in it."

Charlie's voice echoed over the silence. He was watching me anxiously. "Sir John Hannay and Lady Roberta Hannay."

I took my stick and with an ill grace limped up to the head of the receiving line. The Marquess of Cheltenham, clearly bored by the whole shooting match, was murmuring to a stout, middle–aged man who wore his dinner jacket with the self–assured pomposity of one who expects to be recognised. As I made my bow, I caught a glimpse of their eyes suddenly gleaming with interest. I straightened while Robbi was still curtseying deeply and noted with amusement that I was now no longer the centre of interest. I risked a quick glimpse round the room. The whole room was staring at us. A photographer from the local paper crouched, flashed and clicked as the Marchioness stepped forward and took Robbi by the hand.

"Lady Hannay, this is such a pleasure. I have heard so much about you and it appears to be all true. What a beautiful dress. Where did you get it?"

The Marquess tore his eyes of Robbi as she started to explain the story of the dress and extended his hand to me. "Evenin' Sir John. Good of you to make it at such short notice. Do you know our local member of Parliament, Sir George Ashgrove, Secretary of State for Housing?"

I bowed my head in the direction of the Minister who smirked at me in an ingratiating manner. "Well, you may not know me, Sir John, but you, of course, are now nationally famous after your session in front of the select committee."

"Just so long as the Member for Sittingbourne isn't a friend of yours, Minister."

The Marquess was peering at my face. He pointed at my scar. "That where the hunt chappie caught you with his whip?"

I nodded.

"Strange behaviour. Strange behaviour. I mean I agree your attitude is damned odd for a country landowner, but a chap attacking you on your own land? Poor show, eh, eh? Your family lived there long, have they?"

"Seven generations on my mother's side, my lord. I take it that you hunt?"

"Of course, Sir John, of course. This blasted ban on hunting with dogs don't mean a thing, if you see what I mean. Do you shoot?"

"Badly. I have been known to cast the occasional rod though."

"Ah, well. That's something I suppose, but I, Sir John, am the caricature of a country gent – huntin', shootin' n' fishin'. Couldn't live without 'em."

His eyes burned with genuine passion. I changed the subject. "May I present my wife, my Lord, Secretary of State? Lady Roberta Hannay."

The two men simpered at her until the ever–present Hugh Digby recalled the Marquess to his duty. I led Robbi into the crowd nodding at the more friendly faces – of which, by the way, there weren't many. Extraordinary too how many of the women were far more interested in Lady Hannay's dress than in me! I took her across to study the seating plan for dinner. We weren't on the top table I was relieved to find, but close enough, damn it. There appeared to be two separate dining rooms at the far end of the ballroom, a smaller one with the Marquess' table, our table and one other and on the other side of the ballroom stage what appeared to be a much larger room with fifteen large tables for the hoi polloi. I didn't recognise any of the guests on our table until a finger tapped me on the shoulder and pointed at his name.

"Didn't know you'd been invited, John. In fact, I was led to believe you hated events like this. Cuts healing alright?"

I smiled at Nick Maitland. For a Master of Fox Hounds, he was a decent man and he'd come round to apologise to me in person after the attack by the hunt which spoke of a conscience as well as some personal courage. Robbi turned to smile at him too. "Hello, Nick. Is your wife here too?"

"Right behind you, Robbi. I wouldn't have dared come and say hello if she hadn't been determined to ask about your dress. Rosemary – Robbi – John."

I bowed once more and listened with half an ear to Rosemary's detailed questions and Robbi's shy answers. Another woman arrived and then another and soon Robbi was, yet again, the centre of female attention, laughing and nattering away happily while her dress was examined, the stitching analysed and the fabric admired. I pulled out my phone and backed to the window to take a photo of the happy gathering. I noticed one of the thugs walking towards me and called out.

"Ladies, this way, please and... cheese!"

The thug hesitated giving me time to take another photo of the general lay out. I glanced at my watch and WhatsApped the photo at the agreed time. Ten minutes to the next one. I turned and peered out of the window but could see nothing – maybe they could see me. Charlie banged his staff on the floor.

"My Lord Marquess, Lady Marchioness, Secretary of State, Sir John and Lady Hannay, Ladies and Gentlemen please take your seats at your tables for dinner."

I limped in talking to Nick, watching the security men watching me. I sat down and dropped my walking stick noisily. Robbi bent down, picked it up and leaned to kiss me lovingly. "All three of them reached for guns, John."

I kissed her back, smiling. "I've put my phone on your thigh. Text them that bit of info, will you."

She touched my cheek, looked at me adoringly and murmured in my ear. "If I have to give you any more loving looks, I'm going to throw up in the consommé."

I picked up my spoon. A moment later and she was murmuring at me again.

"There's no reception, John."

No reception – shit! "Knock my arm."

I may have said it before, but the joy having married into an army family... She laughed at me and jerked my arm roughly. The consommé sloshed off my spoon and on to my trousers. She jumped up, wiped frantically, ran to the door for some water and was back in a minute wiping again with her napkin.

"I'm the world's clumsiest..."

I stopped her vigorous wiping from getting too near to my groinal region. "And dumbest..."

We smiled at each other some more and I listened to her breathed whisper: "asked your friend Charlie to send it. He was delighted to help." Rosemary Maitland leaned across the table.

"So how on earth did you two meet? I mean I saw John's version at the Select Committee on the TV, but were you both working in the same brokers?"

"Good Lord no, Rosemary. She's far too common to have been allowed on the floor at BTD."

Robbi smiled broadly at me and I felt unreasoningly happy as she pinched my wrist and answered the question. "Living dangerously, John Hannay, living dangerously. Actually Rosemary, I hate to say it but it was so romantic. John was on the run from some rather dreadful people and he was hiding out at Continental

Atlantic, the brokers where I was the general manager. He was disguised as a penniless Australian trader."

Another wife leaned forward as the doors opened to admit a waiter guiding a latecomer to the top table. I pressed my foot against Robbi's ankle and she glanced round casually and glanced back at me. Neither of us had seen the latecomer in the flesh before, but the last time we had seen his photo, his maid, Sampaguita, had been snoring drunkenly in her bed at the top of his enormous house in St Anne's Gate. As for the waiter, well he went under various names, one of them being Superintendent Walker and another being Major Alan Cummins of MI5. The leaning wife was intrigued by the story.

"Sir John was on the run? My goodness, what had you done?"

I smiled and wondered how Robbi would handle this one. "You mean, is he a master criminal? No, no, no. You need brains for that. If you live locally you may have heard about his grandfather, the First World War hero."

There was a murmured chorus of yesses. I bet they'd heard of him and I bet they also knew all about me. I noticed that Nick Maitland and Rosemary were shaking their heads and joined in. "He was a Brigadier – Sir Richard Hannay."

Robbi cut across me. "And after the First War he helped the government out on various secret cases right up until the next war. And he made a lot of enemies who were very powerful. And they've been trying to get revenge ever since. They killed John's parents, they tortured John when he was a child..." Her eyes filled with tears and she clutched the back of my hand. Judging by the reaction from the faces round the table the tears were having the right effect. "... and it still carries on, right up to today. Remember the hunt, Nick?"

Nick Maitland was looking amazed. He turned to me. "Robbi being serious, John? Not taking the piss or anything?"

I shook my head and smiled slightly, waiting for the hovering Hugh Digby to butt in. Clearly this wasn't going quite as planned. He coughed behind Nick. "Is everything good here?"

There was a general and slightly sheepish nodding from around the table. "I didn't realise you were a friend of Sir John's, Mr Maitland."

"Good Lord, friend of John Hannay? Absolutely not. Have you got any friends, John?"

"None who hunt, Nick, thanks. Primitive, murderous bastards the lot of you."

He laughed and I noticed the beginnings of smiles round the table. And these were the men who had backed Medina? Seriously? The entree was served – overcooked venison, overcooked vegetables and something going under the misnomer of gravy – at least it gave me the opportunity to reprimand our new waiter for clumsiness which gave me a great deal of private pleasure. I pushed pieces of meat and veg around my plate and waited for the next move until I decided that what I needed was a wee. I pulled myself to my feet with Robbi fussing round me, grabbed my stick and asked the nearest thug where the lavatories were. He panicked, his eyes flicking to the top table helplessly. I tapped him on the chest with the top of my stick – not wearing a Kevlar vest then, good – and spoke slower and louder. The room listened.

"Could you please tell me where the lavatories are – the loos, rest rooms, toilets, comfort stations, bogs, khasies, dunnies? Good Grief! Sprechen zie English?"

I pushed past him, Robbi calling over her shoulder. "Grab us two puddings, please, Rosemary. I'll get him back asap." And to me as we left the room: "Well they weren't expecting you to do that, John."

I nodded. "Keep 'em off balance. It's all we can hope for. Let's hope the Godfather ploy has worked. You notice they've closed the door on the other diners. My guess is we were supposed to be trapped in there, but they made a mistake when they invited Nick Maitland. They assumed he would be an enemy of ours because of the hunt attack."

"Thank God he's a gent. Rosemary's nice too. We must have them round for supper."

"If we live through this evening."

I dived into the Gents, counted along three cubicles, stepped in and reached above the ledge behind the lavatory, my heart beating wildly. It was there – Palmer's Godfather ploy had worked. I grabbed the small handgun with its muzzle suppressor already fitted and stepped back out, passing the gun straight to Robbi who slipped it into her clutch bag.

We walked back along the short corridor and I opened the door, stepping aside to let Robbi lead the way back into the ballroom. She stopped dead and I cannoned into her back, knocking her forward and then grabbing at her arm to hold her up. The side of the ballroom outside the toilet block was full of the guests from our dining room. At a quick glance they were all there, thugs to the fore, Marquess to the rear and Nick and Rosemary Maitland hovering on the outskirts looking very worried... and our waiter too, pressed against the far wall, his right hand behind his back. Nick Maitland caught my eye and shook his head in confusion. I walked forward smiling at him

"Don't worry, Nick. I know this is nothing to do with you."

I had gained five yards. The three thugs in front of Edgar Alain–Despenser, ninth Marquess of Cheltenham, closed up. They really were amateurs.

"What's the time, Robbi?"

"Eight fifty-one."

"Keep an eye on my stick, will you. I don't want to lose it."

She nodded and I knew she was calculating angles. I'd learnt quite a lot from her and her brother, recently hadn't I? The point now, however, was whether I could remember what I had learnt twenty-five years ago. I'd been good then – good enough for the England junior team. Two more paces if they'd let me. I limped the two steps heavily and leaned on my stick, twisting the handle and pressing at a point directly beneath the grip. It took some practice to get this right, but I'd played with my grandfather's sword stick since I was a child. I stopped, trailed the stick, smiled at the thugs and then turned to include James Bullivant, the Lord Artinswell in my general bonhomie.

"Evening, James. Glad you could make it."

He flinched and turned towards his host.

I whipped into the en garde, advanced, appelled, lunged, and drove my sword through the shoulder of the middle thug, pulling back and flicking the razor-sharp point of the blade across the face of the thug on the left – unorthodox move, I thought fleetingly – but highly effective. Blood sprayed from the slashes – crimson on the white dress shirts around him. He clutched at the flap of cheek. The thug to the right was still reaching into his jacket when my Flèche Coupé caught him in the stomach and he staggered back, clawing at his bleeding gut. Two more quick steps and the point of my blade was at the Marquess' throat. Robbi was round and behind him in an instant, the scrape and click of the magazine sounding loud in the dead silence as she pushed the barrel of the gun up beneath his left ear. I turned, tapped the blade on the floor to flick the blood off and came back to the en garde.

"James, join us. You too, Minister. Chop–chop."

I flexed the sword blade and watched them as I spoke to the Marquess.

"You know what I don't understand, Edgar, is how abysmal your research is. Yes, I have a limp, and yes it was caused by the two men you know all about who tortured and raped me when I was eight, but I scarcely ever use a stick. Nick?"

Nick Maitland watched me.

"You and Rosemary should go now. You're a good man – apart from the hunting bit, of course – and I don't want you to get caught in this..."

I waved the sword blade in a half circle. "Minister, hustle please – over here by Edgar. My Lady, please step aside. I cannot believe that a lady such as yourself would be tied up with something as nasty as this. Nick? Seriously, leave now! Robbi, anyone dangerous?"

"Apart from the hired gunnies, not really, although I think that waiter by the wall should come over here and I'm not sure about the pretty boy who was standing beside your friend Artinswell."

"Probably his latest boyfriend. Pop a cap in him if he moves. You see ladies and gentlemen, I'm a crap shot. My wife says I couldn't hit a barn door at two feet, but she on the other hand..."

The pretty boy moved, Robbi sighted on his foot, fired and had the smoking barrel back in the Marquess' throat before anyone had even begun to react – and I was over the boy with my hand across his mouth. I raised a finger warningly before he could scream.

"Shhhhh... is a marksman. Or woman... person, perhaps."

Robbi smiled with her mouth – her eyes flicking round the room. "Marksman will do, thank you, John."

I stepped round behind the crowd, watching the thugs. Alan Cummins, in his waiter garb, was standing by the Marquess with his hands in the air. "Back over to the wall with them, Robbi. Use them as shields."

We shuffled back until my shoulders touched the panelled wall. "You can put your hands down, waiter."

Alan lowered his arms slowly, put his left hand behind his back and tapped the bottom of his jacket. I saw the outline of the Glock, the silenced barrel stuffed down his trousers.

"What's the time, Robbi?"

She checked her watch. "Eight fifty-seven."

Three long minutes to go then. The thugs began to edge forward. I flicked the blade across the aristocratic throat. He squealed and the thugs stopped. Two and a half minutes to go. The thugs moved again. I murmured. "Alan."

He half–nodded once. I kept the blade against the aristocratic throat as Alan reached slowly for the gun in his waistband. I started to count – nine, ten, eleven, twelve. A thug dived. Alan crouched, fired – that by now so familiar cough of a silenced Glock. The gunnie buckled, groaned and slithered across the polished wooden floor, leaving a trail of red behind him. The second and third thugs had covered half the distance to us when there was a tearing crash at the main doors. They were early. Thank God, they were early. Ignoring the intrusion, I took two short steps and made the longest lunge of my life. The blade skewered the third thug's wrist as he reached for Robbi with his knife. Blood spouted into the air. I glanced back over my shoulder and sighed in relief.

A white Ford Transit van with an improvised snow plough welded to its front bumper had rammed through the double doors and men were spilling out of the back doors and climbing over the shattered wood – big, tough men wearing balaclava helmets, carrying shotguns and two men in camouflage gear holding Uzis – one very tall and broad shouldered and one about five foot nine – but all of them deferred to a powerful, bulky man who surveyed the scene through the eyeholes in his balaclava, leaning back against the snow plough.

"Are you alright, Master John, m'lady?"

"Yes, thanks, Mr..."

"No names, Master John. No names, now. Who are we taking? His Lordship I presume. Who are the others?"

I indicated the minister and Artinswell. He nodded, clicked his fingers and the three men were grabbed and frog marched towards the door.

"Her ladyship won't be anything to do with this, Master John."

He glanced at Dave and Paul. "Gentlemen, will you be getting the photos and names of the others now? You'll be having to come for them sooner or later."

Dave moved from person to person with the digital camera and a notepad. Paul rounded up mobile phones. Robbi passed me the ebony sheath for my sword stick and I glanced at Mr Baptista questioningly. The old gypsy nodded at Dave who straightened and addressed the frightened diners. "You lot lost your money because you backed Dominick Medina. You lost it because John realised that what you were doing was wrong and immoral and motivated only by greed. He made a very good speech about that on the trading floor of BTD at the time, I remember. It stuck in my mind and I wondered if I'd ever get to meet any of the people who'd backed Medina. Well now I have and you had just better hope I never meet any of you again, because if I do, I'll be the last person you ever see."

Robbi had been watching me. She took my arm and led me to the main doors. The Transit van bumped back down the steps. Jehan Hearnes helped me climb in the back and sat me on one of the benches that ran down either side of van. Palmer glanced up from binding, gagging and hooding the three captives and nodded at me. He clamped ear defenders over their heads. When the last of the Gypsies was in, the van reversed fast into a three-point turn and then headed back up the drive. It braked by the lake and Paul slung the bin liner full of phones as far out into the water as he could. He climbed back in and slid a bag towards me on the floor.

"Your clothes. The Bentley's back at Fosse."

I pulled off my dinner jacket and dress shirt and rummaged in the bag for the tracksuit. I chucked Robbi's to her. She looked up at the men opposite to her and raised her eyebrows. With one accord they turned their faces away as she slipped out of the dress and pulled her tracksuit on. A voice spoke in Romany and there were some half–hidden chuckles. Her head emerged from the neck of the tracksuit top, glaring.

"Antoni Buckland, if that's the Romany for 'her collar and cuffs match' I shall give you such a smack round the ear and I'll tell Granny Baptista."

The men roared their approval and I saw Mr Baptista was also laughing on the front bench seat. I smiled and shook my head. Mistake – my ears buzzed.

"Dave, how long before they get choppers up?"

"Half an hour earliest."

Alan leaned over the back of the front seat. "Mr Baptista, I reckon you've five minutes max if they've called the police out. How far to your exit?"

Mr Baptista shrugged. "Two minutes, Major."

I know I was not alone in listening for the distant wail of a siren. Mr Baptista tapped Jacobo Wanne's arm and he eased his foot off the accelerator and let the van coast to a halt, Paul pushing the back doors open and jumping down. Palmer joined him. The night was starless, moonless. The wind howled between the trees and a sudden rain squall battered the side of the van, the drops shining red in the rear brake lights as Jacobo started to reverse, swinging the van round so its lights shone into the trees on the right side of the road. Caspar Smith threw one end of a rope at Dave and the entire group pushed it through the Transit's front windows and pulled the van until it tilted slowly down onto the slope beyond the verge. Jacobo touched the accelerator and the van rolled slowly down thirty yards to stop in front of a small stream. I sat on the rear step and watched the Gypsies replace the trees and shrubs they had pulled out earlier, sprinkle dead leaves from black rubbish bags they had hidden behind a tree and pour water on the verge by the road. Within a minute there was no sign of any disturbance to the green and pleasant land.

Another squall thrashed across the road. Dave looked up, listened, clicked his fingers once and the men dived down the slope and waited. The flash of lights from a car travelling at extreme high speed, under–lit the trees and was gone. One of the Gypsies moved. Dave's hiss stopped him. A second vehicle was following the first car, travelling more slowly, a flashlight swinging from right to left. It passed and still Dave didn't move. The Gypsies watched him, recognising and respecting his battle skills. A beat. Then from a tree above us the single click of Paul's fingers. The Gypsies flattened themselves against the earth. I could just see Dave moving into a crouch, his knife a black shadow in his right hand. A third car was ghosting along the road, its lights and engine off. It passed – slower and slower – halting a hundred yards beyond us. Thin beams of light touched tree trunks and bounced off branches. A sudden flash, a rumble of thunder – another squall. The torches went off. Dave was staring at a point on the road above, his knife arm slowly moving back above his shoulder. For two minutes he stayed fixed in that position, watching. A car engine started two or three hundred yards away. Still, he waited. A shout from up the road; a movement above us as a torch flashed on and a voice:

"No, nothing to report. Next section then."

The torch went off and still Dave didn't move. I could see the Gypsies' faces turning towards him, but their discipline held. Another minute: then a scrape and a conversational voice.

"This is wasting time. Post one man every hundred metres down this road and let's see what the damage is at the hotel."

Footsteps. Silence. Paul dropped to the ground and sheathed his knife. He glanced at Dave. Dave glanced at Alan. "Pros."

Alan nodded silently. I studied him. "Anyone you know, Alan?"

He shook his head slowly. "No, but I think I know where they come from and it's close to home, John, very close to home."

Jacobo turned the ignition key and we walked beside the van as he drove it gingerly along the narrow track beside the river. Two of the Gypsies walked backwards behind us dragging a weighted rug, obscuring the tyre tracks. Within five minutes the van turned on to a well–used forest track and we climbed back in, Palmer swinging his parabolic reflector microphone round slowly, listening for any activity. He paused for a second, shook his head and removed the earphones. "Animal, not human."

Jacobo put on Dave's image intensifying goggles and with the lights off drove slowly along the forest path. I had no idea of where we were or where we were going. I felt I had done my bit for the night. I tried to sit upright and slumped back down. Robbi held me close, staring into my face anxiously. I focused on her. She blurred, swam into focus again and out. She pulled me to her. I heard her voice echoing in the distance.

"Dave? Dave?"

A hand touched my head and there was a shuffling and I found myself lying down with my head in her lap and Alan was watching me and the world was black and white and then white and whiter and I grabbed her hand and squeezed.

CHAPTER TWENTY-ONE

I woke to a soothing murmur and a stroking hand. I listened to my heart's steady beat and opened my eyes. She smiled at me in the dim light of a small torch.

"Better?"

"I'm sorry, Robbi."

"You do know you're an idiot, don't you?"

"Well as you tell me I am at least three times a day, I think I am beginning to realise."

I looked round. The van was almost empty. "Where are we?"

"No idea. Mr Baptista's keeping things pretty close to his chest. He has an agenda here, John. Do you know what it is?"

I shook my head and indicated the still bound, gagged and hooded Marquess. "It's something to do with him, but I don't know what."

Caspar knocked on the open back door. "Is he awake m'lady?"

"Yes, he is, Caspar."

"We're ready then."

I pulled myself upright and sat for a moment waiting for the world to slow down to its normal thousand miles per hour spin. Caspar and two others dragged the prisoners to the back door and pushed them to the ground. I followed. A few stars were now flickering through rents in the cloud cover and after my eyes had become accustomed to the darkness, I could make out a group of men in a hollow beyond the van. I watched as they made their way back up, realising that there were steps cut up the side and that the rear of the hollow was a stone wall – a faint splash in the distance in front of me then a distant, irritated quacking of a Mallard disturbed by a nocturnal prowler – this was a man-made lake. There was only one figure I could recognise in the darkness. His bulk was currently obscuring the few remaining stars as Alan undid the side windows and tied back the rear doors. This time Jacobo didn't turn on the engine – a muffled grunt from Dave. "On three. One." They rocked the van forward and let it fall back. "Two." They repeated the action. "And... three."

They heaved. The van rolled forward over the bank and slid into the water with scarcely a splash – bubbles and more bubbles, a dark stain of mud, a final stream of small bubbles, water lapping up over the bank. Then nothing. The bank was tidied and Alan led the way, climbing back down the steps and across the hollow towards what appeared to be a tunnel beneath the lake.

Palmer hissed. We stood silent and then I heard it. The distant beat of a helicopter. There was a final rush across the hollow to the tunnel entrance. A metal grid across the front had been lifted off its hinges. As I ran inside, Dave was lifting the grid single–handed. He lowered it back on to the hinges while Paul re–fitted the padlock. The helicopter was nearer, a searchlight swinging in great arcs below its body. It passed and it was pitch black inside the tunnel again; at least Bilbo

Baggins had the fire of Smaug's breath to see in the distance – and a magic ring of invisibility too, the lucky hobbit bastard. Alan took control.

"Try the torches."

The torches came on and pointed up the brick lined tunnel. Tree roots had pushed through where the brickwork had crumbled, cobwebs stretched across the tunnel at every height, the floor was rubble strewn, puddled and muddy near the entrance, drying as it rose steadily towards a bend three hundred feet or so ahead. Alan spoke again.

"Mr Baptista, do you know what is at the far end of the tunnel? Is it a grill like this one or a door?"

"A door, Major."

"So, we can use the torches?"

The old Gypsy murmured assent, rucksacks were picked up and we set off, Robbi and I holding hands, bringing up the rear. And I still had no idea of where we were or what we were doing here – wherever here was.

It took five minutes to walk through the tunnel and another thirty seconds for Paul to pick the old lock on the solid wooden door. It opened on to a courtyard with a stone wall of a house on the far side, actually more like a castle than a house... a castle – a castle, of course! We were chez Marquess. My brain started to work. Robbi let go of my hand and I saw her smile in the dim light. She knew I was functioning once again.

I never would have thought that a six-foot six-inch man could flit, but Dave could. He flitted across the courtyard – a giant shadow runner. Then Paul was beside him. Dave cupped his hands. Paul placed his right foot in the cupped hands. Dave crouched, glanced up once, paused and then threw Paul up into the ivy on the corner of the castle wall. Paul turned in mid-air, caught a trunk of the ivy and swung himself up until he was below a stone balcony. Alan was beside Dave now, catching the rope thrown by Paul and swinging himself up hand over hand. The men beside me nodded appreciatively. Then Dave was back with us, hustling us across the courtyard in ones and twos to the corner. By the time it was my turn, the door had been opened from the inside and the prisoners were being carried up the staircase, two on Dave's shoulders and one swung across Jehan's back. We trudged, trotted or crept (according to our various energy levels) up the forty steps to the floor where Palmer had found the Marquess' study. It was a comfortable room, book lined on two walls, with tapestries hanging on the third wall, either side of the fireplace. Heavy curtains were pulled across the window recess and the embers of a wood fire glowed behind the fire screen in front of a deep hearth. Palmer disappeared behind the curtains and backed out a minute later trailing a wire and a video monitor.

"The side of the balcony overlooks the main entrance. I've put a camera out there. Should give us some warning if someone turns up."

He placed the monitor on the long table as a grandfather clock chimed eleven. The last of the prisoners was dumped on the rug by the fire and the heavy door closed and re–locked. Alan placed three office chairs side by side and Dave leaned down to pick up the Minister. I put out my hand.

"Wait, Dave." They all looked at me. "Before they are able to hear us, tell me what's going on, Mr Baptista. I haven't asked you anything about this, but I think you should tell me now."

The old Gypsy seated himself on the corner of the table. Even in the dim lighting of the old room he looked tired – not surprising really when you think about it. He was more than thirty years older than me and I'd had the advantage of being unconscious for half the evening.

"There's something bad about this man and this place. It is something to do with children. Whatever it is, I think he plots it here in this room. I told Mr Palmer to look for a private study when he came here as a tourist yesterday. I won't say anything more until we hear from him."

He indicated the body on the floor. I nodded.

"Dave, just the Marquess first please then. Palmer, sit right in front of him and watch him closely. Try and see which direction he looks in when he realises where he is. It just may show us where something might be hidden."

I tailed off, shrugging. Dave humped the body roughly onto the chair, taping him to its back. At a word from Mr Baptista the Gypsies pulled their balaclavas down over their faces. Alan followed suit. Dave glanced round to make sure everything was ready then lifted the ear defenders off the head and pulled up the hood. The Marquess' face was white; his eyes flicked round the room, widened when they saw where he was and he almost managed to stop a quick, desperate glance to one side – almost. Dave pulled the hood back down and clamped the ear defenders back on ignoring the muffled screams. Palmer walked backwards away from the seated aristocrat, the Gypsies clearing the way behind him. He reached the wall.

"It was here, John. This is what he was looking for – give or take an inch."

Palmer was standing in front of one of the floor–to–ceiling bookshelves: history by the look of it and personal history too, mostly unread, although the spine of the history of the Alain-Despenser family showed usage. I stepped back and squinted. Only one other book stood out as having been handled. I peered at it. The History of The Act of Union, February 1st, 1801, by Frederick Alain-Despenser, 1st Marquess of Cheltenham. I smiled to myself.

"OK, it's here – whatever it is I mean. These two books."

Robbi peered at the books. "Alright you smug git, why?"

I smiled – smugly. "Because, as every schoolboy knows, that particular Act bringing Ireland into the Union passed into law on the first of *January* 1801 not the first of February."

Robbi growled. "God, you are so annoying. Couldn't it be a mistake?"

"Doubt it. 1791 was when the first Alain-Despenser was created Marquess of Cheltenham. Pitt the Younger was Prime Minister and it was Pitt who brought about the 1801 Act of Union so they wouldn't have got that one wrong."

She reached out to touch the book. I put my hand on her arm. "Better let Palmer have a look first, Robbi."

I pulled her to me and we watched. Palmer completed an electronic scan of the bookshelf, shrugged and then raised his eyebrows at Alan who was touching various parts of the shelves. He shrugged back. "My guess is that if there's a hidden compartment it would be mechanical – but it's just a guess. You can reach both books easily if you stand in front of them."

He demonstrated. Dave placed his stethoscope on the history of the family and shook his head. Alan sighed.

"Well, as I'm the one wearing Kevlar..."

He stood in front of the shelves while the rest of us cowered back. He pulled both books out of the shelves at the same time. Nothing. He shook his head in irritation, pushed them back in and turned away. A section of shelving creaked. Paul leapt forward, pushing and pulling in either direction. The shelving creaked again and swung slowly round into the wall. I pressed the old Bakelite light switch down behind the shelves and a dull bulb glowed in the ceiling of the short corridor. Dave tip–toed forward, checking for pressure–on alarms on the floor. The door at the far end of the corridor wasn't even locked and opened at a touch. We entered the small, circular room. It was like something out of the film *Where Eagles Dare*. Massive stone walls, ninety thirties decor, a bare, zinc topped table, a metal filing cabinet – the desktop computer the only anachronism – but Broadsword wasn't calling Danny Boy. Palmer sat down in front of the computer, tapped the keyboard to wake it, looked at the screen and grimaced: the banality of evil.

Photos of children, some as young as nine or ten, the oldest in their mid-teens, standing together in what looked like a forest clearing. Nothing sexual, nothing so obvious, nothing on the surface apart from the haunted faces and the fear in their eyes. They were in small groups – different children photographed at different times of the year. And behind them, broken–open shotguns over forearms, was the Marquess and a coterie of other men. I peered at the faces more closely. I knew them. I had been in a dining room with some of them three hours ago.

"Oh Christ!"

Palmer jumped and I realised I had spoken aloud. I turned to Mr Baptista. "He hunts children?"

He nodded, his head down.

"He fucking hunts children? From the Children's Home?"

"Yes, Master John. From the Home."

"And the dinner tonight was for the charity which keeps the Home going!" I turned to the door, almost blind with rage, pushing through the crowded room until a hand on my chest brought me up. "How could he, Dave? How could that bastard do it?"

The red mist faded behind my eyes. I could see again, although my heart still hammered behind my ribs. I looked at Alan. He was still staring at the screen in shock.

"This all news to you, Alan?"

"Yes, John. Yes, it is. Have you seen these faces? Have you seen who's here?" He shook his head in disbelief. "Palmer can you get everything on to a hard drive. This is..." He waved his hands in the air, lost for words. "Oh, Christ!"

CHAPTER TWENTY-TWO

A hiss sounded loud in the silence. Jehan was beckoning us urgently back into the study. He was pointing at the monitor which showed a car in front of the castle and lights were going on forty feet below us on the ground floor. Palmer flicked off the lights in the room and Dave and he crept out behind the curtains on to the balcony. We waited. The Marquess struggled to move. I hit him. No one stopped me. He didn't move again. Palmer slipped back in through the curtains.

"Dave's keeping watch, but you can see it all on the monitor. It's the wife and the secretary. Dave wants to know if you think the secretary is in on it, John."

I frowned and raised my eyebrows in Robbi's direction. She shrugged. "Probably not. I have no idea why I'm saying that though. There's no evidence either way."

Dave peered back in through the curtains. "Car's gone. Paul, have a scout round downstairs. Make sure we aren't going to be disturbed."

We waited – two minutes and then a movement outside. Seven knives appeared – three irregularly spaced taps on the door and Dave grunted. "That's Paul."

Jacobo opened the door and Hugh Digby was thrown in. Paul followed, shutting and locking the door. Digby opened his mouth – probably to protest – the same seven knives re–appeared. His mouth closed. I stood in front of him. "Sit up Digby."

He sat up.

"Do you know why we're here?"

"No. Yes. Maybe. I don't know." He looked round the circle of grim faces. "It's something to do with what your brokerage, BTD, did to Medina Trading earlier this year. The Marquess wants his money back."

I pulled a chair forward and sat down. "And how much did the Marquess lose?"

"I don't have access to the accounts, but it was something like twenty million – more maybe."

"Why on earth did he do it in the first place?"

Digby looked uncomfortable. "It was his friend, Sir George Ashgrove, the Minister for Housing. I don't know what they expected to happen." He looked at me enquiringly.

"You'll have to forgive me, Digby, but I have become a little bored by the effort of having to explain the rudiments of money trading to every financial incompetent I meet. Medina wanted to destroy the UK's economy. The Edgar Alain–Despensers of this world are just nasty, greedy little inside traders. Mix the two together and then add in the third element of the best trading house in the world and Medina gets destroyed and morons like his Lordship lose their money. How much did the Minister loose?"

He shrugged. "I don't know but judging by the way he was carrying on this afternoon it was a lot more than he could afford."

"And what about the secret room?"

If he was acting then he was damn good – genuine puzzlement. I raised my eyes at Alan wondering whether he had any idea about our next move. He shook his head at me. I looked at Mr Baptista. He smiled and copied Alan. Lot of help. I walked slowly up and down the silent room. The Minister struggled to sit up. I kicked him and momentarily felt better. "Alan, if it's OK with you, I think Digby can stay, but he needs to have his mouth taped just in case."

I raised my eyebrows. He nodded. Dave tied the unresisting Digby to a chair in the corner of the room by the window and taped his mouth. I carried on thinking. OK, we were getting nearer to the person or persons who wished to destroy my friends and me. Nearer wasn't near enough of course. Surely these clowns – I looked at the men on the floor – couldn't have run a whelk stall let alone organise gangs of highly trained killers to kidnap my wife. I felt the anger begin to bubble. I prowled the floor. And who were the men in the cars on the road earlier this evening? Alan thought he knew and it had worried him. Who the hell could I trust – outside this room? The only men I should have been able to trust were the men who had promised my grandfather they would protect me. One of them was dead; one of them was in hospital in Sweden recovering very slowly from a broken neck – Anna Haraldsen; one of them was a traitor and lay bound and gagged on the floor in front of me – Artinswell; which left Ludo Arbuthnot and one other. If I knew who the one other was it might have helped.

"I need to talk to my lawyer, Alan – Marcus Wethers. You know that there were friends of my grandfather who attended a meeting during World War Two and promised to try and protect the family after he died – five of them. I know who four of them were. That bastard there's father..." I indicated the figure of Artinswell on the floor. "...was supposed to be one of them. Uncle Marcus was trying to contact the fifth man, but he said he was difficult to track down. I'm just hoping he managed to reach him. He may know something."

"He does, but not as much as you might be hoping for, Master John."

I glanced at Mr Baptista, wondering what he was talking about as Robbi stiffened and stared at him.

"Your father was a friend of Sir Richard Hannay, Mr Baptista, wasn't he?"

"And my grandfather, m'lady."

He looked at me steadily. "My father was at that meeting, Master John. It was during the war at your grandfather's club." He smiled. "I don't think they quite knew what to do when a Gypsy turned up at the main entrance. But he was a big man, my father. He said he looked down at them and then just sat in the hall and waited for them to fetch Sir Richard." He smiled again. "He said your granda' was furious. Gave the men in the hall such a roasting. Then he took my father up to a meeting room of some sort and he told them all about Medina and asked them to look out for his son – your father – and all his heirs."

I wondered what 'look out for' entailed. "So, when I first met you, you were looking out for me then?"

"The first time you wouldn't remember, Master John. You were only two. I wanted to check out the area, find out who was who. Your father was very polite, showed me round, but I was pretty sure he didn't want any help. We kept an eye on him, though – an oath's an oath. It's easy for a Romany to get information too so like I say we kept tabs. But the year they killed your father, we were north at the big fair in Appleby. One of my cousins got word to me and I left the fair and came south on my own."

He sighed deeply and stared at the fire. "I thought I'd find all the others there, but there was only one – him, Artinswell." He indicated the figure on the floor. 'I hadn't met him before. I didn't like him. He must have been in his late twenties then, but he was very pleased with himself – arrogant. Anyway, he told me that your father's death had been an accident and that he'd be looking after your mother and you so there'd be no need for me to worry any more. But I did worry. And I made a mistake. I worried too much. It was me who advised your mother to move back to London."

He sat down and looked at the floor. "Romanies can't operate easily in London. It's not our natural..."

He waved his arm. I smiled. "Milieu?"

Mr Baptista snorted quietly. "That would not be the word of my choosing, Master John. But, yes, in the country we can hide – blend in – survive. In London we're taken for beggars or burglars. We couldn't watch your mother's flat. We watched you though, when you were away at your school in the country. While you were at school you were safe, John."

"But, of course, I didn't take account of the fact that you were a Hannay. We didn't spot you running away. We were more concerned to watch out for anyone who tried to break in and attack you. By the time we realised you were gone it was too late."

He looked across at the younger Gypsies and seemed to be addressing them rather than me. "My father took a blood oath to help the Hannay family. It wasn't something he did lightly, but Sir Richard had been good to us. Found us places to camp, like Master John did for us this year." He nodded in my direction. "Stopped one of my uncles being imprisoned unjustly; stood up to a gang of the local bullies who were up for a lynching. Protected us against all the silly country folk who hated us for no other reason than we were different."

He turned back to the Gypsies. "Nerves like steel Sir Richard had, just like his grandson here. He was a man who you'd take a blood oath to protect. Just like you would to his grandson. Caspar Smith, step forward."

I'm not sure who was more embarrassed, me for being informed (erroneously) that I was as brave as my grandfather, or Caspar Smith for being called out in front of his peers. "This is a difficult job we've got here, boys. One or two of us may get hurt... or worse. Anyone want to pull out, there's the door, no retribution. Now, if anything happens to me, anyone object to Caspar leading you next?"

The Gypsies shook their heads as one. Mr Baptista looked at each of them in turn, nodded, pulled his knife from its sheath and held his hand out to Caspar. The room was suddenly solemn. And I got dragged into it too. Mr Baptista called me forward and beckoned me to hold out my hand. He nicked my thumb with the razor-sharp edge of his knife, the blood on our hands mixed and blended and Caspar Smith took on the burden of my grandfather's oath. Mr Baptista still held the floor.

"Caspar, you need to get back and take care of the families. Mr Lord's men will be there at the moment, but we have to assume that those men in the cars we saw earlier will head to Fosse. Sergeant Browby? Your wife is there. All of you go with him."

Within two minutes Caspar and the rest of the younger Gypsies had headed off with Paul driving them the long way round via Chipping Norton. I realised suddenly that I was very tired – scarcely surprising, I suppose. Apart from making me meditative, had this strange ritual got us anywhere further forward? Yes, a few more pieces of my family jigsaw had been fitted in, but...

"Who were the ringleaders of the local people who hated your tribe, Mr Baptista?"

"A man called Harker, Master John. The father of the one who's your tenant at Glebe Farm." He was still watching me, waiting for me to make a connection.

"Why did the son become the tenant farmer? The Harkers never had been before. When was it? Oh."

He didn't answer. I stared blankly at the dying embers in the fire. "I see."

He nodded. Robbi poked my arm. I carried on. "I was looking at the deeds of Glebe Farm the other day. Harker took over twenty-eight years ago, three weeks after my mother was killed, while I was still in hospital. They've had a man on the inside at Fosse all my life, just watching and waiting."

Robbi shivered at the thought. Mr Baptista smiled at her. "But, m'lady, Master John's also had us watching too. We've always been there, just not as obvious as a tenant farmer. We're here now too and your brother and his men. We're here to protect him and you too now, m'lady. Especially you, m'lady. Especially now."

Robbi's eyes widened and she reddened. He patted her gently on the cheek and changed the subject. "So, what now, Master John?"

"Three things, Mr Baptista – and in no particular order. One: who were the men in the cars in the road, Alan? Two: are they the same as the men who kidnapped Robbi? Three: how do we interrogate this lot?"

We all looked at Alan. He stood up and stretched and addressed Dave. "Who do you think they were, Mr Lord?"

Dave shrugged. "Special forces, sir, well trained."

I was curious. "Why?"

"'Cos one of them felt something wasn't quite right which is why they waited. Instinct, but you have to be trained to produce that level of instinct."

Alan nodded his agreement. "So, trained by who?"

"Someone rather like you, sir."

Alan nodded again. He kept his gaze fixed on Dave, holding his hands up. "Not me, Mr Lord. Not me. Promise. So, you can put that knife down."

Dave didn't move and I realised that his right hand was by his side, palm down beside his leg.

"Can you prove that, Sir?"

"No, Mr Lord. No, I can't. It's OK, I'm not going to move. I just need to think. I'm sure I knew that voice. The voice on the road. Didn't you?"

"Yes, sir."

Alan blinked up at him.

"Ask my sister, Major. She never forgets voices."

Robbi frowned. "Why would I know a voice like that? Which voice, anyway, Alan?"

"The last one. The one who said to set up watchers every hundred metres."

Robbi looked through me into the distance. None of us moved. Her eyes refocused. She glanced at Dave and then across at Alan. "Sergeant Skinner, Alan. The man who came to our flat when John was shot at."

Alan's jaw dropped. He turned to Palmer. "Got a phone I can use?"

Palmer rummaged in his bag and tossed one across. "I'm calling the night duty officer. Hallo? Voice recognition check, please. Thank you." He paused, ear pressed to the mobile phone. "Major Alan Cummins." He paused again and then went through a brief exchange. Then: "Where is Sergeant Skinner deployed at the moment?"

He listened. "Since when?" He listened some more. "On whose authority? And you have this in writing? Why not? That is a breach of standing orders, Lieutenant. Give me the exact time this authority was given. Very good. Lieutenant? You and I have not spoken this evening. Is that clear? No. No you will not log this call. Yes. Good night."

He pressed the off button, passed the phone back to Palmer who removed the Sim card and threw it on the fire. "Well, he may log it. Do you know Lieutenant Parker, Mr Lord?"

Dave relaxed and pushed the throwing knife back into its sheath. Alan smiled at him wryly. "Lieutenant Parker is a snobby little shit, sir, but he won't log the call. What were you supposed to have authorised and when, sir?"

"I was supposed to have authorised the temporary transfer of Sergeant Skinner and his unit to something called Centre Point Military Services on Thursday at 11:07 hours."

I thought about this. I'd been on the phone with Alan on Thursday morning. I checked my phone's call log. "At seven minutes past eleven, Major Cummins, I believe I was on the phone to you telling you about the ball this evening. I sent you an email when the call finished."

I span through the sent box on my laptop. "I sent it at just before ten past eleven. Which means you couldn't have made the call. Which means that someone at MI5 is in on this little plot."

"In or above, John."

Palmer looked up from his laptop and cleared his throat. "Centre Point Military Services. Founded in 2003. Original non–executive directors include one James, Lord Artinswell, and the chairman was, guess who?"

Robbi pointed at the figure of the Marquess. Palmer nodded. "Coconut for her Ladyship."

He looked at the screen and read. "Under the About Us tab it says: 'at CPM we're ready to respond whenever the military needs us... blah, blah, blah... the world's armed forces don't think twice whenever duty calls. And neither do we.' Strangely enough, though, it doesn't say anything about co–opting Special Forces for the private purpose of threatening a peer of the realm."

Robbi stage whispered to him. "Baronets aren't peers. I understand from one who knows that they're common – although one or two of them do get to marry above their station."

I sighed. She grinned. "Which of them first, Alan?"

"Artinswell. He'll be the weakest one. Let me handle the interrogation. It's what I do."

Dave lifted the body off the floor. "It's what the Major does."

Alan moved the desk light so it was shining on the chair. The rest of us moved back into the shadows and squatted on the floor. Dave removed Artinswell's ear defenders and hood. The wretched man blinked in the light and tried to squint past it. Alan waited for five seconds and then spoke quietly.

"Lord Artinswell, I'm interested in your involvement with Centre Point Military Services. I'm willing to take the tape off your mouth, but if you try and shout or scream the rather large gentleman beside you might become aggressive. Carry on, Sergeant Major."

Dave ripped the tape off Artinswell's mouth and stood over him menacingly. Artinswell licked his lips.

"I er, it's a military services company which was set up as a UK subsidiary to one of the big American players during the Iraq war. It, er, provides logistical assistance to the British army both here and abroad."

Alan waited and then continued in the same quiet voice. "And what kind of services does it provide in this country?"

"Up to now it has been housing." He spoke in a rush, helpful, ingratiating. "We identify sites and then contract with house builders. These are homes for soldiers, built at a price they can afford, close to their bases."

"Not on military land then."

"No."

And the Housing Minister was here. Hmmm. How much land did the Marquess own that was near a military base? Alan continued. "Where were you on September the nineteenth, Lord Artinswell?"

Artinswell licked his lips again. "Without my diary I can't be sure... Sorry."

I whispered to Robbi who whispered to Palmer who tapped quietly on his iPad for a moment and passed it across. Artinswell was still blathering on. I slid the iPad on to Alan's lap. It lit his face from beneath, giving him a child's Halloween mask of a face. He studied the screen briefly, smiled and looked up again. "Did CPM build any military housing near Salisbury, Lord Artinswell?"

"Yes, yes it did. It was a PFI – private finance initiative – you know."

"How many houses was it?"

"Over a hundred – I couldn't be more exact than that."

Alan paused, scrolling down the screen. "And on whose land were these houses built?"

"Er... Oh. I would have to check."

"Who is EL?"

"Sorry?"

"Or PO?"

Recognition flickered in his eyes. Alan changed tack back again. "Did you first meet the Marquess of Cheltenham on the sale of his land to CPM for the house building project?"

"No, no. It was at er, at a shoot."

"So, it was his land?"

"Yes, yes, I think so."

"So, you shoot, do you?"

Artinswell started to nod and stopped himself.

"Occasionally, yes."

"With the Marquess?"

"Yes, er, yes, I have done."

"And who is EY?"

Artinswell all but cringed.

"I can't..."

Alan watched him. "Is there anyone you need to tell that you will be out of circulation for a while?" He held up his hand. "And I don't mean the Whip's Office in the House of Lords. Your colleagues there have already been informed of this enquiry. I mean anyone personal to you – your maid, Sampaguita, for instance?"

"Sampaguita? Nothing will happen to Sam will it?"

"Why should it? What has she done?"

"Nothing, nothing at all. She is here on a visa. It's all perfectly legal." His voice trailed off. "If you could let her know I won't be coming home, I would be grateful. She's a very good girl."

Robbi nudged me. Alan paused and continued. "You are not the main object of this enquiry."

Faint hope stirred in Artinswell's eyes.

"But you have committed crimes. Do you need me to list them for you?"

Artinswell shook his head, looking down at his knees, silent.

"Do you want to list them for me?"

Artinswell shook his head again.

"The most serious crime is murder."

Artinswell jerked back in his seat. "No, no. I never... I didn't realise what they were... No. No."

He shook his head more firmly, his jowls wobbling. "The second most serious charge is accessory to murder and then..." He continued over Artinswell's bleatings. "... we get down to fraud, misrepresentation, attempted theft. It's quite a long list."

Alan nodded at Dave who re–taped Artinswell's mouth hooded him, replaced his ear defenders and deposited him back in the corner of the room. Alan stood, stretched and looked at his watch.

"Nearly midnight. That went well enough, but then again, we had enough different pieces of dirt on him that it was relatively simple to keep him on the back foot. Incidentally, not that it matters, but I do believe he didn't kill any of the children."

I reached a hand out to Palmer who pulled me to my feet and returned to his default position hunched over his laptop. Robbi stayed on the floor looking up at me. I shrugged at her and spoke what words of wisdom I could come up with. "I think we have to continue with these two for another hour. All we've got for definite on the Minister is that he's in the photos where the children were being hunted. But we don't know where it took place and we don't know how they disposed of the bodies. Jesus, those poor, poor kids! I just can't stop thinking about them."

Robbi stood up, slipped her arm through mine and looked at Palmer. "What you got, Palmer?"

Palmer looked up. "You know there are times when I wish I wasn't your chief geek. This hasn't been a lot of fun. Right. I've been through the hard drive on that computer and someone actually shot some video on one of those hunts. It's wobbly, but given facial recognition I think we'll be able to see some people we know. There's also definite proof that at least one of the children was killed – there's a body and I'm assuming that the people lifting the body into the back of a tractor work for the Marquess. The other thing is that it didn't happen here – more like about ten – fifteen miles away in your direction, John. There's an iPhone photo in there and it's got the co–ordinates on it."

Alan was watching Palmer. "So, we know where to start digging then."

I shook my head. "Not necessarily. Palmer said the body was loaded on to a tractor."

I gestured at the three bound men. "Why don't we rattle the Minister's cage? Show him some of the photos. Make it clear just how deep the shit is that he's in. I have the feeling that our Edgar's going to be a much harder nut to crack. One, he's pretty stupid and two, he's mighty arrogant. You've got to remember that he's not only the ninth Marquess, but the thirty first baron – the family literally came over in 1066 with William the Conqueror, so he probably thinks the world revolves around him."

I paused. Who could we trust outside this room? Who could help us? Emma 'the Boss' Fitzgerald? No. Peter

Bibby MP of the select committee? Maybe, but what could he do? My wealth manager Tony McElroy? No, he was an adviser, not a man of action. Ludo Clanroyden or Marcus Wethers then? Yes, but not enough influence. Mr Holroyd – the secret civil servant? No... not yet. We hadn't quite got to where he wanted and he had his own agenda I was sure. Sir Ian Hamilton? He was definitely retired now, but once you've been the head of MI5... I stopped walking and looked at Alan. "We need to bring Sir Ian Hamilton in on this and Ludo Clanroyden and Uncle Marcus as well."

Robbi was incredulous. "You can't trust Ian, for God's sake, John. Look what happened last time when ffitch got at him."

I kept my eyes on Alan. He was nodding. "I've been through the same thought process, Robbi, and I've reached the same conclusion. We have to reel 'em in slowly and if we could get Sir Ian down here in the morning he'd understand."

Robbi shook her head, unconvinced. Palmer rummaged in his rucksack and passed Alan a mobile phone. Alan started to dial. I stopped him. "We have to keep his Lordship on ice for a few days."

Alan waited for me to continue. I looked towards Hugh Digby. Alan followed my gaze. He nodded. I looked at Robbi. She nodded too. Dave walked across, pulled the tape from Digby's mouth and cut the plastic ties round his wrists with his throwing knife. Digby massaged his wrists, his eyes flicking between us. Palmer swung the laptop on the table towards him. We watched his face as he saw the photos.

"What is this?"

He glanced up at Palmer who just pointed to the screen. A jerky home video started to play. Digby's hand went to his mouth. He saw the body on the tractor. His face was white as he staggered to the small bathroom off the study. The noise of vomiting was followed by a flush and then water running. He came back into the study wiping his mouth and sat down. His hands were shaking. "The children, they were from the Home?"

Palmer nodded agreement. I sat across the table from him. "Digby, your boss is a monster. The men on that hunt are monsters. They must be stopped. The children, well, that's the worst crime, but those men and others have been poisonous leeches on this country for far too long. I repeat: they must be stopped."

He nodded his head violently. Palmer shut the laptop down. Digby continued to stare at the lid in horror. "How can I help?"

Alan took over. "We need to keep his Lordship hidden for two or three days. Artinswell and even the Minister we can move, but your man is too well connected."

Digby nodded some more. "He most certainly is. When I started work here, he boasted he could call anyone in the country. And I've seen him do it – prime minister, any member of the royal household, CEOs of FTSE 100 companies. But Sir John's right, he is both stupid and arrogant. Whatever's been going on here he wouldn't have been in charge. I mean he would have been for the hunting. That has to have been his idea – Oh God!"

Alan called Sir Ian. I called Uncle Marcus, apologising for the lateness of the hour. He said he would call Ludo and collect Sir Ian. Dave went to lift the Minister of State off the floor. Alan tapped his arm to stop him. "This is going to be quick and dirty. I want him up and in that chair with earphones and hood off in one move. OK? Palmer, get that laptop over here. I need one still and then the home movie. Ready?"

Palmer tapped the keyboard twice and nodded. Dave lifted the minister bodily off the floor, dumped him in the chair, wrenched off his ear protectors and tore off the hood. Alan leaned straight into the Minister's face. "You sick bastard. Did you think you could actually get away with this?"

He swung the laptop screen round to face the minister and showed him the photo where he was standing beside the Marquess, smiling, with his gun over his forearm. I watched his face closely. He was half expecting this. Palmer left clicked the mouse pad and the movie started. Now this he wasn't expecting. Dave gripped his head and forced him to watch it. Three expressions crossed his face in eight seconds – fear, terror, guilt. I could have shot him dead. Actually, I could have beaten him, strangled him, stamped on his head, anything to make him suffer, die and obliterate his memory from the world of humanity. Alan stopped the video and leaned over the table again, pushing himself right into the Minister's face. "You know what we're doing now?"

He glared into the man's eyes. "Well, do you? Take a guess."

The terrified Minister shook his head from side to side. "We're digging up the bodies."

He turned away, paused for a second, then reached over the table, pulling the man forward by his dinner jacket lapels. "And in case you wonder who I am and what I am doing here..."

He reached into his pocket and pulled out a warrant card. "Superintendent Walker, SO15. To be clichéd, you're nicked – you sick fuck!"

He leaned back on his chair and gestured at Dave who immediately pulled the hood down over the Minister's head and pushed the ear protectors back on. I stood and applauded. Robbi jumped up and hugged him from behind, kissing him on the cheek. Alan grinned at Palmer. "I must do this again you know, Palmer."

Palmer gave that twisted smile of his back at him. "If you have a go at the Marquess, do you reckon she'll snog you properly – you know, with tongue?"

Robbi slapped him on the head and looked in my direction. "You do know you're supposed to defend my honour against these sexist pigs, don't you?"

I nodded in what I hope she believed to be a supportive manner, still letting thoughts tick over. "Digby, the Marquess, here. Does he have any other vices? Alcohol? Women? Bondage?"

Digby studied the snoring figure on the floor with contempt. "All of the above. I had to buy some poor girl's silence six months ago. He claimed she'd agreed to it, but I saw the rope marks on her wrists and neck. He's a sadist, I suppose. Just laughed when I told him I thought his behaviour was unacceptable." He paused, shook his head and looked round the room. "I'm very sorry. I should have done something before, I know. He even got me here on false pretences; held out the opportunity to take over the tenancy on one of the estate farms. I know now... that was never going to happen."

I patted his arm, sat down on the floor and yawned. "We'd better get some sleep. Digby, I'm sorry, but you're staying here. Mr Baptista, please take the chair."

Dave lay across the door, Robbi curled up beside me like the cat I was sure she had somewhere in her ancestry. She leaned in to me and I waited to hear her purr. She whispered instead. "Why did you ask about his other vices?"

"Because I thought he might have them and you may remember that we know a very beautiful lady who could probably out–drink him and can be pretty cruel, don't we?"

She rested her head on my shoulder and closed her eyes. "You are a clever little baronet, aren't you? Em's no lady though."

CHAPTER TWENTY-THREE

I was eight years old. I was terrified. I was running through a forest. Men holding shotguns were stalking me. I kept glancing back over my shoulder as I ran. I could see them now. They were smiling. They were walking slowly. They were silent. I tried to run faster. They were closer. I ran faster. They walked slower. The slower they walked the nearer they got. They were going to catch me. I could hear them whispering to each other now: "John, John, John. John!"

I forced my eyes open. They drooped shut. It was Robbi whispering in my ear – repeating my three favourite words again and again.

I tore myself away from my nightmare, wiped the sweat off my forehead, uncurled my clenched fingers, kissed her on the forehead and clutched her to me with shaking hands as she continued to whisper into my ear. My heart began to slow. I peered round the room. They were all watching me: Dave standing up, Alan crouched forward, Palmer lying on his side and Digby against the wall. I supposed some sort of explanation was required. "I'm sorry. I, er, I've had nightmares ever since I was a kid. You know, after Medina... It was the kids being hunted. It just brought it all back again. Sorry. Did I make a lot of noise?"

Palmer yawned. "You mean apart from the screaming – no not a lot."

Robbi hugged me. "One of his school teachers told me that he found out he used to stuff a handkerchief into his mouth so they wouldn't hear him when he screamed."

Palmer looked almost sympathetic. "Did you have the nightmares a lot, then?"

I shook my head. Robbi punched me. "Oh, only about three or four nights a week since he was eight, since the time Medina tortured and raped him. Why do you think he works so hard all the time? He's just trying to exhaust himself so he sleeps without dreaming."

So, she'd worked that one out. Dave stirred. Oh God, they were all going to ask me about my childhood. "What about all the child psychologists you saw?"

"What about them?"

"Didn't they try and help?"

I snorted. "Well, the first one was a paedophile. He assaulted me – sexually, I mean. The second was useless, the third one tried a bit, but I was ten by then and could run rings round all of them. Took me a while to realise there were a few adults you could trust."

I closed my eyes so I wouldn't have to watch them staring at me. Pity wasn't something that interested me much. The damage had been done far too long ago. Anyway, I had her now. I didn't need anyone's pity. I leaned my head against her shoulder. She whispered again. I breathed out.

* * *

It was nine thirty in the morning by the time the three men arrived in Ludo's Rolls, driven as always by

Lockhart. Digby was on hand to welcome them, show Lockhart to the kitchen and lead the others to the study. The prisoners had been taken to the lavatory and given water to drink although they were still blindfolded, bound and gagged. Alan, Dave and Paul came to attention as Ian entered the room. He didn't look happy, but on the other hand he didn't look as though he was about to explode. Alan started in with the report about Sergeant Skinner and then back tracked into the story and left me to fill in the gaps. I started with Robbi's kidnapping and didn't spare the details. By ten I had pretty much finished and Lockhart had arrived with breakfast. Marcus spoke before Ian could say a word. "He was always good at fencing, wasn't he Ludo? Foils more than épées though wasn't it?"

Ludo glanced sideways at me. "Well, he made the England junior team, didn't he?"

Robbi stopped chewing and stared at me. "You never told me you fenced for England."

"Junior and you never asked."

Palmer pushed his laptop across the table and tapped the mouse pad. The three men watched the screen and winced. Marcus whitened and looked away as the home movie played. Ludo put his head in his hands. Only Ian stayed the course. The danger of explosion had passed. He rose, stared out of the window, hands behind his ramrod straight back. He spoke without turning. "Major Cummins, get Skinner and his team here now."

Alan used one of Palmer's phones. Ian swung back round. "Marcus, we're going to need Counsel's advice on this immediately. Someone you trust implicitly.

Someone who is not part of the establishment. Someone who is not 'one of us'. Ludo, do you know any of his friends?"

He indicated the supine Marquess with distaste.

Ludo shrugged. "No one, Ian. No one who isn't part of his set. I've met him a couple of times on shoots – he's a marksman by the way – but he mixes with a younger crowd than I do – younger than him too. Not my sort."

Palmer stopped chewing and turned the laptop towards Ian. "He sits on one hell of a lot of boards. Not FTSE One Hundreds either. I reckon he's doing it for the cash. What's a non–exec chairman of a listed company earn, John?"

I shrugged. "Anything from a minimum of twenty-four k a year to a hundred and fifty and a lot more. A proper chair would put in a weekly conference call, a monthly board meeting and investor meetings too. A crap one would just lend his name and do the monthly board meeting."

Palmer counted. "Well, he's on a minimum of two hundred and eighty-eight thousand a year then."

Ian was staring at the laptop. "Mr Palmer, did any of those boards have Medina on them too?"

Palmer pulled the laptop closer. Robbi picked up the iPad. I looked at Digby. "Hugh?"

He looked startled at the use of his Christian name.

"The estate accounts – positive or negative cash flow?"

He held his right hand up, palm down, waggling it from side to side uncertainly. "I don't get to see the accounts of the whole estate, but the farms aren't bringing in enough revenue. The castle is National Trust – sold by his father to pay death duties. I don't know about the timber business, the shoots or the rents from all the property he owns."

"Would two hundred and eighty-eight k a year help?"

"From what I've seen of his lifestyle it wouldn't even touch the sides."

"How many farms?"

"Four."

"Well, they could have buried the bodies of the children on any of them. Fuck!"

Alan's phone rang. He looked across at Ian. "Sergeant Skinner's here, sir."

Palmer stretched and cracked his knuckles – disgusting habit. "You're spot on with the boards, Sir Ian. Four out of seven so far."

Ian turned to Alan and nodded in Marcus' direction. "We're going to need an analysis of every board member on every board, Mr Palmer, and as you're best connected in the City, Marcus, you'd better keep an eye on the findings."

Dave passed a mobile phone across to Ian. "The photos of all the people at the ball last night, sir."

"Good, good. Now let's see if we can do some proper analysis and find out what's going on here."

I tried not to yawn. He smiled grimly. "Roberta, even your beauty is a thought tarnished this morning and your husband looks all but beyond repair. Take him somewhere quiet for twenty-four hours and somewhere which is s–a–f–e! That does not include Fosse Manor or your favourite hotel in London."

I started to protest. Robbi put a hand over my mouth and pulled me away. "I'll take him somewhere very safe, Ian, don't worry."

She could have taken me to the moon for all I knew about it. One of Skinner's squad was seconded to drive us back to London. I can remember stumbling down the forty steps from that vile room and being half–lifted into the back seat and then blackness, nightmares and blackness.

* * *

I drifted back to the surface. I was in a bed – good. New sheets – better. A small snore: hers – best. I lay in the half darkness of what looked like an attic bedroom listening for sound clues as to our whereabouts, but the double glazing must have been too good. All I could hear was her soft breathing. I turned over slowly to watch her sleep – a recent and now favourite activity. Her left arm was stretched out towards me, her hand palm up, the fingers half curled. I decided I was bored. No matter that she had probably been awake half the night worrying about me – I was now awake and so she must be too. I lay still for a further five minutes before giving into my selfishness. I reached across and tickled the palm of her hand with my fingers. She stirred. I tickled again and in an instant her fingers clamped round mine. She smiled through half closed eyes.

"Hello, John Richard. You're feeling better then?"

I pulled her towards me. She pushed back. "Oh no you don't. I've had to change the sheets twice 'cos of you dripping sweat, so you can bugger off and have a shower before you get anywhere near me."

"Where are we, Robbi?"

Her eyes opened wide. "I'm not going to tell you yet and you have to promise me you won't open the curtains or leave this room."

She pinched the back of my hand.

"Ow! All right, all right. Vicious woman."

I showered. She showered. We went back to bed. The bedclothes were messed up again. We showered once more. I stared at the mound of sheets. "Is there a washing machine in this building wherever this building is?"

I hesitated not wanting to ruin her game. "You can't have bought a new place in London so quickly. Anyway, it's too quiet."

She smirked and pointed at the wardrobe. "There are clothes for you in there. Get dressed."

I pulled on a tee shirt and Levis while she hustled into a short skirt and a roll neck pullover, wrapping a towel round her damp hair and showing the suspicion of a tendency to bounce.

"Come on. Come on."

She grabbed my hand and led me out of the bedroom on to a small landing and down a steep flight of stairs to the floor below. "I haven't had time to do any decorating."

She watched me anxiously while I looked at the bedrooms and the bathroom across the landing from them. "They're just guest rooms, but we could use one as a study."

I nodded and held out my hand. I was led down a further flight of stairs and into a panelled drawing room with shuttered windows in deep window recesses. It was all very familiar. There was an early Victorian fireplace with bookshelves on either side of it full of books from the family flat. My grandfather's portrait hung over the fireplace and the furniture – from sofa to drinks cabinet – could have been installed eighty years ago. I smiled. She sighed with relief and I was led on down to the ground floor with a dining room and reception room. My grandfather's grandfather clock ticked solemnly. I smiled again and was pulled down to the basement and an ultra-modern kitchen. I liked it.

"So where are we, Robbi?"

"You have to guess."

"Well, it ain't Mayfair. The proportions of the house are all wrong for Mayfair. It could be somewhere in Hoxton where my restaurant was, but..." I paused at the distant sound of a full Westminster chime. "We're in Westminster. You wonderful creature! Can I go and undo the shutters now?"

She smiled happily and ran up the stairs ahead of me, opening the shutters to the right of the front door. I peered out into the semi darkness of the sodium lit city, blinked and stared again. We were in Lord North Street, right on the corner of Smith Square. I turned and grabbed her – mainly to stop the bouncing. "You genius. How?"

"I told Angela Arbuthnot we were looking for somewhere here. She put the word out. The person who lived here had wanted to move out for some time and said yes and we got it with no estate agent fees. I am a genius, aren't I? Don't you want to know how much it cost?"

"Not really. I love it."

She looked at her watch and bounced again. "And the takeaway should be here any minute now along with our guest."

"Guest? On our first night here? I thought it would be a quick snack and then more shagging."

"Ha! Think again, Hannay."

The bell rang. It was the takeaway. Leaving her to pay I carried the heavy box down to the kitchen and opened the heaviest of the bags in it – three bottles of Chateau Musar 1999. That was going some for a takeaway. I found a big glass jug, decanted two of the bottles and turned back to the bags. I sniffed and smiled. She'd managed to get a takeaway from Maroush. I emptied the bags of Lebanese food into containers and put them in the oven to keep warm while I set the table. I could hear Robbi singing upstairs. She really was a genius – at least at making me happy. The doorbell bell rang and I heard more female laughter, then high heels on the stairs. Robbi led the way, dressed now in leggings and one of my shirts (yet again) and carrying the pile of sheets. Behind her was The Boss – tanned, elegant and relaxed.

"Em!"

I hugged her while Robbi stuffed sheets into the washing machine. "So where have you been hiding, Em? How did you avoid the select committee hearing and how did Robbi find you?"

"Been travelling, John. I was on Necker when I saw a report of your appearance at the committee. Then I saw it on You Tube – pissed myself. You were so angry: 'you mean, as in 've ask ze qvestions'. So, I kept in touch with

Robbi on emails from different accounts. Safer than you knowing anything about it. You're such a control freak anyway. Now pour us a glass of that wine and catch me up."

Robbi hugged her from behind and kissed her on the neck. Em grinned mockingly. "Unless you're after a threesome? But you'd be out of luck there – I don't do skinny has–beens and slappers!"

Robbi bit her ear.

It took us an hour and all the food and wine to bring her up to speed. She sat back while I shoved dishes into the too small dishwasher. Robbi grabbed glasses and I followed them up the sitting room where she had lit the fire earlier. I used the bellows and watched the smokeless coal glow. Em swilled Armagnac round her glass.

"So, you want me to go and seduce this Marquess and find out who he's working with and if he's still killing children."

"Pretty much."

"It'll be safe will it?"

"Dave and Paul will be as close as they can get – which is close."

She walked over to look up at the portrait of my grandfather. "You know the older you get the more like him you look. Don't you think, Robbi?"

Robbi smiled. I waited. She turned away, held out her glass for a top up and sat down again. "All right, I'll do it. I've been thinking for a while that I should get stuck in so this could be my moment in the sun. Don't tell anyone about me doing this, John – apart from Dave and

Paul, I mean. Alan would try and stop me. You won't know me if we happen to meet. OK?"

She stood up. Robbi hugged her. She left. I yawned. We slept.

CHAPTER TWENTY-FOUR

Hiatus, lull, gap, pause.

Two days back at Fosse Manor when nothing happened to us – see, I can say 'us' now, not 'me' – when life was normal. We rode both mornings. The dogs came with us and nearly behaved properly despite Robbi's previous training. I ate what was put in front of me. I had no nightmares. On the third morning I had just started in on the accounts again, trying to get to the bottom of precisely how much (or little) Glebe Farm had contributed to the estate, when I heard angry voices raised in the hall. Robbi had gone Christmas shopping in Burford with Miranda so it must be Margaret – worryingly out of character. I slid open the drawer of the old desk, unclamped the Glock from its magnet and waited. A tap at the door – a red faced Margaret and two thin, unkempt men lurking behind her in the corridor.

"John, I'm very sorry, but these two men are demanding to see you. They refused to leave without seeing you."

I nodded at her. She mouthed 'I'll get Paul' and stepped aside. The two men barged forward – mottled faces, worn, red veined, poorly shaved, scarcely washed. I kept my hand in the drawer. "What can I do for you, Mr Harker? Is this your son?"

"None of that Hannay. You know why I'm here!"

"You've come to pay the rent owing on the farm?"

"Don't try and be clever with me, Hannay. I know your games."

"Perhaps you would care to elucidate."

He glowered and looked round for a chair. I made no attempt to move the paperwork from any of the available seating.

"What d'you mean by putting Gypsies on my farm, Hannay? Bloody vermin the lot of 'em. I'll take my shotgun to 'em if I sees them anywhere near the house or my livestock."

"No, you won't, Mr Harker. You'll not break the law, I'm sure, especially as you well know that they were not on or near your land. Now, I'm glad you've come round as I wanted to talk to you about these."

I took my hand off the Glock and tossed the copies of the deeds of sale between him and Mallin onto the desk in front of him. He pretended to squint at them. "What the hell are they, then?"

I turned the top agreement over to the signature page and pointed. "You should know, Mr Harker. There's your signature. I know it's yours because it's just the same as the one on the last cheque you wrote for the rent on your farm. Although maybe it might have changed since then as the last cheque you wrote was more than fifteen years ago."

"What are you playing at Hannay?"

He leaned menacingly over the desk, his son puffing out his chest and cracking his knuckles. It was laughable. So, I laughed. "So far as I am aware this is the first time I have spoken to you since I was twelve, so I don't know what games you think I play. As a matter of fact, I don't ever play games. I think I'm quite well known for my lack of game playing." I sat forward so my face was directly in front of his. "Mr Harker, you owe me at least fifteen years rent on your farm. You have been selling parcels of my land without my knowledge or permission; you have ignored the drainage on four of your fields to the detriment of pasture on Home Farm and you have made no attempt to maintain either the stock proof fencing on Mill field, the woods by the stream or the fabric of the farm buildings themselves."

The son started to push past the father, waving his fist at me. "Don't you start coming it all high and mighty with my dad, Hannay. I'll..."

I smacked away his hand. "Stand back, young man, and learn some manners. It's Sir John to you, not Hannay and I was speaking to the organ grinder, not the monkey."

I swung back to his father pointing my finger in his face. "Now you, Mr Harker, will listen to me. You have a choice. Either I call the police now and have you arrested for attempted assault and fraud and then I will have you evicted from your farm immediately... or, and I want you to think hard about this, Mr Harker, I will pay you the sum of one hundred and fifty thousand pounds now into your bank account and you will leave Glebe Farm tomorrow morning having signed an agreement releasing you from the terms of the tenancy."

He started to speak. I pressed my face to within an inch of his. "Did it look as though I had finished speaking?"

I paused and sat back. I could see that he was trying to work out what was happening. I carried on, speaking more quietly. "Maybe you think I don't why your father became the tenant after my father was killed, Mr Harker. Maybe you think I don't know about your relationship with Mallin. Maybe you think someone's going to murder me, just like people you know all about murdered my parents and maybe you think you'll just carry on living at the farm, paying no rent for as long as you want."

I paused again and leaned forward, tapping the now silent farmer on the chest. "I don't play games, Mr Harker. I don't know how to. They murdered my parents before I'd learned much about playing. But I do know about fighting. I've fought all my life since I was eight and what I've learned is how not to lose. Now, if I *were* playing a game, I would say... your call."

His son started to say something to him, but he waved him into silence staring at me, muttering to himself. "How do I know you'll keep your word?"

I picked up the phone and pressed a short code. Both men watched me. I saw a shadow in the doorway and raised a hand as Paul entered. The two men looked round at him. "Sir John Hannay for Mr Wethers, please."

Paul picked up some of the papers I had declined to move from one of the chairs and pointed to it. The son sat down immediately. Paul's reputation had reached Glebe Farm.

"Morning, Uncle Marcus. Very well, thank you. No, she's Christmas shopping. Oh, and she wants to know when you'll be arriving for Christmas and how long you'll be staying. Right, OK, I'll tell her."

I made a note on my pad.

"Uncle Marcus, I've got a very urgent request I'm afraid. I'm with Michael Harker, the tenant farmer on Glebe Farm. I have just made him an offer of one hundred and fifty thousand pounds to quit the tenancy immediately and leave the farm tomorrow. I'm going to put you on speaker phone so you can speak to him direct."

I put the phone in its cradle and sat back. We could hear Marcus calling through to his secretary to bring in a property associate. He spoke directly into the phone.

"Harker? Can you hear me?"

"I can hear you."

"Do you have a solicitor?"

"I use Old Mr Harford of Harford and Stone."

"Good. I know him."

So did I. A lovely old buffer who had long acted for the family in various capacities when Uncle Marcus wasn't available. Marcus was calling to his secretary again.

"Fiona, get me Harford and Stone in Burford. I want Geoffrey Harford. Put him into a conference call immediately."

Within forty seconds the conference call had started. I repeated my statement, making it clear that I didn't much care if I brought the police in immediately to deal with the illegalities. Paul faxed through the land sale documents to both lawyers. We could hear the rustling of papers. Harker bit his nails and wouldn't meet my eyes. I heard Harford sotto voce.

"Good Lord."

He spoke into his phone. "Marcus, have you got someone who can draw up the deed?"

"Being done now, Geoffrey. I've got your DX number, but why don't we fax and sign and exchange hard copies tomorrow. Would your client accept that?"

"Under the circumstances, Marcus, I wouldn't give him an alternative. Harker, can you hear me?"

"Yes."

"I am astounded, Harker, astounded. I know perfectly well that you've sailed close to the wind in the past, but this is blatant criminality. I have no idea why Sir John is being so lenient with you, but I advise you in the strongest possible terms to accept his offer."

The old farmer wriggled. "Ow do I know he'll pay up?"

There was a sharp intake of breath from both lawyers. I intervened. "I can bring one more caller in on this conference, gentlemen. Just one moment."

I dialled my wealth manager.

"Morning, John."

"Tony, I've just brought you in on a conference call with Marcus Wethers and another lawyer, a Mr Geoffrey Harford, who represents one of my tenants. I have just made an offer to this tenant of one hundred and fifty thousand pounds in exchange for giving up his tenancy immediately."

There was the slightest of pauses. "Very well, John. Morning, Marcus, I take it you've advised on this. Morning Mr Harford. I can transfer the amount into your escrow account now if you'll give me the details. You'll see the transaction in a moment. You paying the bank charges, John?"

"Yep. Thanks, Tony. Email me the transaction too, would you?"

"Very well, John."

He collected the account details and left the conference call. Harker was still biting his nails, convinced he was missing something. He pointed at me. "You'll be paying the legal fees."

Before I could open my mouth, Harford was shouting down the phone. "Harker, you listen to me. You'll damn well pay my fees on this transaction and it'll be the last time I deal with you or your rotten family. How much do you think I can charge for an hour's work, anyway?"

His voice died away, but we could still hear him muttering. "Ridiculous. Who the devil does he think he is?"

His voice came through louder. "Got the email, Marcus, thanks. Your chap works fast."

I opened the email on my iMac and pressed print to run off two copies of the contract. Paul passed one to Harker. He read it laboriously. I stared at the ceiling and concentrated on slowing my heart rate. I glanced at Paul and moved my eyes to the two men. He nodded. It took a further ten minutes to check through the agreement. I signed two copies without even having read them. Harker wiped his hands across his trousers, bit his nails again, squinted at me suspiciously and finally signed. Paul faxed the documents to both lawyers. Geoffrey Harford checked his account. "Harker, the money has arrived. You'd better come in here and give me your account details. Bring a copy of the agreement with you. Goodbye, John. Hope to see you soon. Cheerio, Marcus."

The phones went down. Young Harker stood nervously, completely out of his depth. Old man Harker was still watching me, still sure I had conned him out of something.

"Paul, shut the door."

Paul moved and blocked the exit.

"You will be out by twelve thirty tomorrow. You will never again come anywhere near my land."

Paul tapped the old man on his shoulder making him jump.

"And if I ever see you again on John's land, Mr Harker, you will regret it. Please don't think I'm threatening you. I never make threats. Same goes for you son. Listen to your dad on this one as I don't reckon you've inherited his brains."

He took a step forward.

"I'll also be watching you for the next twenty-four hours so do try not to be clever. I would hate to think that there might be an accidental little fire or anything like that at Glebe Farm. Tread carefully, boys."

He escorted them to the front door. I picked up my mobile and dialled.

"Hugh?"

"Yes, John. Are you better now?"

"I'm fine, thanks. Can you come over to Fosse tomorrow?"

"Er, yes. Any particular reason?"

"Just be here at one."

I put the phone down. Paul came back in followed by Margaret with coffee. She was worried. Laughter from the kitchen – I smiled immediately, relief flooding through me. Margaret nudged Paul. "Look at him. The second he hears her, he's happy again."

She called through the door. "In the study, Robbi."

She came in, still laughing over shoulder at Miranda. She stopped dead and stared at me.

"What's happened, John?"

She grabbed my wrist to take my pulse. I opened my mouth to explain. She put her hand over it and turned to Paul. I licked her palm. She shook her head at me. "You're not that bad then."

Paul explained. I showed her the agreement. She sat down, read it and tidied the papers on the desk absently, standing up to file the contracts, shutting the drawer of the filing cabinet. We watched her. "OK. OK. Probably for the best although, frankly, I would've preferred Paul to sort him out."

Margaret nodded vehemently. "Me too."

Miranda was looking nervous.

"What's the matter, Mimi?"

"You're not going to ask me to run Glebe Farm are you, John?"

I smiled at her. "No Mimi, I'm not. I have an idea who could though. Paul you'd better get over to Glebe Farm and keep an eye on them. Mimi, can you prepare an outline of all the works that need to be done there. We'll go over tomorrow when Paul says it's clear.

* * *

Paul had called at twelve thirty-one. He was still laughing at the terror in Harker junior's eyes when he had dropped down from a tree in front of their house at exactly twelve thirty, clad in full camouflage gear and carrying his sniper rifle. Digby arrived early at twelve forty-seven. As Miranda was in the study, I took him through to the kitchen.

"How's things back at the castle, Hugh?"

"I don't know, John. His Lordship's carrying on as if nothing has happened. After you'd gone Sir Ian revealed himself to the Secretary of State and Lord Artinswell and then ordered Sergeant Skinner to take them away to a secret location. Sir Ian started on dear Edgar after that and he wasn't exactly apologetic to him either. Just told him in front of me that certain very important people had requested his release and that they had been ordered to do nothing further at this stage, but..."

"But what?"

"Well, Edgar just swelled with self-importance. After Sir Ian had gone, he rushed off up to his study and came back down looking even more pleased with himself. It was all I could do not to punch him in the face."

Robbi came in from the stable yard with Grace. I called for Miranda to join us. She came through from the study scratching her head over the outline of works to be done, saw Digby, did a double take, blushed, dropped the papers, scrabbled on the floor for them and banged heads with him as he stooped to help. They both stepped back rubbing their foreheads and looking at each other thoughtfully. I ushered them in the direction of the Landrover while Robbi and Grace fluttered their eyelids, clutched their hands to their hearts and made kissy noises.

I had deliberately avoided Glebe Farm since I had returned to Fosse six months ago and as I braked to a halt outside the farmhouse, I was glad I had. It was depressing. What could have been a pretty Cotswold stone farmhouse was decaying, unkempt, broken windowed and filthy – absolutely filthy. I watched Digby's reaction to the venue. He looked interested, excited. Hmm, maybe my palate was just jaded. I tried to look at the building as though it didn't represent twenty-eight years of misery – through what Seamus Heaney had called 'rinsed eyes'. I failed. Robbi rolled her eyes in my direction.

"What are you squinting at, Hannay?"

I shook my head at her as Paul came out of the front door brushing dirt off his hands. He nodded at Digby and spoke to Miranda.

"I wouldn't go in there, Mimi, unless you have to. They've left it in a right two 'n eight."

Digby turned to me, grinning cheerfully.

"Do you need a hand sorting it out, John? His Lordship owes me some holiday. Happy to help if that's what you want. It'd be good to get my hands dirty again."

I stepped back physically and metaphorically, gesturing towards Robbi who smiled at me pityingly.

"Hugh, John had something more permanent in mind. Jack Cartwright is the tenant on Home Farm; Paul's our gamekeeper (among other things); Miranda here's our estate manager, but as of twelve thirty this morning we need a tenant farmer for Glebe Farm. Interested?"

He stared at her, mouth open, looked at Paul who was grinning at his discomfiture, then at Miranda who was watching him thoughtfully and then, finally, at me. "Are you serious?"

"Is he ever not serious?"

Miranda laughed. Digby blushed and stammered. Robbi put a hand in Miranda's back and pushed her forward.

"Well, before you say yes or no, Hugh, you'd better let Miranda show you the mess the whole farm's in. There's her list of the problems. First of all, though, why don't we look at those parcels of land that Harker sold, in inverted commas, to Mallin?

Paul found the Collies chasing rats in the tumbledown barn, ordered them back into the Landrover and we set out with Miranda navigating from the deeds on her lap. It took us an hour to survey all the patches of land. They'd all been turned over and then re–covered. Digby stared at the last patch of scrub and scratched his ear. "You haven't got coal or shale gas or oil or something round here have you, John? You know, for fracking."

"No, that was my first thought. Nothing. Geology is all wrong."

Miranda stepped back and peered at the piece of land through half closed eyes. "Well, if they weren't so recent it would look like ancient burial sites."

I snorted and headed back towards the vehicle. Paul called the dogs who were sniffing and scratching on the far side of the plot. We drove back to the Manor with Robbi uncharacteristically silent and headed into the kitchen where the dogs lapped noisily at their water bowls and she sat at the table filing her nails with almost manic concentration. I waited. She threw down the emery board, stared at me and burst into tears. I went to comfort her, but she held up her hands, palms towards me. "It's what Miranda said." She wiped her thumbs over her eyes and fixed me with an angst-ridden stare. "If they weren't so recent it would look like ancient burial sites...."

I stared at her blankly. The penny dropped. I sat down. "The children from the home? He buried the children they murdered on Fosse land so he could implicate me. Oh God, those poor, poor children."

I looked at her in horror. She reached across the table and gripped my hands. I didn't hear the back door open. I didn't see the two men enter until one of them cleared his throat in a noisy, irritated fashion. I looked up to see Ian and Alan glaring at me. Ian started.

"What the devil do you mean bringing Emma Fitzgerald into this, John. Can't you ever learn discipline?"

I stared at him dully, half hearing, half despairing. "John? John? Roberta, what is he...? What are you?"

I pulled myself together. "I er... We..."

Robbi took over. "We know where the bodies of the children are buried, Ian."

They joined us at the table all thought of Em forgotten – thankfully. I brought a map of the estate through from the study and showed them. He studied the locations in silence. He could see the implications as well as I could. He looked up at me. "Well?"

I shrugged. "We either do it privately or publicly. If we do it publicly, I have to announce we have found some graves, bring in the local plods who will bring in the Met and then where are we? For all we know, Edgar has planted a shotgun somewhere with my fingerprints on. If we do it privately no one can know anything about it, but we already know that Mallin and Harker must have had more than an inkling. Christ this bloody Marquess has some clout."

They watched me. Robbi blew her nose. "I know this sounds ridiculous, but...". She stopped, shook her head. "Doesn't matter."

I kicked her under the table. "What?"

"Well, it's just that Dorothy is going to start a fund to restore the floor in the old Lady chapel. Could we bury the children there and have her read a burial service? She's completely trustworthy."

I nodded slowly. "Dorothy's our vicar."

Ian sat down and waited for me to continue. "If we do it privately, Ian... disinter the bodies, take them to the church, rebury them and lay the floor over them then there's no evidence. We'd have to film the disinterment I suppose. I'll get going on replacing the stock fencing immediately afterwards."

Robbi blew her nose again and put more coffee in the pot. I rolled up the map of the estate. "Ian, about Emma Fitzgerald? Yes, we had dinner with her three nights ago. She's been travelling for the last couple of months so I brought her up to speed, but you don't seriously think I can influence any course of action she chooses to make do you? She's the Boss! You want to try telling her what to do?"

He grimaced. "I just did."

"And?"

"I was told to fuck off and set up a committee."

Robbi smiled wanly. Alan joined the conversation.

"You sure your vicar can be trusted?"

"Oh absolutely. She's seriously discreet. Can we help with the disinterment, Ian?"

Disinterment sounded so much better than 'digging up the decomposing bodies of murdered children'.

"No. It's best you stay well away from the sites. It won't be pleasant and I'm sure Alan can put together a specialist team – by tonight I think, Alan?"

"Do you need to borrow a video camera? There's one in the study."

Sergeant Skinner was summoned, the camera borrowed and the small team left to do their dirty business. I was ashamed how relieved I was not to have to accompany them. That night after Robbi had fallen asleep I slid out of bed, curled up on the floor with a handkerchief stuffed in my mouth, dreamed my awful dreams and shook, shivered and sweated. Before she could wake and upbraid me, I was in the shower and trying to whistle. She wasn't fooled. She just lay in bed and watched my every move.

"You are an idiot, John."

"I know."

"I want to be with you when you're having nightmares. I can help. Don't you understand?"

"I'm sorry."

"No, you're not."

And I wasn't either. Her eyes, so hot, haunted and red the night before, were clear and rested now. And I had lived with my nightmares for twenty-eight years – one more night would make no difference.

CHAPTER TWENTY-FIVE

Another day, another disaster – another night, another nightmare. I struggled out of bed at six, showered, fed the dogs and horses, mucked out and still felt shitty. I went to find Robbi and made my proposal.

She wrinkled her nose at me. "All right, but I'm not going anywhere with you until you stop smelling of horsey pooh."

I showered again while she made the phone call, dressed in a pin stripe suit, picked my sword stick out of the cupboard and waited for Robbi to finish in the bathroom. She emerged wearing the Stella McCartney trouser suit. I may have revealed something of my feelings about the way she looked in such attire as I found myself in receipt of one of her looks.

"You're a disgusting pervert. Come along."

I went along. We took the Bentley, drove up on to the A429 and eventually arrived at the children's special home, St Christopher's School, in time for morning break. I'm not sure what I expected really – a mixture of DotheBoys Hall and the Rugby of Tom Brown's School Days, populated by psychopathic teachers and a sadistic headmaster's wife. It wasn't like that at all. It was a pleasant, mid Victorian, Cotswold stone pile with some thirty children ranging in age from ten to sixteen and a charming if somewhat doddery head teacher who was delighted to welcome us following the phone call from our friend, Catherine Symonds, of our local Academy school – the call that Robbi had arranged earlier. I left her to do the talking while we walked round the school and watched some of the activities.

"I hope you don't mind my asking about fire escapes and such like, headmaster?"

Robbi reacted immediately, putting her hand on his arm and talking confidentially. "John was caught in a fire in an office block once and is paranoid about it."

What a little chuckle we had about that. There were three fire escape doors on the ground floor, only one of which was suitable for what I had in mind. It looked out onto a sunken path at the side of the building. "I suppose it's permanently alarmed is it?"

"No, not at all. The alarms only go on when the children are in bed at ten."

I nodded and sneezed suddenly, reaching for a handkerchief and blowing my nose. "Sorry – allergic to house dust."

We walked back up the steps and I sneezed again, fumbling into my pocket for the handkerchief. I kept my hand in front of my face and cursed. "Must have dropped my handkerchief back there. I'll be straight back."

I hurried back round the corner and down the steps to the door. It took four seconds to cut the wire leading to the alarm, pick up my handkerchief, sprint back along the corridor and limp slowly up the steps and round the corner, wiping my nose.

We stayed for lunch and I watched the children watching us: all so normal... until the pudding course.

One of the older boys, who hadn't been able to take his eyes off Robbi, dropped a plate. Time slowed. I watched the shards of ceramic fly out from the splashing, red–cored semolina and flicked a glance at the culprit. Terrified, he stared in abject fear at someone directly behind me. I had time for a momentary glimpse of the head teacher. He hadn't even raised his head, just carried on sucking at the glutinous mess of his pudding.

Robbi was on her feet immediately, hurrying to help the fear–stricken boy. I reached for my stick, knocked it back clumsily and stooped to peer behind and under my arm. A thin, bent, elderly woman was turning back towards a door hidden behind a floor to ceiling curtain. I caught a glimpse of an embittered, vicious face, jagged scarred across the bridge of her nose, then a thickly muscled, tattooed arm pulled the door closed in front of her. I blinked, looked back at the room and read the scene from a new script. The head teacher wasn't a sweet old man; he was venal, cold, without empathy or feeling. The child psychologist (how could I, of all people, have missed this?) was the psychopath, the games teacher – the sadist; the two sleek priests – paedophiles; the remaining teachers, stupid and uninterested.

The children cowered in their seats while Robbi laughed at the mess and helped the desperately frightened and embarrassed boy to pick up the pieces of plate and wipe the stickiness off the floor.

"Come along, Finn, let's find the bathroom and get you cleaned up."

She walked to the door as I limped down from the platform, collected the last couple of shards and put them in the bin by the door. I walked back to the dais and smiled up at the teachers.

"Poor lad, he looked terrified. Hope you won't be too hard on him. Look, I've seen a great deal today which is very impressive. I'll report back to Catherine Symonds that I think St Christopher's would be a great addition to what we're doing and I'll pop back over in a couple of days with a confidentiality agreement so we can discuss things in more detail. A bit more financing can never go amiss, don't you think?"

The old man positively beamed at me and even the stupid teachers looked interested at the thought of 'financing'. Robbi re–entered with young Finn, smiling at the room in general – a smile which, I could tell, contained nothing but danger for the assembled adults. Finn was looking mystified and a lot less petrified. We made our excuses and left. She drove. I sat sideways, looking at the building as she reversed the long car carefully and turned to go down the drive.

"That boy Finn, John, he said they'll punish him tonight."

Her knuckles whitened as she squeezed the steering wheel. I thought for a second. "We're going back then. I'll try and raise Paul or Dave. They should be nearby if they're keeping an eye on Em." I stared at the house, memorising the layout. A face moved away from a window on the top floor and even from this distance I could see the scar across her nose.

* * *

Robbi drove us home via Cheltenham, which seemed a strange way to go. We parked on one of those once graceful, Georgian side streets in which most of the houses were now offices and most of the gardens, car parks. Now, you know how much progress I had been making – what with listening to her, holding hands in public and even letting her snuggle up in bed, but shopping – please – and in Cheltenham? It turned out to be a cycle shop, but one so very different from the cycle shops of my youth – six thousand pounds for an electric bike; five thousand for a front and rear fork suspensioned, mountain bike, drop handlebar, fixed wheel racers you could lift with one finger and Lycra, endless stretches of Lycra – leggings, shirts, hats, in branded fluorescent orange, purple, green, yellow – all of it positively ghastly. She informed me that I sounded like the Prince of Wales and we left with Lycra 'stuff'. At least it was black.

Back at Fosse I spent the rest of the afternoon on Google Earth looking for places to leave a car by the school, digging out my grandfather's woodworking tools and trying to raise Paul and Dave; even, after careful consideration, Ian and Alan. No one responded.

I made supper for Robbi and Margaret. By nine I realised that we were going to be on our own and, with considerable reluctance, squeezed into the Lycra cycle kit. Robbi nudged Margaret and they giggled cruelly at me especially after I donned the balaclava. Robbi tucked her shining, golden hair under her balaclava and slotted a Glock into her hip holster. I admired the effect – purely for aesthetic reasons. With Margaret promising to keep phoning Paul, I tossed a full rucksack on to the back seat of Miranda's ancient Beetle and we chugged back towards the school.

The main gates were still open. Robbi spent two careful minutes with the night glasses searching for CCTV camera or wires. Eventually she shrugged at me and we slipped through the gate and ran for the shelter of the trees. The grass was wet and cold and my new, black trainers were soaked in seconds. We ran again, keeping in the shadow of the Cedars, the ground drier underfoot. Robbi darted forward, stopped and held up her hand to stop me. She tiptoed backwards towards me and tilted her chin to murmur in my ear. "We're not the only ones here, John."

"What do you mean?"

"There's someone else in the grounds, I'm sure. Keep your eyes open."

I put the image intensifiers on and scanned our near horizon carefully. "No one near, so far as I can tell." I peered at my watch. "Come on. We'd better be inside before they activate the alarms."

I took a bearing on the house and we trotted on more slowly, Robbi's Glock held ready, safety off. I caught a hint of movement ahead and jerked her back to me. She nodded. We crept forward. A click. A sobbing breath. Someone trying to break out... or in? I adjusted the image intensifier. A figure hunched in front of the fire escape. A scrabbling noise. A muttered curse. It was a break in. A friend? I squeezed Robbi's Glock–free hand and pointed. We separated and closed in on our prey. I reached him first. Across his shoulder I could see Robbi slithering down the far bank. I pulled the image intensifier off my head, took two more short steps and reached for him as he straightened. My fingers clamped round his neck. Robbi's gun was at his mouth. I whispered in his ear – neat little ear – slender neck too. "Em? What the fuck are you doing here?"

The figure shuddered, sobbed and threw her arms round my neck. Robbi closed up behind her, hugging her from behind.

"John? Robbi? God, you scared me."

She shuddered again and relaxed against me, reaching to stroke Robbi's arm by her side. Incongruously she chuckled. "About that threesome. I could be persuaded to change my mind."

I slapped the top of her head and left Robbi hugging her while I stooped over my rucksack and pulled out the brace and bit. I laid a cloth on the ground, lined it up opposite the push bar on the inside of the door and drilled through the wooden frame with the razor-sharp bit in seconds. I glanced at my watch – just under three minutes before the alarms went on. I pushed the hook through the hole, manoeuvred it under the push bar and tugged hard. The bar dropped with a click and the door swung towards me. I held my breath, but there was only silence. I glanced at my watch. A distant bell rang. It was ten p.m. and we were on the inside. Spotlights came on in the grounds, casting long, white shadows across the drive.

"So, Em, what are you doing here? Where's Dave?"

"I'm sorry."

Well, that was a first. An apology from the Boss. Robbi hugged her again. "Don't be silly, Em. He's just worried about you."

Em kissed me on the cheek. I'd have bet my last billion that there wasn't any hugging and kissing on an SAS managed operation.

"It was the ghastly Edgar. I heard him on the phone saying he'd come over. I asked where he was going and he said he was going to a school where he was one of the governors – responsible for the moral welfare of the children. Then he burst out laughing. He is such a sick bastard. Anyway, I realised this meant he was coming here... so I followed him. I know I don't know what to do, but I couldn't call anyone and I knew I couldn't let him do something horrible to any more children."

Robbi took charge. Shoes off and in the rucksack: Robbi leading the way, Em in the middle, me watching our backs. Thirty seconds passed; Robbi hesitating at the bottom of the main stairs and then flitting across to the dining hall, through the doors; Em running, slipping on the polished parquet; me, poised to go. A step in the corridor behind me. I slid behind the balustrade; footsteps above me on the stairs – voices. The steps from the corridor stopped. Then a rush of air, a presence beside me – a big presence and a big hand over my mouth. Thank God. Dave took his hand away and patted my shoulder. The voices faded.

"Seen Paul, John?"

I shook my head and pointed. "No, Dave. Robbi and Emma are through there. You have no idea how relieved I am to see you."

I saw his half smile in the half light. We walked across to the dining hall. After further hugging and a palpable release of tension I brought Dave up to speed. He summarised – action points as ever.

"So, headmaster's not going to cause trouble. One man with big tattooed arms – dangerous; old woman, probably dangerous; maybe a couple more teachers and the Marquess – who's an unknown quantity regarding action but probably dangerous when cornered."

The half-smile... "So – odds in our favour then. Where's this door?"

I pointed.

"Wonder where Paul is – he'd like to be in on this. Didn't take to the Marquess did our Paul."

He vaulted up on to the stage, listened at the heavy crimson curtain, shrugged, lifted it from the bottom and disappeared. We huddled on the floor beneath the stage. The curtain was rucked up again and a hand beckoned us forward. Robbi jumped up, turned to pull Em up, leaving me to clamber up behind them. Dave hurried us. The room behind the door behind the curtain was an ante–chamber. Bucket and mop in one corner, stacked chairs beside them, a trestle table on its side, all lit by an ancient ten-watt bulb. Dave was already by the inner door listening with his ever-present stethoscope. He looked back towards us; his eyes unfocussed. "Voices."

He squinted, frowned, closed his eyes and straightened.

"Four people talking. Could be more in there not talking, obviously."

Robbi waved her hand frantically – steps sounding on the platform, the far side of the curtain. We scrabbled for the cover of the trestle table. I could feel Em shivering against me. Dave peered round the corner, throwing knife in hand. I saw his teeth as he smiled. The door closed. "Our friend the Marquess. Shhh."

I strained my ears and heard the faintest of movements on the platform. Dave clicked his fingers once – an answering click and Paul's head came through the door. He looked from one to the other and grunted.

"Next time leave slightly more obvious indicators, Dave, I could scarcely see the knife cut in the curtain."

"It's your eyes, Paul. Told you. You need bifocals."

Paul growled. "Anyway, I did see the Marquess – so I followed him. Briefing?"

It took less than a minute. I handed the camera to Em, showed her how to operate it and followed Robbi and our two soldiers through into what appeared to be some sort of gallery over a small hall. I know now that the school had originally been built for an eminent nineteenth century surgeon and this room had been his private operating theatre and dissection room. The students had sat in the gallery where we now crouched above the central table. This evening the body it contained was in need neither of an operation nor of an autopsy, just comfort. It was poor, terrified Finn, the plate smasher from lunch, strapped face down by his wrists and ankles. I tore my eyes away from him, glanced at Em to make sure she was filming and took in the rest of the scene. One of the two priests, 'entertaining' a teenage girl on his lap; the headmaster, seated apart from the rest in a high-backed chair, chin on hand, sipping what looked like a glass of Port; the back of the tattooed, big armed thug; the scar nosed profile of the older woman and the full face of his Lordship, Edgar Alain–Despenser, ninth Marquess of Cheltenham, standing at the table above Finn's head, flexing a cane, swishing it through the air, smiling, silent. I slithered back to where Dave was murmuring in Paul's ear. Dave turned to me, leaning in close.

"We need two minutes to get into position. Can you cause a distraction?"

I nodded and crawled across to where Robbi was crouched by Em.

"Robbi, can you hit that cane with a bullet if it looks as though he is going to use it?"

"Why?"

"I'm going to cause a diversion while Dave and Paul get in position."

She nodded grimly and lay full length, face down, heels tilted towards the floor in approved military style, elbows on the floor, Glock held firmly between two hands. I patted Em's shoulder. "Stop videoing when I start talking, Em."

I straightened, stretched my back to ease the stiffness in the lumbar region and strolled down the stairs as Edgar raised the cane. "Ooh I say, Edgar, I wouldn't do that you know. There's laws against corporal punishment these days."

The tableau froze.

"Evening headmaster. Good vintage? Hello padre, offering first communion, are we?"

I could see now where Finn had wet the top of the table in his fear. The cold fury and hatred bit into my stomach. I wanted to hit, kick, bite, tear, scream. Instead, I leaned against a pillar, folded my arms and smiled. The Marquess closed his mouth, lowered the cane slowly and looked up at the gallery, turning slowly on his heel.

He saw nothing, but as his gaze settled on me again, out of the corner of my eye I caught the faintest movement over his head. He cleared his throat and turned to the stunned headmaster.

"So, you've met Sir John before have you?"

His voice was harsh, grating. The headmaster's arm jerked, sloshing dark, red wine on to his trousers. "I er. I... He came to see the school earlier. I..."

His voice grew stronger. "He came highly recommended by Catherine Symonds, the headmistress of our nearest academy school. She said he was developing a charity for local educational needs and you cannot deny that we need the money. Your own efforts at fund raising have been little more than a miserable failure."

Edgar strutted towards him all thoughts of me forgotten momentarily in his irritation at criticism of any sort. He paused, glanced towards the tattooed thug who had caught up with proceedings and nodded towards me in a meaningful kind of way. Then he laughed, turned away and raised the cane high above his head to strike at the boy's buttocks. In those strange acoustics the shot was a more of a bark or a rasp than a cough... and the cane shattered in the Marquess' hand, fragments of wood showering out and down over the body on the table which jerked reflexively.

Edgar stared at the frayed ends in his hand in bemusement – and then Dave arrived. He dropped from the gallery onto the tattooed thug like a seventeen stone feather. I heard the crack of the spine breaking as the thug hit the floor with a huge and heavy thud. Dave rolled away to one side in a single move. I glanced towards the scarred woman, who was beginning to raise a knife in my direction. Then she lost interest in proceedings, staring down at her chest where the point of Paul's long bladed throwing knife was protruding through her beige cardigan. The Marquess made his break for freedom. Paul came out his crouch ten feet behind the woman. He wrenched the knife back, leaving the woman to crumple to the floor and hurled the bloodied blade once more. It sang past my ear and thudded into the edge of the closing door. The Marquess was through and away. Robbi was running down the stairs holding out her gun for him to take.

"Get him, Paul. He mustn't get away."

He shook his head.

"The knife will do just fine. Coming, Dave?"

They ran. The door slammed behind them, jerking the priest out of his catatonic state. He lumbered to his feet and Robbi's Glock slammed into his groin. He collapsed forward on to his knees, groaning. She stood over him pressing the gun hard into his crotch. "I would so love to squeeze this trigger, so do try not to give me an excuse."

I pulled plastic ties and duct tape out of my rucksack and secured the men. Robbi and Em took take care of the two disturbed and distressed children while I covered the dead bodies on the floor.

It was quarter to eleven when Dave and Paul returned. I raised my eyebrows. They nodded. I looked at the two bound men. Dave crossed the floor and found the carotid arteries. Their heads slumped forward. I stood up.

"OK, before you start telling me that officers have ideas, this is as far as I've got."

I glanced up. Robbi had squatted on the floor by the door to the anteroom watching us. I indicated the table and the teachers.

"If we let the authorities know about this then there'll be a huge scandal which the children will be caught up in. They'll all get sent to different homes and for all we know it'll start all over again. You remember the property deal that the idiot Miles Scowcroft was involved in?"

They nodded.

"Well, we own the property now. It is about forty self–contained units being developed as a care home for the elderly. Want me to join up the dots?"

They nodded. "OK. In chronological order... we get the headmaster here to sign a paper agreeing to let the children be taken care of by us. We get the staff to sign some kind of confession. We talk to the head teacher of the local Academy school. We get properly qualified staff in. Then, tomorrow, we start a fire." I tapped the floor with my right foot. "We start a fire right here and we 'rescue' the kids. We take them to Fosse. Some of the teaching staff may not survive the fire."

"Got to be careful though," Paul said. "Forensics can tell if it was started deliberately."

"Look at those electrics," I said. Picked at the cabling on the wall. "Ancient."

Robbi called down. "What's the score with the Marquess?"

Dave gave the half smile. "Tripped over a root in the dark and broke his neck."

I smiled at Paul's emphatic nod. "Dave, can you get him straight back over to the castle before rigor mortis sets in? I just checked online and you've got…"

"Three to four hours. We have seen dead bodies before, John."

Paul smiled. I carried on. "Leave him out in the park with a shotgun. Make it look as though he tripped up in the dark."

Dave left and we got to work.

CHAPTER TWENTY-SIX

I accept it's a cliché to say that NCOs are the backbone of the British army, but they are. And without Paul there we wouldn't have made it. Young Finn had regained a modicum of confidence although he still clung to Em's hand and the girl, whose name I discovered was Jay, clung to Robbi's while Paul listened to their high–pitched whispers. He nodded and in a lower pitch whispered instructions to me. I tore duct tape into strips and picked out plastic ties.

The first bedroom door belonged to the Gym teacher. Paul squirted WD40 onto the hinges and the door handle and slowly, gently, eased the door open. I heard a snore. Paul slithered forward until he was beside the bed. I saw the outline of his body as he raised himself into a crouch and then stood over the body looking down. He beckoned me in. When I was in position, he shone his torch up into his face, highlighting the wicked scar on his jaw, tapped the sleeping man on the shoulder and waited. The teacher stirred, the pitch of his snoring changed and he muttered. Suddenly his eyes flicked open and he stared up in horror at the grotesquely lit face over him. I stepped out of the shadows and clamped the duct tape over his mouth.

Paul placed his Glock against the man's forehead and raised a finger to his lips, then whispered. "Hold out your hands."

The hands came out from beneath the sheet. I whipped the plastic tie round the wrists and pulled it tight not caring if it cut off the circulation.

"Feet."

The feet emerged. I tied them.

"On the floor."

He managed to roll himself out of bed, naked, and knelt on the floor. Paul turned to me.

"Bed."

We picked up the heavy bed and pushed it up against the kneeling man. If he pushed back, we would hear him.

The other rooms should have been easier, but the second priest thought he would put up a fight. It lasted three seconds. We waited in silence, but no one had heard. They must be used to the sounds of violence in the bedrooms. My anger rose again. The child psychologist had a guest in his bed, a cowering, half–drugged, ten-year-old boy. I took a photo on my phone and carried the boy along the landing to Robbi and rejoined Paul. The psychologist tried to smile at me ingratiatingly. The sight of the young boy... memories of my own childhood... I lashed out and hit him hard on the nose, blood spurting. My knuckles hurt. I raised my fist again. Paul's outstretched hand stopped me. The red haze faded.

By the time the fifth and final teacher was being bound Dave had returned. He took in the situation with a single glance and a half sentence from Paul.

We brought the teachers out of their rooms, Dave emerging from the Gym teacher's room, dragging the naked man behind him by his wrists. He collected the child psychologist in the same way and hauled them both towards the stairs. They stumbled, staggered and tried to get to their feet. Dave didn't pause. He bounced them down the steps and across the hall to the dining room. The remaining teachers went quietly.

By eleven thirty the resident staff had all signed the generic admission dictated by Emma and typed by Robbi. By midnight their rooms had been tidied, their beds made and the children's files had been removed. Paul and Dave had worked on the electrical wiring in the anteroom to the torture room. Then we dozed fitfully until six the next morning when the cook and her staff arrived. Em headed into the kitchen. Paul and I waited outside the door while Robbi and Dave went to help the children wash and dress. As ever, listening to Em's management style was an education.

"I don't give a shit what you normally prepare for the children – and that's 'children' not 'brats!' How dare you! Today they will have bacon and fried eggs and baked beans and as much toast as they want. Sorry? Then go and fucking buy some bacon. You! Here's some money – enough bacon and eggs for thirty-four children. And if you should decide to take the money and not return, may I suggest you think again. In fact, my colleague will accompany you to ensure your swift return. Paul?"

Paul's small throwing knife appeared in his hand as if by magic. He spun the blade through his fingers, watching the kitchen hand all the time. "Oh, he'll come back, Boss. Trust me on that."

And he did. In the interim the cook had squared up to Em, backed down and walked, followed by the rest of the kitchen staff – Em had held the door open for them. I had taken over. By the time the children arrived in the dining hall, piles of crisp bacon, fried eggs and a tureen full of baked beans had been carried through from the kitchen. They stared at the food in awe as I deposited the final plateful of hot buttered toast on the table. Em smiled with genuine warmth.

"Come on, you lot! Tuck in. There's lots more for those who want it."

And they did. And there was. And they helped wash up. Em addressed the children.

"Right. We know you've been having a horrible time. Just to be clear – we know everything... everything. I am – we are – so terribly, terribly sorry. But from now on it's going to be different. We're going to take you to a new place and we'll be in charge and you will never – never – see any of your old teachers again. Now it doesn't mean that everything's going to be perfect because it never is. In fact, I'm going to have to spend half the day on the phone ordering beds for you in the new place. We're all going to have to work hard, but it will be fun. Hard work can be fun, you know. I promise. Any questions?"

Finn nudged the tall girl beside him. She glared at him, but another hand pushed her forward. She blushed bright red. "Please Miss, what about the Lord? Will we have to see him again?"

"First off, my name is Emma Fitzgerald, but everyone calls me The Boss... 'cos I am. And in answer to your question, no, you won't. Patricia, wasn't it?"

The girl nodded, pleased to have been remembered.

"I can assure you, Patricia and all the rest of you, that you will never have to see his Lordship again. Regimental Sergeant Major Lord and Staff Sergeant Browby have made sure of this."

The children silently looked towards the two men. Dave smiled gently and spoke in his deep rumble. "Kids, the boss is right. We know what he did to some of your friends, but I promise that he will never come near any of you again. And I keep my promises."

A small hand went up. Em smiled. "Yes?"

It was Finn. "Please, Boss, we want to know what happened to our friends."

Em turned to me, but it was Dave who stepped forward to the front of the stage. "I don't like not telling the truth. It's my army training. You heard the Boss call me Regimental Sergeant Major Lord, well I'm from the SAS. We're the people who clear up nasty messes in odd parts of the world. We do all sorts of undercover operations, so I know a lot about death and I can tell you that we found seven bodies buried near John's house. I'm sorry, kids, but they were your friends. They've now been given a proper burial in the church in John's village. You can visit them there. There's a plaque with their names on the floor there. Now, Robbi here is my sister and she's married to John over there...". He pointed to where I sat on the edge of the stage. "... and John is now going to tell you what happened to him when he was a kid... like you. John?

I straightened my back and looked out at the kids. "What happened to your friends has been going on a long time now. It nearly happened to me when I was a child. I was eight."

I breathed deeply and hid my trembling hands. It still hurt to talk about this. Robbi squeezed my arm and as I turned to smile at her I saw the door at the back of the hall swing open and Sir Ian entered quietly followed by Alan and Sergeant Skinner. I raised a hand at them half–heartedly and carried on talking, wondering how he would take this. "The people who killed your friends and have allowed all these horrible things to happen to you here have been around a long time. The father of one of their leaders murdered my father when I was six."

Ian sat down.

"When I was eight, he murdered my mother and then tortured me and beat me and raped me. I was lucky. The police came before... Anyway, I was sent away to school and I had child psychologists and no one ever found out what they did to me." I looked out at them. "You understand?" I could see the nods and hear the murmured 'yeses'. "I er, I had nightmares, lots of nightmares – still do. And I soon discovered that the easiest thing was to sleep on the floor, curled up in the corner of the room with a handkerchief in your mouth so no one heard you screaming and of course it was easy to wash out pyjamas if you had sweated in them all night or wet them when you were so frightened. They beat you when you wet the bed, don't they?"

They nodded again. One of the older girls was crying and Robbi jumped down from the stage to go and hug her. She spoke with her arm round the girl. "Our parents were killed in a war zone, so I know what it's like to lose family, but I was dead lucky. I had a big brother. She turned and grinned down at the girl. "And when I say big, I mean huuuge!" The children all laughed. Even Ian smiled. "Anyway, you need to look at John as an example of what can be achieved even with the rottenest start in life. He worked so hard that he became the one of the top traders in the City of London – Emma, there, was his boss. And much, much, much more importantly he had the incredibly good luck to marry me. Moi!"

She stood and swept a deep curtsy. The children all laughed and cheered. Em stood up again. "Right, bags packed. Robbi, Paul, Dave, can you help?"

They filed out, one of the younger boys pausing to look up at me. "Is that why you limp? 'Cos they hurt you?"

I patted his head. "You got it. Yes, that's why I limp."

He nodded thoughtfully. "You'll be alright now, John. We'll take care of you."

I crouched down and looked into his eyes. "Thank you, Sean. Thank you."

I stood up, trying not make an exhibition of myself by crying. Ian was watching me. I held out my hand.

"John, I'm very sorry about last night. We had decided to round up everyone involved in this ghastly affair as information was leaking out all over the place. We had all comms switched off to protect the operation."

"Did you get them all?"

"All apart from his lordship, yes."

"Well, he'll be back at his castle. He was here last night but managed to escape while we were rounding up all the rest of the scum."

He looked at me quizzically, but if there's one thing my wreck of a childhood had taught me to do, it was to look innocent in the face of the most damning evidence. I passed him the camera Em had used the night before. He held it out so Alan could see the small screen. They both grimaced. I passed him the teachers' signed admissions of liability.

He nodded. "Hmmm. Very well, John, very well. Um... his Lordship was found half drowned in a stream near the castle this morning. He appeared to have been climbing over a dry-stone wall and slipped. A heavy stone caught him on the back of the neck. He was dead."

I nodded and tried to look both surprised and satisfied. "Good."

He looked at the floor and half smiled. "John, you will remember our first meeting at Marcus Wethers' house."

"Yes, of course."

"Well, if there was one thing I learned about you then, it was that you were able to tell half-truths or even bare faced lies without moving a facial muscle."

He patted my upper arm. "Having heard what you just told the children, though, I think I can begin to understand why. In any event, the Marquess now being out of the way is, quite frankly, most satisfactory. Now, how are you going to manage the children and the teachers here?"

"Teachers are up to you, Ian. But the children...". I told him about the care home I now owned and about the fact that Councillor Miles Scowcroft would do anything to keep me happy, that Catherine Symonds the local head teacher was an ally, that I would be footing the entire bill and that I would have good coverage in the local press.

"So, I think I can handle the objections to a children's home from the local authority if you can get Whitehall onside."

He smiled sourly and turned to Alan who was grinning broadly. Even Sergeant Skinner was smiling. "Dear oh dear. You wouldn't have lasted five minutes inside Whitehall. They'd have you murdered in your sleep just to stop you climbing to the top. I assume you want me to release Mr Scowcroft on condition that he delivers what you want?" He indicated the video camera. "Now, where have you kept the teachers who are on here?"

I pointed towards the door at the back of the stage as the voices of children, of happy children, drifted down the stairs, half drowned by the clatter of their shoes on the wooden steps. Em directed them to the front door and they headed out into the cold December morning. I glanced at my watch and explained to Ian.

"I ordered a coach to be here for ten thirty. Want to see them off?"

We joined the rear guard and I managed a surreptitious glance at my watch. Timing was everything now!

I propped the front door open as George's old coach pulled into the drive. The children cheered. Right now, I think, however, they would have cheered anything. Dave and Paul organised them into ranks, barking orders as if they were in the army. The children loved it and shuffled up together, right arms outstretched for 'dressing by the right' in rows, giggling when they were informed that they were "'horrible little men".

Em walked over to Ian to apologise for her rudeness to him the previous week and I managed finally to turn casually and look back as if for the last time.

A movement on the hill to the left of the house caught my attention – a man running. No, two men running. A third stepped out from behind a tree and stood still, looking straight at me. As he turned away, I caught a glint of the earring in his left ear. I thought about this for a moment, then turned back to stare at the house again. Was that a heat haze above the windows of the central dome over the torture room? Was that a tiny plume of smoke? No, my eyes were just watering. I blinked the tears away and began to turn when I heard the faint tinkle of glass breaking. The heat haze reddened – hints of flame licking up out of the glazed cupola.

The Gypsies had administered justice.

I walked back over to Ian and Em, my heart pounding. I didn't dare look at Robbi. Just let the fire catch properly. Just let it catch. Two more minutes – the children were just beginning to board the coach – a piece of ash landed on Ian's sleeve. He brushed it off and continued his conversation with Em. One landed on my eyebrow. Another landed on his sleeve. He looked up sharply. I swung round towards the building and yelled. "Christ, it's caught fire. Call the fire brigade, Robbi. Quick, Dave. Quick."

We pelted back to the open front door, but the heat from the dining hall, fanned by the cold air from outside, was way too intense. I peered through the glass doors as the crimson curtain at the back of the stage disintegrated into a shower of blazing sparks and the wooden stage floor crackled and buckled. Flames were now racing across the dining room floor and Dave grabbed and half carried me outside. By the coach the children were cheering themselves hoarse. I shook my head and coughed to get rid of the stench. I retched. Through the chaos I heard Dave's voice.

"It may be my fault, sir. When I went to check up on them this morning, they moaned about being cold so I let them have an electric fire. The electrics were pretty ancient."

Ian looked from Dave to me. I coughed and turned back once more. The children's wing was now ablaze. And did I care that I had sentenced half a dozen men to a horrible death? I thought about this for a moment. No. No I didn't. Not one jot, tittle or iota. I half wished I was a Catholic so I could believe they would burn in hell for eternity for what they had done to the children. Robbi took my hand and we climbed aboard the bus.

I had forgotten what it was like working for Em. On the coach I called Catherine Symonds and warned her what was afoot and then tuned into Em's phone conversation.

"Sorry, you are a bed maker. Yes? Excellent. That means you make beds. Yes? Good! I need forty of your single beds to be at an address near Northleach in Oxfordshire – the county in which you have your factory – tomorrow. I will pay in advance by Chaps direct into your account in one hour. Now, can you deliver or not? What do you mean you think so? It's a simple question, give me a simple answer or I'll go to another supplier. Oh, for the love of God. Put me on to your Managing Director."

It took her two minutes to give the MD the whole story of the children's home burning down, the excellent P.R. that could be made out of this etc, etc... P.R. – I called Luke Warburton at the North Cotswold Gazette. By the end of the call, he was talking to me on the run as he ran to his car in order to get to the Manor before the coach.

The rest of the day is still a blur: photo ops, ordering deliveries of thirty-four portions of fast food for lunch and supper; arranging mattresses and sleeping bags for thirty-four in the dining hall; Em visiting the sheltered housing I had bought off Miles Scowcroft; Robbi talking to Catherine Symonds, and eventually sitting in the kitchen with Robbi, two dogs, a dumpling stew and a couple of decanted bottles of Chateau Palmer with which to celebrate. There was a discreet tap at the scullery door. As the dogs only trotted towards it wagging their tails, I just called out that it was open. Hugh Digby peered round. "Sorry, John, just had that soil analysis for Miranda so thought I'd drop it round."

Robbi smiled at him. "Come and have some stew, Hugh. John always makes miles more than we can eat."

I waved away his protests, pointed at the bowls on the dresser and pushed the decanter in his direction. He sat and ate.

"Your old boss is dead, Hugh."

He stared at us. The door to the hall swung open and Em reversed in carrying the children's files.

"Fucking hell, are kids always this knackering? Pour us a really big glass of wine, Robbi, will you. Evening Mr Digby."

Hugh's mouth was hanging open, stew dripping off his spoon, unnoticed. I smiled at his horror.

"Hugh, I would like you to meet Emma Fitzgerald, our closest friend and my old boss."

He looked from one of us to the other. Em nicked my bowl and Robbi's spoon.

"Mmmm. Love dumplings. They made of semolina?"

I nodded. She slurped.

"Such good grub. Sorry, Digby, I couldn't tell you about any of this because I really didn't know where you stood. Anyway, did John tell you that the ghastly shit is dead?"

She turned to me.

"I'll have to go and visit Betty – that's his wife – tomorrow and celebrate with her. She caught on very quickly that I was playing him for a sucker. Nice lady, Betty. Reckon I could get her in as a patron of the new children's home. That would be irony for you wouldn't it? Push the stew over, Digby, there's a good boy. Where's the bread?"

Hugh recovered slowly and ate on, but I could see him looking at us with new respect. And the next day I began to think we'd deserved it. I don't care what you say, moving thirty-four children aged between nine and sixteen into a new home with no food, no beds and no furniture and with heating, phone and broadband promised by British utility companies... But we did have a secret weapon – Emma, the Boss, Fitzgerald. Over breakfast she had remembered that I had once invested in a British feature film. Dreadful film it was too – full of Mockney gangsters calling each other 'slaaags'. At least I only put in the gap finance – last in, first out. I got my money back... the only one who did.

"Location caterers, John. Remember? You visited the set to make sure it was legit and you told me the food was fab."

"But it means I'll have to phone that dreadful producer bloke, Dowson. He'll only start trying to pitch me his next project and he will go on and on and on..."

"Just speak to that sexy little secretary of his. You know she'd lurve to hear from you."

I put my head in my hands.

"Oops, sorry, did I say something wrong in front of Robbi? Deary me. Me and my big mouth."

I risked a peek through my fingers. Robbi and Em were high fiving each other and laughing silently. Women – a cruel and unremitting sex. The upshot was a call made with Robbi listening in. I could hear the dreaded Dowson shouting at someone in the background, but I got through the entire experience unsullied and emerged with a phone number. Robbi made the call to the caterers. It being nearly Christmas they weren't working and seemed quite amused by the whole idea. They promised to be at the home by tea time.

CHAPTER TWENTY-SEVEN

Four days of chaos – the chaos that only thirty-four children with years of psychological, sexual and physical abuse could create. Apart from the feeding, the clothing, the bedding, the teaching, the caring – God, the caring!

One of the girls had been found in a pub in Carterton with an older man and two of the boys had picked a fight with half a dozen lads from the local school. On day three a deputation of some of the most reactionary neighbours arrived. It was their intention to have the home closed without delay as these were young criminals who should be in prison or deported or in the workhouse or beheaded – who knows? I had been there, watching quietly in the background, stopping the children from doing anything too extreme by way of swearing or hurling abuse. But seriously? Watching those poor, middle class, deluded men and women – lambs to the slaughter. The Boss greeted them and charmed them. Robbi brought them tea and glamourised them. Then the Marchioness made her entrance and patronised them. Then the children sang them a carol. The concerned became the converted. They departed wiping sentimental tears from their eyes in a twitter of contentment and admiration, at least three having agreed to come in on mornings and read with the younger children.

But not a word from Ian or Alan. They didn't answer their phones so I didn't know where they'd gone. I didn't know how many people they had rounded up. I didn't know if I was safe now. I didn't even know if I was of any importance anymore. I decided to visit the Gypsies. The least I could do would be to say thank you. I took the Landrover and bumped over the fields with the Collies in the back, heads stuck out of the side windows, tongues lolling, noses twitching, eyes everywhere. I could see a spiral of smoke twisting up through the trees, but as I rounded the final bend, I saw there was nothing left – just a skip full of rubbish and a camp fire smouldering in the centre of the clearing. They had struck camp and left for God knows where.

For a moment I was hurt, but as the dogs sniffed round the skip and dived off into the bushes, I thought about what they had done for me: the risks they had taken, the respect they had shown Robbi, the care they had taken of us both. I walked back to the Landrover, whistled up the dogs, texted Paul to get the skip removed and drove home.

An official black car was parked in the drive by the front door and Sir Ian Hamilton was waiting patiently in the kitchen. The dogs sniffed and wagged at him.

"I let myself in, John. Your security has become somewhat lax."

"Sorry, Ian, you should have called me on the mobile. I'd have come straight back. Anyway, I thought you'd rounded everyone up so I didn't require security anymore."

He sipped the mug of tea I passed him, nodded approvingly, placed the cup on the old table and looked at me. "It's never as simple as that though is it?"

He sipped his tea again and I knew he was waiting for me to draw conclusions. I sighed. "You still don't know who's behind it, do you? You still don't know if I am *a* target or *the* target. And if I'm not the target you still don't know what they are after. Right?"

He cocked his head. "Nearly right. I think I can say that you're definitely safe for the moment. Whoever is behind it is currently laying very low. We have them on the run for the moment."

"So, it's 'they' not 'he' or 'she'?"

"There's many more than one, yes, but at the very top there'll be just one. There always is eventually. Now listen, John. We rounded up nine men and women in that raid we carried out. It's taken all this time to interrogate them and we're still at it. They were all, more or less, actively involved in the plot to extract money out of you. Seven of them believe that is the sole aim of their little conspiracy. Four of those seven are convinced you beat Medina by foul means."

I shrugged. "Sounds like the QAnon branch of the GOP after Trump lost the 2020 election."

Ian flicked imaginary crumbs from the table. "Quite so. They are not of interest to us. They were smug and self-important little people, but they have now become very frightened and chastened little people."

"And the other two – Artinswell and who?"

He smiled. "I apologise. I continue to underestimate you, don't I? Artinswell is remarkably subtle. He appears to be genuinely contrite, most desirous of helping, determined to repent of his deeds, but..."

I could see that Ian had been shifting in his seat for some time. He was a man who thought on his feet. He stood up and paced to the door and back. "We have cameras in his cell. One of them is quite obvious – up in the corner where he can see it, but the most useful is one in the wall beside his bed."

He held up a USB stick and pointed at the laptop on the dresser. I booted it up and pushed the drive in. Ian continued with the narrative. "This was taken immediately after a two-hour interrogation last night. He was in tears by the end of it. Now look. He comes straight back into the cell."

He pointed at the screen. "That's him on the camera in the corner. See. He's still snivelling. Now watch. He rinses his face then lies down and we cut to the camera in the wall."

A close up of His Lordship's face filled the screen. The snivels slowed and stopped and he started to breathe heavily as if sleep were approaching. He snored. But his eyes were wide open and a slow, self–satisfied smile spread across his jowly face. I ejected the USB stick and returned it.

"Who's the second man, Ian?"

He smiled grimly and changed the subject. "The men who kidnapped Roberta?"

I went through an eyebrow raising exercise.

"FSB. Ukrainian though. They seemed to have been paid a great deal of money to do the job. They were also the ones in the Ford Mondeo, by the way. We managed to take three of them alive and you know what the strange thing was?"

I raised my eyebrows even higher and tried to look my most encouraging.

"They didn't understand why anyone er, associated shall we say, with MI5 would have been out to stop them. It's not easy to get information out of special forces personnel, you understand. They're trained to handle the most severe forms of enhanced interrogation. But in this case, they were happy to help, just puzzled."

He frowned at the table while I waited for him to continue. He looked directly at me. "According to them they had been paid to do the job by MI5. Cleared at the highest level, they said. The trouble is, of course, you can't exactly ask them for a receipt or a bank statement, can you?"

I thought about this. "Who else knows about this, Ian?"

"Exactly, John. Exactly. Who else knows?"

His chin went down on to his chest. How old was he? I reminded myself to ask Uncle Marcus. In any event why had he come to see me? Had I finally reassured him that I was to be trusted? Possibly. Was there no one else he could trust? Probably. So, I was a last resort? Definitely.

"How much does Major Cummins know about this, Ian?"

"*Colonel* Cummins is no longer seconded to MI5. He is back with the regiment along with Sergeant *Major* Skinner. These are significant promotions."

So, Ian had no one to play with now. Would that worry him? I stared at the prominent veins on the back of his right hand and then up at his lean, lined face. "You think they're going to kill you next, don't you, Ian?"

He smiled. "I was talking to Emma Fitzgerald about you, John. She said that working with you is a nightmare, but once you get beyond the sheer brainpower and work capability and the inability to take orders or even contemplate working as a member of a team, what is really interesting is that you have remarkable insights. I think I may just be beginning to get beyond the nightmare stage."

I shrugged dismissively. I suppose it was always pleasant to receive compliments, however backhanded, but I'd not really had much time for touchy–feely stuff since the age of eight. "It's the second man who's made you think this, isn't it, Ian?"

He leaned forward and tapped the table with his bony ring finger. "John, you may be very good at dissembling, but I am even better at seeing through dissimulation. I've made a career of it. You've been holding out on me for quite a while."

He pointed the bony finger at me. "You tell... He tapped his chest with the same finger. "I'll tell."

What had I got to lose? But if only Robbi were here to advise. I smiled at him wryly. That's why he had waited for me today. He wanted me on his own, on my territory, but on his terms. He smiled back.

"She won't be back for another half hour, John. Well?"

"Mr Holroyd."

He thought about that for a moment. "I have heard rumours of a Mr Holroyd. Explain."

I explained as briefly as I could – which wasn't briefly at all. He thought. "It's possible, of course. When I said I had heard rumours of a Holroyd, well there've been rumours among spooks of such a person for many years.

I first heard it mooted when I was in my twenties. Mr Holroyd. Mmmm. And did you ask Alan how he'd met him – why he knew him and I didn't?"

I shook my head, irritated at my stupidity. He nodded slowly and continued.

Well then. Fair's fair I suppose." He stood and walked to the Aga again. "The ninth person is, well, actually it's two names and one of them you're not going to like one bit – Julian ffitch."

"But I thought Alan was using him as bait. I thought that was why I got summoned to the Treasury Select Committee. I thought that was how the select committee got such crap information on me..."

"It was. We have, we have – ah – misjudged ffitch, John. He isn't as stupid as you think."

He passed me another USB stick. I pushed it into the side of the laptop and watched the repulsive ffitch being interrogated. I sat forward. He was right. This wasn't the ffitch I thought I knew. He was sitting across the table from the interrogator, a chess board with a half–played game between them. He was answering each question between moves, thoughtfully, carefully and (possibly) even honestly. He understood now that he had been under the influence of Dominick Medina. Yes, he understood that he had been used by Medina to work against the interests of the Treasury, but he still felt, even now, on balance that Medina's analysis had been correct.

"I think I need to apologise to John Hannay too..."

I stared at the screen. Really? Not sure I wanted that.

"It's just that he is so damn superior. He was like it at school..."

That was more like it.

"Never interested in making any friends. Passed every exam without even trying. Best fencer they'd ever had and he just didn't seem to care."

Probably because I didn't and anyway, I'd worked bloody hard to pass those exams.

"Not frightened of anything or anybody – they stopped him from doing martial arts because he nearly killed one of the school bullies."

Now that was a blatant lie. All I did was keep hitting him just hard enough not to knock him out, but so he felt the pain – really felt the pain. He didn't bully anybody after that, I can tell you. And it worked for me. I got left alone which was all I'd ever asked.

"So why should anyone like him?"

No reason at all, ffitch. No reason at all. The interrogator sat in the shadows, studying the chess board, rarely questioning, just nodding slight encouragement from time to time. But ffitch wasn't addressing him. He was talking to himself, listening to himself, judging himself. Justifying himself? Probably. His carefully constructed world had disintegrated in front of him. He had lost not just his present position, but his entire life plan, his raison d'être. Ian leant across and pressed the pause button on the laptop. He sat back, folded his arms and waited.

"A while ago, Ian, I asked Major – sorry, Colonel – Cummins how important I was in all this." I waved my arm around in a rough circle. Ian didn't move. "He seemed to think I was very important. I don't like that, Ian. I don't like being important. I've tried not to be important all my life."

"Why?"

I shrugged. That was simple. "Because when someone thinks you're important they hurt you. At least they hurt me. I used not to care about this. You heard what I said to the children at that school. But then I met her, Ian..."

On cue the sound of Robbi's laughter echoed in from the hall. She had taken to using the front door since the Christmas tree had gone up so she could see it and all the mad decorations.

"I would do anything to protect her from being hurt, Ian. Anything."

The Collies were barking, the door burst open and it was chaos again – a happy chaos. And that was the adjective that came to mind every time. She was happy. She made me and everyone around her happy. Even Ian was smiling at her like an indulgent uncle. And she had no idea – as unconscious of this as she was of the impact of her beauty. I mean if you asked her whether she thought she was beautiful or happy she would have agreed... happily. She knew it, but it had no impact on her behaviour or her ego – unaffected was the word. She put shopping bags on the dresser, kissed Ian, hugged the dogs, asked why I hadn't offered her a cup of tea and just touched the back of my hand with her fingers. Ian refused another cup of tea and retrieved his USB sticks. I walked him out to his car.

"How come you still have an official car and a driver, Ian?"

"Perhaps because I'm more official than I let on."

"Are you, Ian? Are you indeed? Ian?"

"Yes?"

"Mr Holroyd plays chess. He mentioned the Chicago gambit. Robbi had to look it up."

Ian paused, one foot in the car. He lowered himself slowly on to the seat. "But the Chicago gambit's a very weak opening isn't it? Why would he mention that?"

"Because he kept on mentioning pawns and I asked him why. ffitch didn't play chess at Eton, Ian. I played a bit. So why was he playing chess with the interrogator?"

"He asked to. He told them it helped him think."

I stared at the toe of Ian's polished brogue.

"Do you have complete faith in your interrogator, Ian?"

He pulled the door too. It closed with a reassuringly expensive clunk and the interior light went off. The electric window wound down and I peered at him through the gloom of the evening and the half–light from the open door of the manor.

"I want to see that chess game, Ian. I want to know the moves."

He nodded slowly.

"Very well. I think I understand you."

He tapped the back of the seat in front of him and as the car moved away, I saw him reaching for his mobile phone. I shouted. "Ian? Wait!"

The car braked. I ran inside to the study, grabbed one of Palmer's phones from the desk and ran back out. I passed the phone through the window and spoke quietly.

"Don't use your phone, Ian. Don't use a mobile in your car. I'll tell Palmer to call you on that phone."

He studied me impassively. I whispered. "Don't die, Ian. I've lost too many friends. Don't die because of me. I'm really not worth it. Honestly."

He smiled at me and held out his hand. I shook it.

"Someone thinks you are, John and someone was prepared to let the country go down the plughole because of that. Chicago gambit, indeed. I think we need a counter–gambit. Yes, that's what we need."

He laughed. "The Latvian gambit would do nicely, I think. Don't forget that and don't worry, I'll be even more careful than normal. I promise."

He tapped the back of the driver's seat again and the window closed. The rear lights had disappeared round the corner before I realised I hadn't asked him who the second person was.

CHAPTER TWENTY-EIGHT

If she said another word about Christmas, I swear...

There was still a week to go so what was it with this constant planning and re–planning – and all these people coming? I muttered darkly, but she watched me out of the corner of her eye, judged my mood to a millimetre, smiled her happy smile and sailed on regardless. The worst thing was I was defenceless. Digby and Paul were slumming it at Glebe Farm so I was a man alone and under siege. The Christmas tree had arrived a week ago from the plantation, the decorations from the attic, the geese yesterday from Home Farm – I didn't care where the sprouts and potatoes were going to come from.

Grace had already moved in to one of the small bedroom suites on the top floor, Miranda was camping out in the stable block, Margaret was totally complicit in the whole bloody conspiracy and the worst thing was... I really didn't mind at all. From the moment I awoke to the moment my head hit the pillow I was surrounded by female laughter, warmth and excitement. To my horror I looked in the mirror while shaving at the beginning of the week and found myself smiling.

I mean normally, as any man will tell you, you don't look at yourself when you're shaving – just at the bits that need to be shaved; but when you have to stop smiling in order not to cut your cheek – well, it brings you up short! On the Tuesday I escaped to Oxford ostensibly under instructions to purchase more decorations, but primarily in order to collect Robbi's present. I drove back on the A40 contemplating my existence. So far as I could recall, the last Christmas I had celebrated had been five years ago at the Sandy Lane hotel on Barbados – alone. I hadn't enjoyed it much. I hadn't slept well. I'm not really suited to a tropical climate.

I diverted to visit the parish church – tentatively. I hoped the floor of the Lady Chapel had been completed and it had – the Victorian tiles replaced and in the exact centre of the floor the extract from the poem I had thought most appropriate, inscribed in brass, an eternal memorial to those poor, unloved children with a list of their names carved below the well known poem.

> They are not long, the weeping and the laughter,
> Love and desire and hate:
> I think they have no portion in us after
> We pass the gate.
> They are not long, the days of wine and roses:
> Out of a misty dream
> Our path emerges for a while, then closes
> Within a dream.

I drove on to Glebe Farm. Digby and Paul were finishing positioning the last of the posts for the stock fence by the woods. Paul jumped down from the tractor and walked over towards me, tilting his head and pointing with his jaw along the fence line to where I could see how the tractor tyres had crossed and re–crossed the erstwhile graves of the children, obscuring their contours, coating them with unrecognisable, rain-soaked earth. I nodded.

"Seen the church floor yet, Paul?"

He patted my shoulder. "I'll look in on the way home, John."

He pointed to where Digby was smacking down the last of the posts with the tractor bucket.

"Good man. Works very hard. Knows his stuff. He'll do."

"Good. Thanks, Paul."

My phone buzzed in my pocket.

"I'd better get back to the insanity."

And insanity it was. Before the Landrover had even slowed to a stop, Grace was running up with the dogs beside her and hunting for the decorations. She whispered to me while she was scrabbling in the back.

"Did you pick up Robbi's present, John? Can I see it? Please? Please?"

I smiled, leaned over the back of the seat and showed her. She gasped.

"Oh, it's beautiful."

I showed her how to open it with the catch. She gasped again.

"She'll love it, John."

She gave me a quick peck on the cheek and ran back to the house with the dogs barking and jumping round her. I thought about how much she had changed over the last six months – how happy she was here. I thought about how much I hoped she would like her gifts from us. I tucked

Robbi's present into my pocket and headed surreptitiously towards the kitchen. An impossibility – Grace had already informed her ladyship of my presence and I was requested (for 'requested' read 'ordered') to help with the Christmas tree... and so went the rest of the week.

* * *

The day before Christmas Eve.

I got up in the dark, carried my clothes downstairs to the kitchen, dressed, ate, mucked out the horses, showered, dressed again and walked towards the Lodge House to see if Paul could come out to play. He was tightening his gaiters on the back step.

"Coming shooting, John? I need to keep the Pheasants down on the Plantation."

"No thanks, Paul. I was hoping for a bit of male company, though. I think I'm being emasculated."

He laughed. "Incidentally, John, Mimi's got the report on the biomass proposal for the plantation and Mill woods. It's not bad you know, not bad at all. If you plant Hazel or some other fast-growing crop you could turn a pretty penny."

"Paul, no one has 'turned a pretty penny' since nineteen thirty-two. Get with the now daddy–oh!"

He grinned, gave me the finger, crooked another finger at his dog and departed. I wandered back up the drive. The Manor looked warm and sleepy, with the early morning sun glancing off the individual panes of the mullioned windows on the top floor, a small spiral of smoke twisting into the still, cold air from the chimneys in the roof high above the drawing room. I stopped and stared at the rambling old building feeling an answering warmth of my own – my home... our home – God, at the moment home to half a dozen females (if you included the dogs) and a hitherto uncalculated quantity of guests.

I started to add up Christmas lunch numbers on my fingers: Aunt Mary and Uncle Marcus, Ludo and Angela Arbuthnot, Grace, Paul, Margaret, Dave, Joan and Jack Cartwright, Mrs Trudgeon – her and me, of course. I'd run out of fingers. Anyone else? Miranda would be back with her family, Hugh too. Em? What about Em? I opened the door. Light flickered and danced off the baubles on the ten-foot-high Christmas tree. I stepped over the threshold, heard a giggle, looked up, caught a glimpse of an unspecified piece of greenery (I was informed later that it was 'mistletoe, stupid') and a golden-haired woman jumped on top of me from the chair behind the door on which she had been hiding, demanding a kiss. I slung her over my shoulder and carried her into the kitchen. Order was restored.

"What about Em, Robbi? What's she doing for Christmas?"

"She's staying at the school with the children. I don't think she can bear to leave them. Betty is staying there too."

We looked at each other.

"If we have breakfast and pressies here and then go over there for Christmas lunch, do you think Ludo, Angela and everybody else will mind?"

I didn't even need to think. "Of course, they won't. I was going to be there tomorrow anyway to prepare the food. You know Em's been rehearsing a carol service with them for the last week. Is it too late to get them to the village church for an early midnight mass tomorrow?"

She clapped her hands with pleasure, got on the phone and half an hour later it was all arranged. I shook my head. It would never have occurred to me that it could be that easy. I would have hidden behind potential negatives and probable indifference, but the village seemed to be delighted with the idea.

And the next day the church was even more crowded than at our wedding; and after the children had sung the last carol and the last tear had been wiped from the cheek of the last parishioner, I took the thirty-four kids into the Lady Chapel to see the plaque on the floor. Em wiped another tear away.

"Days of wine and roses. Come on kids. Time for bed. John and Robbi and all the rest of the Fosse mob are coming for lunch tomorrow."

* * *

Christmas morning.

I opened an eye. It was still dark. The alarm clock showed it was six o'clock. Robbi turned over and smiled at me. I went to the bathroom and came back with only one thought on my mind. She ran to the bathroom before I could act on the thought. I heard something moving on the landing and realised I had to dismiss the thought. I called out. "Grace Harker, what are you up to? Come in here immediately."

The door opened. A head peered in – Grace in pyjamas. Robbi slid back into bed beside me, passed me some pyjama bottoms and beckoned. "Come on Grace, jump into bed before you catch your death."

She made room between us and Grace clambered in. I gave her a Christmas hug and went to find a dressing gown. The night attire theme continued over breakfast in the drawing room and then it was present time with Grace bouncing from person to person handing them out as we oohed and aahed politely. Eventually, I called her over to where I sat on my grandfather's old armchair with Robbi tucked in beside me. She looked at us expectantly, nervously. Robbi handed her an envelope. She opened it looking from one of us to the other, gasped and turned to Aunt Mary.

"They've given me Mavis as a present. They've given me a pony."

She hugged us both. I passed her another envelope and we watched her. She read through the legal document and then dropped it on the floor. She stared at us in amazement, burst into floods of racking sobs and threw herself into Robbi's arms. I heard Uncle Marcus explaining to Ludo and Angela.

"They've made her their ward and the other document changes her name by deed poll from Harker to Hannay. Lovely thought isn't it."

What with the wealth of over–emotion I was almost scared that my present to Robbi would be a let-down. Grace was still draped over our laps. "Don't be soft, John. She'll love it."

I passed the chamois leather pouch across to her and waited. She opened it and put her hand to her mouth. It was a cloisonné enamel locket holding a piece of perfect jade set in gold with the words of that remarkable medieval prioress, Julian of Norwich, carved in the centre.

> All Shall Be
> Well; and All
> Shall Be
> Well; and All
> Manner of
> Thing
> Shall be
> Well

And it was Robbi's turn to wipe away a tear. The locket was passed from hand to hand although I suspect that only Ludo knew its true value. He smiled across at me and shook his head in admiration. Grace hung it round Robbi's neck and together they stared at it and stroked it. Eventually Robbi reached behind her.

"And now it's my turn. Your present must have cost you a fortune, John, but mine... well it's priceless I think."

Out of the corner of my eye I saw Joan Cartwright smile at Jack and then Robbi was putting an A5 envelope in my hand. I opened it and what looked like a small photo dropped out on to my lap. I picked it up and tried to puzzle it out. I glanced up. The room was silent. I was the centre of attention again – God how I still hated that. Robbi was biting her lip nervously and Grace was staring at the photo. And the penny dropped. It wasn't a photo. It was an ultra–sound picture – a picture of a tiny baby in a mother's womb. I was going to be a father! Two images flashed through my brain. Mr Baptista patting her cheek: 'especially now, m'Lady', Granny Baptista smiling at her. The gypsies had known long before I had the faintest idea. I came back to earth and smiled at her. "So Robbi is going to have a baby, then."

She pulled herself into my arms. "No, Robbi's going to have *your* baby." She leaned back from me and looked up into my eyes. "Um, actually? It's more like Robbi's going to have two of your babies..."

And Grace was squeaking and Aunt Mary and Uncle Marcus were patting me on the back and Ludo was applauding and Angela was crying and I felt a tsunami of happiness wash over me. I went to find the champagne from the cellar. I came back up with three bottles in a basket and was passing the phone in the hall when it rang. I picked it up expecting it to be Em, but it was Alan's voice.

"John? John? Are you listening? I have to tell you about Ian."

THE END

THE FORTIETH STEP TRILOGY
VOLUME 3

PROMISE

STEPHEN TIMMINS

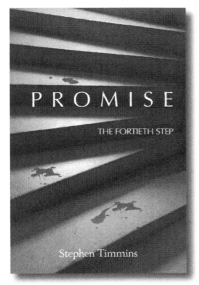

At last, John Hannay comes face to face with his nemesis, the man who has vowed to destroy not only John's family but also the country that generations of Hannays have loved and served. It is a fight to the death – the final encounter. One that John has to win.

diamondbooks.co.uk

DIAMOND
CRIME

DIAMOND
BOOKS

Printed in Great Britain
by Amazon

74421727R00199